The Summer Posy

The Liverpool Brides, Book 4

Michelle Vernal

Copyright © 2022 The Summer Posy, Book 4 in the Liverpool Brides series by Michelle Vernal

All rights reserved.

No portion of this book may be reproduced in any form without written permission from the publisher or author, except as permitted by U.S. copyright law.

For Brian Minns the coolest cousin there ever was

x

Compendium of Liverpudlian Words

Donkey stoning the step – Vigorous rubbing of the front doorstep with a stone manufactured by a firm in Wigan. The stones were stamped with a donkey hence the term.

Bevvie – Alcoholic beverage
Judy - Girl
Pea-souper – Thick fog
Wabs – Weed
Meff – Idiot
Clobber - Clothes
Cob on – In a mood
Gaff – House
Arlarse – Someone who is out of order

Prologue

EVELYN, LIVERPOOL, 1925

Evelyn Flooks lay wide eyed in the bed she'd shared with her three sisters her entire life waiting to see how the land lay. She was hungry, and her tummy was protesting the watery stew they'd had for supper. Her eyes burned from staring up at the ceiling, which served to distract her from the gnawing pangs. She held her breath, waiting for the skittering shadows she'd once thought to be ghosts to chase across it. To count the shadows was a game she played to while away the time until her father came home. All those years ago, though, when she'd thundered down the stairs, convinced the ghosts were going to take her Violet and Bea, she'd been told she'd too much imagination for her own good.

She recalled her mother, who'd been hunched over her pride and joy, the Singer sewing machine, finishing the seam she was in the middle of before taking her foot off the treadle with a sigh. Evelyn had stood shivering in the doorway of the boxy parlour, lit only by a single gas lamp where her mother would toil until her father came home, in floods of tears as she sobbed out her story of the ghosties.

'You'll be the death of me, Evelyn Flooks.' Lizzy had swivelled around in her seat and rubbed her eyes before giving her temples a quick massage.

Evelyn had known her mother's head was hurting from squinting at the fine work she was doing in the poor light. Her mam worked long and hard, and she'd had even less to eat than she and her sisters had. She'd been more concerned with her current plight though as she'd cried, 'Don't let them take us, Mam!'

She must have looked a ghostly apparition herself in her white nightgown that had once fit Violet, Evelyn mused now. She remembered her mother telling her she took after her not only in looks but with her imagination too, and she'd inspected her through red-rimmed, watery eyes for proof of this.

She'd have liked her hair to be long like her mam's so she could twist it in a bun, but it was kept trimmed short to her chin, being easier to comb through for the nits. She did like the bow she got to tie in it for church though. When her father was in good humour, he'd say her mam's hair reminded him of toffee, but the locks that escaped during the day, which she'd tuck behind her ears impatiently, had turned silver, seemingly overnight. While Evelyn liked having hair the colour of toffee, she wasn't sure about the silver. Would her eyes, a curious mix of green and brown identical to her mam's, lose their sharpness and be framed by lines one day too?

'It's a curse and a gift, an imagination, Evie,' Lizzy had said that long ago night. She'd gestured to the simple house dress that was the cause of her headache. It was splayed on the fold-out wings of the sewing cabinet with the cotton waiting to be snipped. 'I'd not be able to sew and make what I make without one. To create things, you need to see the garment in your mind's eye, our Evie. You've got that gift, luv. Mark my words, in another year or so, you'll be helping me with the dressmaking.'

Her mother's skill to make an item of clothing from a bolt of fabric was a source of fascination for Evelyn. Even then, terrified by the spirits she was sure were haunting her and her sisters' bedroom, she'd itched to be allowed a turn sitting at the sewing machine.

Mam was right. She could see what a dress would look like simply by stroking the material. Instead of the plain cotton her mam was whipping into an everyday dress she'd pictured it embellished with lace and ribbons because she liked pretty things. She'd not realised she had a gift, and the thought that she should have a talent pleased her, but Mam hadn't finished.

'And it's a curse, Evie, because my girl, you see ghosts where there are none. Now c'mon with you. Back up them stairs.'

Evelyn had felt her mother's fingers dig into her bony shoulders as she was frogmarched back up to the small room overlooking Potter Street. She was led straight over to the window, and she stood there shivering as her mam pushed the curtain aside. It did little to keep the light out anyway, she thought as the moody glow of the gas lamp burning outside pooled on the floor of the room.

Evelyn was aware of two sets of eyes peering over the bedcovers as she'd huddled up to her mam, terrified despite her solid presence. She'd managed to frighten her sisters too, with her talk of spirits coming to get them, but Lizzy had banished them by pointing to a man with a derby hat hiding his face who was about to pass under the lamp.

'Watch what happens, Evie,' she said.

Evelyn had watched in wonder as the man's shadow flickered about their room as he strolled under the lamp.

'There's your ghost. Now into bed and no more of your messing.'

Lizzy had waited while Evelyn clambered over Violet and Beatrice before sliding back under the bedclothes.

'Night, Mam.'

'G'night, Evie.'

There was a wistfulness in her mother's tone, Evie had thought as she listened to her light footfall on the stairs.

Now, she remembered how even though the shadows no longer frightened her, she'd still not slept for ages because she'd been waiting to see how the land lay that night too.

The clues as to in what form her father, Jack Flooks, would barge through their front door would be doled out as he turned the corner onto Potter Street. Evelyn knew all would be well if he walked the few hundred metres to their front door whistling. She'd allow her eyes to close upon hearing the familiar shrill tune. Her inner eyelids were imprinted with the image of him swaggering along with his tweed cap pulled low over his brow, hands thrust in his pockets, jangling the winnings inside them. Then, reassured it would be a quiet night, sleep would claim her.

But, living under the same roof as a man like her father was as precarious as the toss of a coin because on those Saturdays when he'd been paid for the three, or four if he were lucky, days' work labouring he'd picked up down at the docks, it could just as easily land the other way.

On the nights the odds weren't in their favour, her body would tense, and her hands ball into fists. She'd hear the maudlin Irish ballads from the homeland Jack Flooks had not seen since he was a babe and knew he'd be scuffing the pavement with the toes of shoes. His expression beneath the peak of his cap would be dark, and the slump in his shoulders suggested the world was out to get him.

Back then, Evelyn hadn't understood the weakness in her dad. All she knew was the singing meant they'd go hungry if mam didn't get the dress she was sewing finished. His wages would be gone—gambled on the horses. The thuds and cries that would echo up the narrow staircase as Jack took his folly out on her mam made Evelyn feel cowardly. All hopes of sleep were dashed until the sounds of Lizzie's sobs subsided.

Evelyn had tried to stop him, but he'd turned on her instead. He might have been a slightly built man, but his wiry frame belied his strength. It was gleaned from the hours spent unloading the cargo of the big ships whose horns would echo eerily through the foggy streets she called home. Her mother had been angry at her for involving herself as she'd tended her bruises. 'What's the point in us both being black and blue, Evie?' She'd made her promise to stay in bed come what may on the nights when it was the singing drifting down Potter Street.

Her mother wouldn't show her battered face outside their tiny, terraced home in the days that followed a beating. It mattered to her that the neighbours didn't think badly of her husband even though the walls of the houses on either side of them were paper thin. So instead, she'd keep one of her daughters home from school to take care of all the daily chores that required venturing outside.

What baffled Evelyn was the excuses her mother made for their father.

It was the war that changed him.

It wasn't his fault.

He didn't mean to lash out, but the drink changed him.

He was a sick man. And so it would go.

The one time Evelyn had asked if gambling was part of that equation too, she'd received a slap. Lizzy had looked as shocked by her actions as Evelyn.

Didn't the Bible say do unto others as you would have them do unto you? Evelyn had thrown at her mother on another occasion. Lizzy had shot back that it also stated we were to forgive as God forgave us and that it wasn't Evelyn's place to question her father. She needed to know her place. Evelyn hadn't forgotten the sting of that slap and had stopped pushing for answers where her dad was concerned. That didn't mean she accepted things though, far from it because she couldn't forgive.

She worried that this made her a bad person in the Lord's eyes. She'd tried, but she couldn't. It would take more than a wink, a joke and a slice of the cake brought home from the new Sayers Bakery that had opened on the Aintree Road to make her giggle like her mam and her sisters. Never mind, it was meat they needed for the scouse, not cake.

She might be a child, but she knew that without what her mam brought in there'd be more nights than not when they'd go to bed hungry. Still, her father complained about the constant humming of the machine shouting about a man's home being his castle, and how he should be able to find peace in it.

There were so many things that bubbled inside Evelyn, words she'd like to hurl at him but would never dare.

Her greatest fear was their mam would die like her friend Lizzy's mam had. Tuberculosis killed her, and Lizzy's family felt her loss keenly. If their mam were to succumb to sickness, Evelyn didn't know how they'd survive without her.

The familiar lyrics of 'Christmas in the Trenches' sounded. They were faint at first but grew steadily louder. Evelyn froze. Her father had a strong voice even when the drink weakened it.

No, she couldn't forgive, and she vowed to find a way to take her sisters and her mother and clamber out of their life here at 46 Potter Street before it was too late.

Something terrible was going to happen if she didn't. Evelyn could feel it in her waters.

Part One

Chapter One

LIVERPOOL, APRIL 1982

The door to Brides of Bold Street jingled open and the gust of wind it let in stirred the silk fabric of the dress on display on the shop floor.

'How're you, Sabs?' Florence bellowed, having forgotten she had her earphones on as she listened to her Walkman.

The Bootle Tootlers had had a whip-round and presented Florence with it to use when she jogged as a thank you for being their manager, but Flo never had the flippin' things off her head, Sabrina mused. Her friend had informed her the gift had put Bossy Bev's nose right out of joint. After all, she was the president of Weight Watcher's Bootle branch, not Florence. The Bootle Tootlers were a breakaway group, and all she'd got by way of a thank you for her dedicated service to the business of weight loss was a Terry's Chocolate Orange. Florence told Sabrina it served her right for being so bossy.

Sabrina swallowed the Opal Fruit she'd been chewing and tapped her ears, indicating Florence's headphones. 'Take them off, girl!' She closed the Vogue Summer Brides pattern book and put it back in its rightful place on the shelf alongside the other heavy bridal fashion books.

Florence gave her a sheepish grin, shouting, 'Sorry!' and pushing stop on the Walkman. She removed the headphones. 'I was listening to Yazoo. Tony loaned their new tape to me. I luv that diary song of theirs.' She began to croon it, but unfortunately, she was no Alison Moyet because another bellowing sounded from the workroom out the back.

'Florence Teesdale, you sound like a cat being strangled, and it's a good job we're closed because you'd frighten customers away with that caterwauling.'

'Sorry, Aunt Evie,' Florence called back, not in the least bit apologetic as she flashed a grin at Sabrina.

'So.' Sabrina smirked. 'Tony loaned you the tape did he?'

'You can cut that out.' Florence's hand came to rest on her ample chest, and she added dramatically. 'Me heart belongs to Tim.'

Sabrina frowned because, be that as it may, Tim's heart didn't belong to Florence. Adam had told her he was getting serious about Linda, who'd moved on from the Farrah Flick and was a fan of the crimping iron these days. She hadn't the heart to tell Flo this, though but wished she'd take the blinkers off. Despite his sprayed-on jeans, Tony was a nice guy. He was good-looking in a quiet way and smitten with her. They got on well too. He made Flo laugh, and there was a lot to be said for a fella who made you laugh.

Whenever Sabrina broached the Tony topic, Florence would trot out her latest horoscope reading in *Cosmo*. She could always interpret something in there that gave her hope. This month would be the month Tim would realise the girl of his dreams was Florence Teesdale.

She appraised her friend's outfit. 'Is that skirt new?'

'Bought it on my lunch break, didn't I, girl.' Florence said.

'Well, you look smashing, and I luv your boots.' She'd been with Flo when she'd hummed and hawed over splurging on them.

Florence struck a pose, and Sabrina laughed.

'What's with the smell?' Florence sniffed the air. 'It's like a florist's shop in here.'

'Chanel No. 5, Giorgio, L'Air du Temps and Oscar. One of our customers had each of her bridesmaids have a squirt of the fragrances she liked at Lewis's before coming here and then asked me to pick one,' Sabrina said, counting them off on her fingers.

'Which did you pick, then?'

'Chanel No. 5 because it's soft and elegant, and this bride's going to need all the help she can get.'

Florence laughed.

'I've still gorra tally up. You can head upstairs if you like. I won't be long.' Sabrina moved towards the antique oak table that served as the counter.

The collection of dainty bone china cups and saucers with delicate patterns arranged on the shelf behind her provided a pretty backdrop. They'd been birthday and Christmas presents for Aunt Evelyn, who refused to drink out of anything else. She was adamant that tea didn't taste the same unless drunk from bone china. Personally, Sabrina thought this a load of rubbish, and she was delighted with the mishappen mug she'd sourced from a thrift shop from which she drank her tea.

Still, she enjoyed hunting out the treasures for her aunt bi-annually. In addition, they provided a talking point with their brides-to-be, which had the bonus of softening the bill when they came to pay!

The interior of Brides of Bold Street had stayed much the same since Aunt Evie opened it as a young woman, but then Sabrina had joined the business. She'd started work in the shop upon leaving school and had bemoaned the antwacky fit-out. Aunt Evie decided it was high time the shop floor had a makeover and told her to go for her life. She'd done just that, transforming the boutique from old-fashioned to quirky, elegant and sumptuous.

The notebook in which she'd not long finished jotting measurements and ideas for one of their summer brides lay open next to the telephone. Tracy Ward of the recommended Chanel No. 5 and backcombed straw-coloured hair was going to be a tricky customer. Sabrina knew the signs.

The first clue had been in the timid behaviour of her bridesmaids, Melanie, Karen and Wendy, who'd not dared voice an opinion when it had come to their dresses. The second had been Tracy's insistence that despite her sturdy frame, Sabrina ensured she looked like the willowy model in the picture snipped from a magazine she'd shoved under her nose. Lastly was the simmering tension beneath the surface, which signalled this bridezilla could blow at any time.

Oh yes, Sabrina knew the signs, but she was well-versed in managing brides-to-be's who were close to the edge. She closed the notebook and slid it in the drawer glancing at the sign in the window. The shop was shut. It was Friday evening, and dappled rays of sunlight were still streaming in through the front window. She was officially off duty now and would soon be out there enjoying the patch of balmy weather they'd been experiencing this last week.

Florence was speaking, she realised, turning her attention to her friend.

'No, you're ahright, queen. I'll have a chat with Aunt Evie while you finish up.'

THE SUMMER POSY

'I won't be long.' Sabrina opened the till to retrieve the wad of pound notes.

Florence wandered through to the workroom where Evelyn was seated at the ancient Singer sewing machine she refused to modernise. The machine whirred and thrummed almost with a life of its own as she fed yellow satin through it. Not wanting to interrupt her, Florence's brown eyes, reminiscent of milk chocolate buttons grazed over her surroundings while she waited for her to finish the seam she was stitching.

A headless mannequin, upon which a full-skirted, fussy, calico toile was draped was posed next to her, and she wondered if that was for the Chanel No. 5 bride Sabrina had mentioned. A row of dresses, protected by plastic sheaths, awaited collection on a rack near the wall, and the shelves were bowed with trays she itched to sift through filled with sequins, crystal, glass beads and pearls. There were reams of rainbow coloured ribbons, fringing and lace applique along with practical spools of cotton, thimbles, tape measures, packets of sewing needles, scissors and a jar chocka full with pens.

The large table used for cutting out patterns dominated the space, and a tray with an empty china cup and saucer along with Sabrina's wonky mug was sat on it. There was also an open packet of Garibaldi biscuits. Florence helped herself. 'I'm starving, me.'

Evelyn reached the end of the seam and Florence observed as she snipped the cotton and turned the stop wheel mechanism towards her to release the dress from the machine. Then, she got up and spread the shiny, yellow monstrosity out on the table.

'A lollipop lady in bad weather if ever there was one, Florence. There's no accounting for taste.' Evelyn pushed the glasses that had slipped down her nose back up.

'That's true, but you're looking luvly in lilac, Aunt Evie.' Florence wished she had a pair of sunglasses she could slip on because that yellow hurt her eyeballs. She pitied the poor bridesmaid who'd be wearing it, and she dragged her gaze back to Aunt Evie. You could mark the days by her shop coats with a different coloured one keeping the days of the working week. Friday's was lilac with a deep purple stripe running through it.

Evelyn peered through the thick lens of her glasses, observing Florence keenly as she gave her the once-over.

Florence braced herself because Aunt Evie didn't hold back.

'I'm surprised your mam let you out of the house showing that much leg, young lady,' Evelyn tutted.

'I'm twenty-two, Aunt Evie, I can wear what I like, and it's not that short.' Despite herself, Florence tugged the back of her new neon pink skirt down. Her mam *would* have had something to say if she'd seen her, as would her dad. 'No daughter of mine's leaving the house looking like she's from

THE SUMMER POSY

Scottie Road.' was what he'd said the last time she'd flounced out of the door in a frilly mini. And Florence would have wished yet again she could save the deposit she needed to get into a flat of her own as she banged the door shut behind her. Things like new clobber, shoes, records, makeup and hair products kept sabotaging her savings though.

So, rather than go home, Florence had come straight from the shipping company's office where she worked, having got changed in the loo. So far as she was concerned, Monday was soon enough to see her boring navy skirt, white shirt and sensible shoes again. Feeling like a butterfly emerging from its chrysalis, she'd stepped forth from the loos, nearly colliding with her boss, Mr Steel. He'd cleared his throat and looked very hot and bothered at the sight of one of the company's secretaries exposing so much leg. Florence had giggled halfway to Bold Street over his flustered manner.

'Well, I hope you didn't pay too much for it, given how little fabric was used,' Evelyn snipped.

'Ra-ras are in fashion, Aunt Evie.' Florence rolled her eyes.

'What's a ra-ra when it's at home?'

'Ignore her,' Sabrina called out before Florence could reply. She was standing behind the till, counting out the coins. 'You're wasting your breath trying to explain. You want to have heard her going on about my new jumpsuit.'

'I can hear you, you know, Sabrina, and in my day, the jumpsuit was something worn to work in the factories during the war, not on an evening out with a young man.' Evelyn shook her head, despairing of the youth of today as she asked Florence, 'Where are you two off to this evening anyway?'

'We're meeting up with the Bootle Tootlers for an early tea at the Golden Dragon in China Town to ask them if they'd like to be part of the modelling gig for Esmerelda. It's in a fortnight, you know.' Florence was looking forward to a chicken chow mein. It always made her feel worldly when she sat in the Chinese restaurant as though it were the sort of thing she did every day instead of twice a year if she was lucky. The meeting was hush-hush because nobody in the group was sure of the calorie count in a Chinese and they didn't want a lecture from Bossy Bev, who was sure to know. 'And then we're off to catch up with the lads down at The Swan.'

'I do know it's only a week away as it happens, Florence. You and Sabrina have mentioned the show every opportunity you've had. Esmerelda's been bending my ear about it for the last however many Wednesday evenings too. So I'll be glad when it's done and dusted.'

Florence grinned, and Evelyn busied herself, carefully rolling the lace lying unravelled on the table. 'Oh, that's gorgeous, that is.'

THE SUMMER POSY

'It's Irish lace.' Evelyn picked it up to place it back on the shelf. 'Hand made with a hook the way it's supposed to be. None of your machine rubbish.'

'Can I have a look?' Florence stepped around the table to stand next to Evelyn.

'It was Queen Victoria who put Irish lace on the world map.' Evelyn repeated what the little Irish woman who supplied it had told her. 'The tool used to make it's called a famine hook. It's a sewing needle with a broken eye in a wooden handle. Crocheting the lace helped many an Irish woman ward off starvation for her family during the potato famine. And see this here.' She rested her hand on the petal-shaped design in the lace. 'These motifs are unique to each family, and they're a closely guarded secret, but it's a dying skill in Ireland these days.' Her grey curls, carefully set each week, bobbed as she shook her head sadly.

'What a shame,' Florence agreed, seeing the intricate work through new eyes. She'd tried to do a tapestry of a kitten once but had got fed up and never finished it. 'I'd luv that on my wedding dress.'

'Have I missed something, Florence?'

Florence laughed, 'Chance would be a fine thing. You'd be the first to know, well, second or third anyway. But, of course, I'd have to tell me mam and dad and Sabs first. It will be her making her way down the aisle before me though. It's only a matter of time before Adam pops the question, I think.' Florence prattled on, and Evelyn turned away so she wouldn't see her frowning as she put the lace away on the shelf.

'So, what have you got planned this evening then, Aunt Evie?'

Evelyn was glad to get off the topic of Adam and Sabrina. She'd not told Sabrina that Adam's father, Ray Taylor had been to see her while she and Adam were gone, having stepped back in time for what Sabrina promised was the last time. He didn't want her to tell Adam and Sabrina the secret they shared. She could understand his reluctance. After all, he'd spent his life distancing himself from the events that had shaped both their lives. Well, almost. He'd not been able to stay away from her. The past bound them together. Now the future looked likely to tie Adam and Sabrina together, and their story needed to be shared. Evelyn wanted a clear conscience, and she knew, deep down, Ray did too.

Thinking about how she'd go about telling Sabrina made her head hurt, and so she thought of the Woodbine ciggy waiting for her upstairs along with a fresh brew instead. 'My slippers and a spot of tele will do me. *The Good Life*'s on at seven. I've a luvly salmon steak to have for dinner too.'

Florence pinched another Garibaldi. 'Me dad likes that programme too, but Mam says it's Felicity Kendall's bum in those jeans of hers he really likes.'

Sabrina appeared then. 'Right, that's me done.' She picked up the tea tray, 'C'mon, youse two.'

Florence dutifully headed towards the stairs outside the workroom that led up to their flat.

'I'll be up in a minute.' Evelyn sat down heavily at the table. Sabrina registered the flash of pain on her aunt's face, and the teacup rattled in its saucer as she hesitated. 'You ahright there, Aunt Evie?'

'I'm a box of birds, Sabrina, don't fuss,' Evelyn flapped her hand. 'It's a touch of housemaid's knee is all.'

'You should get that checked out,' Sabrina admonished because it wasn't the first time she'd noticed her aunt's knee bothering her.

'It's called age, Sabrina. I'm not wasting the doctor's time moaning about my aches and pains. Now, go, you'll be late for your meal if you don't get them upstairs and get yourself changed.'

Knowing better than to argue, Sabrina did as she was told.

Evelyn watched her go. Her knee was bothering her, but it was Florence's throwaway remark about Adam proposing to Sabrina that was bothering her more. It had given her a sense of urgency. Her eyes alighted on the notebook Sabrina used for jotting down ideas and sketches. She'd not been able to start the conversation she needed to have with her, but could she write it down instead?

Chapter Two

Evelyn hauled herself up the stairs. It felt good to have made a decision, and she was oblivious to her knee paining her as with each laboured step, she became more certain writing her story made perfect sense. Things could get jumbled in the telling of a tale, and she wanted Sabrina to understand—needed her to understand the part Ray Taylor had played in her life.

She'd not had much experience when it came to writing, other than the odd letter or two over the years. But how hard could it be to commit her own story to paper? An autobiography of sorts. It would be more colourful than any of those Hollywood stars' tell-alls.

She hobbled into the flat, closing the door separating their little flat from the stairwell with its exit onto Wood Street. A brew was in order, and then she'd dig out a writing pad. Sabrina, bless her, had knocked the kettle on, knowing she'd be up in a moment. By the time she'd hung her shop coat up and discarded her shoes in favour of slippers, it was whistling. She was a good girl, Evelyn thought, running the hot tap until the water heated so she could fill the teapot and let it warm for a moment.

Whatever Florence was on about had Sabrina giggling, she thought, smiling at the laughter from Sabrina's bedroom.

Those two had never been any different; their school reports were a testament to that. If Sabrina spent as much time on her school work as she did giggling with Florence Teesdale, she'd be top of the class the teachers used to write in the comments. Florence's had said much the same. Her smile faded as she poured the boiling water over the teabags. What would it be like when Sabrina left home. It would happen one of these days. She didn't like to think about how empty the place would feel without her in it.

'You managed before, Evelyn Flooks. You'll manage perfectly well again.' she told herself sternly. Indeed, she'd lived here alone in the flat above the bridal shop premises on Bold Street she'd secured as a nineteen year old for years before Sabrina had come into her life. She'd always prided herself on her independence. Oh, but how different her middling years would have been if not for Sabrina. The little girl she'd found outside Cripps, the dressmaker's, had swiftly secured a place in her heart, and before Evelyn had known it, she'd thought of her as a daughter.

Your children are only on loan, Evelyn, Ida had said when Evelyn had been commiserating with her over her daughter. Marie had married and moved to some godforsaken village in the wilds of Wales. That had been years ago now, but the words had never left her because it was true.

Her tea was just how she liked it by the time Sabrina and Florence emerged from Sabrina's bedroom. They wafted into the kitchen in a cloud of that Charlie perfume they were so keen on gassing themselves and everybody in their vicinity with. Sabrina had artfully tousled her hair into the shag cut she favoured these days and had been heavy-handed with the eye makeup too, Evelyn noticed. Her unusual whisky coloured eyes were her best feature, and they didn't need all that muck around them, but who was she to say anything? Sabrina was a grown woman of twenty-two, after all.

'What's that you're wearing, then? It looks like a shirt from him next door,' Evelyn asked, referencing pompous Mr Barlow, who owned the menswear shop wedged next to Brides of Bold Street. She peered at Sabrina's outfit overtop of her glasses much as she'd done Florence earlier and added, 'And one with shoulders to fit an Olympic swimmer to boot.'

'Ta very much, Aunt Evie. It's a shirt dress with shoulder pads for your information,' Sabrina said, adjusting the pads so they sat squarely on her shoulders before fiddling with the wide red belt she'd used to cinch her outfit in around her waist. 'What have you got for your dinner?' she asked, keen to get her off the topic of fashion.

'A nice bit of salmon, and I'll boil those new potatoes to have on the side with some peas.'

'Well enjoy,' Sabrina leaned in and brushed her lips over her aunt's soft, powdery cheek wiping off the glossy red stain she'd left behind, 'And enjoy your programmes too.'

Evelyn wasn't sure she'd have time for *The Good Life* now, not with the project she'd tasked herself with.

Florence gave her a quick squeeze, having forgiven her earlier comments about showing too much leg.

'Enjoy yourselves. And, Sabrina, don't be too late in. You were a bear with a sore head last Saturday, and we're going to be busy tomorrow.'

Sabrina winced at the memory. She'd no wish to repeat it this Saturday, and besides, she was going out for dinner first, that would soak up the pints down The Swan later.

Evelyn had deposited her cuppa on the tray table and was about to sink into her seat when two heads bobbed back in the door.

'What've you forgotten? And why do you look like the cat that got the cream, Florence?'

Florence was beaming from ear to ear. 'Sabs didn't do the light thing, Aunt Evie. Can you believe it?'

'It's true. I didn't,' Sabrina confirmed, a wonderous note in her voice. 'I didn't even realise I hadn't until Flo stopped me halfway down the stairs to say so.'

'You didn't switch the light on and off, you mean?' Evelyn asked, not sure if she believed what she was hearing. She was as used to Sabrina's quirks as she was the humming of her sewing machine or the ticking of the carriage clock on the mantle.

Sabrina reminded Evelyn of that Enid Blyton children's storybook character she'd loved when she was small as she nodded. 'And, now that I think about it, Aunt Evie, I haven't been checking things either, not since Adam and I got back, you know, from nineteen forty-five.' She'd only been home a few weeks, but in that time, her rituals had been abandoned, and it hadn't even dawned on her. The compulsions triggered by panic that something awful would happen if she didn't perform them had upped and left. She no longer needed to flick the lights on and off three times each time she turned them on or to check the heater was off at the wall or the element on the cooktop turned off. Just thinking of them all made her exhausted!

Evelyn forgot about sitting down as she hugged Sabrina, who was dizzy with liberation at the thought of leaving the flat without having to run through her checklist.

'I wonder if it's to do with you finding out what happened to your mam,' Florence mulled.

Sabrina stepped back from Evelyn and shrugged. Perhaps it was down to knowing the truth about what had happened on Bold Street when she was a child. Maybe it was this that had allowed her to shed the anxiety that had plagued her for as long as she could remember. To know she hadn't been abandoned after all but instead separated from her mam by the street's mysterious timeslip forces.

'It doesn't matter why it happened. It only matters it's happened.' Florence said before seeing the time and shrieking, 'Eee, girl, we're going to be late, c'mon.'

'Bye, Aunt Evie,' they called out for the second time, shutting the door behind them.

Evelyn stood there a moment longer, listening to the clatter down the stairs.

It had terrified her each time Sabrina had ventured back to the past searching for her mother. She knew what had happened now and had made her peace with it. It was time for her to do the same. There were things she needed to get off her chest. Secrets held for too long, but first things first, a ciggy and that brew before it got cold.

Chapter Three

Sabrina and Florence chatted as, with their arms linked, they made their way along Duke Street, oblivious to the admiring glances they were on the receiving end of. Well, almost. They had dressed to impress after all. Sabrina had splurged on new slouchy boots too, but unlike Flo who'd thought the spiked heels made her legs look longer, she'd opted for flats, something she was glad about as her friend staggered alongside her.

It was a glorious evening. The sky was a heady blue, and the temperature was that perfect mix between warm and hot. The faces of people walking past reflected good humour thanks to the balmy weather. The soft summer-come-early light was good for the soul, Sabrina decided. It ironed out the wrinkles of winter.

Florence, leaning on Sabrina for balance as much as friendship, was busy filling her in on the injustice of her mam hiding her new Berlin tape.

'Why did she do that, then?' Sabrina asked, avoiding the fresh pigeon dropping that had landed on the pavement a step ahead of her. At least it had missed her head! She'd never understood why it was considered lucky to have bird poo land on your head.

'Nice boots, luv,' a lad whose eyes were hidden behind Wayfarers muttered. He and his mate were walking towards them, and his pal, wearing an identical pair of sunglasses, sniggered as they veered around the girls.

'Do one,' Florence tossed over her shoulder as they grinned back at her. 'The flamin' things are beginning to rub,' she said, turning to Sabrina.

'I've got some plasters in my bag. We'll sort you out when we get to the restaurant. G'won then, tell me why your mam took the tape.'

'Because Shona and Teresa started making sexy noises about the house, that's why. You know from that sex song some of the radio stations have banned. Mam said it was disgusting music, and what would the neighbours think?'

Sabrina giggled, picturing the terrible twins as Flo called her younger sisters getting about the house making rude noises.

'It's not funny, Sabs. I think she's destroyed it because I've looked in all the usual hiding places, and it's not there. I paid nearly eight pounds for it.' Her sigh went all the way down to the pointed tips of her new boots. 'I'm desperate to move out and get a flat of me own where those muppets can't sneak into me room and nick me stuff. I'm a woman of twenty-two whose mam still confiscates me things. It's a tragedy, is what it is.'

'You'll have to stop blowing your wages on new clobber and ankle boots then,' Sabrina stated, knowing full well Flo had it too good at home to move out.

'I want to impress Tim, don't I, kid? And I can't have him seeing me wear the same outfit twice. Do you think he'll like me hair?' The inch of regrowth, now Florence had decided to grow the blonde out, was on-trend, and she'd spiked her newly shortened hair ferociously. It suited her even if the twins said she looked like an angry porcupine.

'Who cares what he thinks. You look gorgeous, girl.'

'I care. And did I tell you, me dad's on about putting a ladder under me window with twenty quid attached to it to tempt the fella's my way because he's sick of my carry-on with the twins? Of course, they thought that was hilarious.' She shook her head. 'I caught them making a cardboard sign to stick in the front room window with Florence loves Tony written on it! They'd coloured in a big red heart and all.'

Sabrina grinned. 'At least you caught them in time.'

'Yeah, that would have been embarrassing. It's tricky enough with Tony because I do like him, and I don't want to hurt his feelings.'

'Unrequited luv,' Sabrina stated.

'Yeah, and don't I know all about that?' Florence said glumly. 'That's why I had to play the sex song. It's the closest I get to the real thing.'

Sabrina squeezed her arm and laughed. 'Sorry, Flo, I shouldn't laugh, but I keep thinking about the twins making you-know-what noises.'

'Orgasm,' Flo said in a voice that made a lad with his collar turned up like a preppy American college student nearly trip over his own feet. 'I tell you, Sabs, it's like being in flamin' MI5 living with them two. I'm exhausted from constantly having to thwart their attacks. If I had a flat, I could play whatever music I like. There'd be no twins to worry about and—'

'You'd have to feed yourself and do your own washing.'

'There is that, and I'd miss Mam's scone's.'

They lapsed into companionable silence. Sabrina thought how much she'd have liked to have siblings to spar with. That didn't mean she didn't love her life with Aunt Evie in the flat above the bridal shop. It was the life she knew, and the flat was home, just as Flo's noisy terraced house was her second home.

Sabrina enjoyed the argy-bargy of family life at the Teesdales'.

Her mind threatened to wander down the path that would lead her to her mother, Fern, and the half-brother and sister, along with a stepfather who would never know she existed. The family whom she'd met in nineteen forty-five the last time she'd wandered back in time seeking answers. Only that last time, she'd had Adam by her side when she'd finally learned the truth of what happened to her mam all those years ago.

But, while she'd solved that mystery, finding the answers she'd looked for had come at a cost because they'd shown her what she'd lost.

Fern had never told her husband, Kenneth, the truth about where she'd come from or about Sabrina. Sabrina had agreed with her that it was best if her siblings, Sarah and Alfie, didn't know their story either. So she'd known when she said goodbye to Fern, she'd never see her or Sarah and Alfie again. She'd never meet Kenneth, the man for whom her mother had given up her life in nineteen eighty-four to build a new one with him, but knew he must be special for her to love him so deeply. There was comfort in knowing she'd been wanted because Fern had begged her to stay and be part of their lives. They could figure it all out, she'd said, but Sabrina had made her decision.

Adam's hand had held hers as they traversed the pocket on Bold Street outside Cripps until fate, for whatever reason, had seen fit to allow them to step back to their own time where they belonged.

Here, now, was where she belonged, she knew this, but still, it was hard to accept the sacrifices she'd had to make.

There was something else she'd figured out too. Fern must have died before time caught up to the day they'd become separated. She couldn't have lived to see nineteen-sixty-three for a second time. If she had, she'd have come and fetched her three-year-old daughter from where she was waiting for her mam outside Cripps. If she'd lived, she'd never have been found by Aunt Evie.

This time, Flo squeezed her arm as she sensed her friend's mood dip. Sabrina squeezed it back and resolved to pack those thoughts away. Didn't she have Aunt Evie, Flo, who was as much a sister as anyone could be, the Teesdales and Adam? Her lovely Adam. She couldn't wait to see him down at The Swan later. It had been three whole days since she'd last seen him because he'd been around at Tim's every evening with Tony.

Tim and Tony were helping him get his Triumph Bonneville up to speed for the Isle of Man TT. They were heading over for Mad Sunday on the first Sunday in June, a free-for-all when bikers could push themselves to the limit on the course that was open to the public for the whole day. Sabrina thought it sounded flippin' mad. Then, they planned on watching the racing for the rest of the week.

She'd never thought she'd have a motorcycle as a love rival either. But at the moment, she was feeling decidedly second best to Adam's Triumph, and she wasn't sure how she felt about him riding the TT circuit. She might not know much about it, but she did know people had been injured, even killed in it. The lads were bound to push themselves to the limit, each determined to outrace the other. It would have been nice to be invited to go with him, but there'd been no mention of this. She could have been his support person, providing him with bananas and water or was that cycling? He clearly preferred the idea of a lads' weekend away though.

It wasn't long before she and Florence reached the enormous, colourful Chinese arch spanning Nelson Street presided over by two bronze lions. Florence was hobbling as they wandered under it and began counting the street numbers of the businesses lining either side of the street.

'I knew I should have worn them about the house for a few nights to break them in.' She glanced at Sabrina's boots enviously. 'This is us.' She came to a halt outside a nondescript three-storey brick building. The two upper floors had sash windows between which an unlit neon sign in Chinese dangled. The ground floor that housed the restaurant was painted cream and could have been home to a corner shop for all its exoticness. A sign in the front window informed them they'd found the Golden Dragon, and Florence yanked the door open. Sabrina followed her in and as it closed behind them, they swapped looks.

'I feel like I've left Liverpool behind,' Florence whispered, not quite sure why she felt the need to lower her voice.

'Me too. It's not what you'd expect from the outside. It's like we've arrived in China.' Sabrina inhaled the unusual spices along with a lungful of cigarette smoke floating above a nearby table of men in business suits. She noted they'd all loosened their ties and slung their jackets over the backs of their chairs. The table was full of empty glasses waiting to be cleared, and one red-faced man of indeterminable years was waving his glass in the direction of the waitress for a refill.

'A Butlins camp in Shanghai.' Florence eyeballed a table filled with children munching wontons they were dunking in a glowing red sauce while their parents picked out the cashew nuts from their chicken dishes.

The Golden Dragon's tables were packed together and the restaurant was busy, which was to be expected on a Friday night. The clientele was a mixed bag. One or two groups gingerly stabbed at the dishes whizzing past on the lazy Susan centrepiece with their chopsticks. There were tables full of work colleagues putting the past week to bed as they helped themselves to plates of sticky sweet chicken. Over in the far corner near the front window, a rowdy group of girls were exclaiming as they read their fortunes from the cookies they were snapping apart.

Sabrina and Florence watched admiringly as a few Chinatown locals clacked their chopsticks with aplomb before oohing over the décor. It was plush and shone boldly with red and gold, the tables were laid with white and red cloths, and red lanterns were strewn about the place. The interior felt authentic compared to the bland exterior, and a plump, gold cat waved its paw at them by the counter.

'They're for luck those.' Sabrina elbowed Florence and pointed to the cat. She wasn't sure how she knew this piece of trivia; she just did.

'There's Janice and the others over there.' Florence headed towards the table near the suits, where Janice was waving at them enthusiastically. You couldn't miss her in her Bootle Tootlers tee shirt. She was a well-endowed woman for one thing, and for another, the shirt was canary yellow with Bootle Tootlers emblazoned in black so she looked like a well-fed bumblebee. One or two other Tootlers seated at the tables, pushed together to accommodate the group's booking, had decided to don their shirts too.

Sabrina would have refused to come if Florence had made noises about them wearing theirs out. Having to jog in them twice a week was bad enough given the nasty, cheap fabric that clung in all the wrong places.

Florence pulled the seat out at the head of the table as befitted her role as manager of the Bootle Tootlers. Sabrina sat next to her, immediately regretting her choice of seating because Sharon on her right was wearing the tee shirt, and she had a thing about deodorant, as in she refused to use it. From the whiff Sabrina was getting, she wouldn't have been surprised to learn Shaz, as everyone called her, had jogged to the Golden Dragon. She'd have to breathe through her mouth for the duration of her meal.

The two girls greeted everybody, and seeing an empty seat still at the table, Sabrina asked, 'Who are we waiting on?'

'Carol,' Joyce, across from her, said. 'She's always late.'

'She's here now. Over here, Caz,' Janice shouted over with much jiggling, causing one of the suits to miss his mouth with his drink.

Carol, whose ambition in joining the weekly jogging group had been to see her toes when she stood in the shower once more beamed as she bounced on over.

'Hiya, Caz,' Florence said, automatically taking charge as the older woman reached their tables. 'How're you?'

Carol did a twirl. 'Fabulous, ta very much. And I'll have youse lot know I'm wearing a dress I haven't fit into since I wore it to our kid's christening.'

Sabrina couldn't help but wonder what year that had been as the zig-zagging orange and brown pattern of the polyester fabric made her eyes go funny. She joined in the clapping, and Carol curtsied before sitting down.

'We haven't ordered yet,' Janice said, raising her glass, 'But my vodka lemonade's hitting the spot. It's very low cal is vodka,' she added wisely.

Nobody mentioned the fizzing lemonade.

'Oi, a girl could die of thirst,' Patty piped up, waving out at one of the waitresses working the room in her uniform of red top and black trousers. Her hair came to her chin in a jet black bob, and it was hard to guess her age, but Sabrina guessed she was probably a student. The dainty young woman cocked her head to one side, introducing herself as Bai, before politely asking what those who didn't already have a beverage in front of them would like to drink.

'Malibu and Coke, ta, luv.'

'Pernod and black, queen.'

'Babycham for me, girl.'

'It's a good job, Bossy Bev's not here,' Florence said. 'She'd be having fits at all the calories you've ordered. I have to say you're a brave woman on the Pernod and black, Gina. Me and Sabs promised we'd never touch the stuff again a few years ago. I'll have a cider, ta, Bai.'

'Me, too, cheers, Bai.' Sabrina nodded, trying not to remember the night she and Florence had got stuck into the Pernod and black and wound up on a table back to back screeching out Pat Benatar's 'Heartbreaker' at some club they'd never had the front to return to. She'd woken up on the floor of Flo's bedroom with the twins standing over her with a whistle. Mr Teesdale had given them special permission to use it as punishment for her and Flo both having thrown up in the front garden on their way in.

Menus were snapped open.

'They've only gone and spelt Pecking Duck wrong,' Peggy announced. 'Flamin' 'eck, I didn't win any prizes in spelling, but even I know there's a 'c' in it.'

'I'm going to have the lemon chicken. I luv lemon chicken me.'

'Fried lice, for me.'

Sabrina and Florence exchanged a glance. Worldly, the Bootle Tootlers were not. Janice of the fried lice thought she was a right comedian, and Sabrina realised she was gritting her teeth when Bai reappeared with their drinks. She only unclenched her jaw when she'd taken their meal orders, and Janice had managed to refrain from making any further witty remarks as she ordered her rice. General chatter resumed as Bai glided off towards the kitchens.

'Right,' Florence said, tapping her glass with a spoon the way her dad did on occasion when he wanted to get their attention. It worked a treat.

'I asked you all along tonight for a reason.'

'Not just to get up Bev's nose then?' Janice piped up with a wink at the other girls, who all dutifully laughed.

'There was that.'

More laugher rippled, and once it had died off, Florence said, 'How would you lot like to take a turn down the catwalk a week this Friday?'

'Wha? Like models, you mean?' Peggy asked.

'Like Faces of the Eighties?' Gina breathed.

'What about me eyebrows?' Janice enquired, and everybody turned to look at her mean little brows.

'What about your eyebrows?' Florence asked, feeling they were getting off track now.

'All them models have caterpillar eyebrows. They didn't pluck them within an inch of their life when they were teenagers.'

Florence thought that 'all them' models were also stick thin and hovering around the six-foot mark, not five foot two and a half. She held her hand up so she could finish what she'd started. 'Do you know Esmerelda's Emporium on Bold Street?'

There was a consensus that yes, they did know it. It was hard to miss, after all, with its vibrant window displays and equally colourful owner.

'Well, Esmerelda's hosting a fashion show for the summer garments she's got coming in at the emporium, and she's asked Sabrina and me to model them, but she needs at least ten to twelve women in total, like, to showcase the new clobber.'

'Will we get paid?' Patsy, who barely said a word most of the time, asked. She had a reputation for disappearing just before it was her turn to get the round in. So Florence would be keeping an eye on her when it came time to split the bill.

'Payment is a silk scarf, and there's a dress rehearsal at her shop this Sunday.'

'Well, I'm in,' said Janice.

'And me,' and so it went until all eyes settled on Patsy.

'I s'pose I could put the scarf away as a Christmas present for me, mam-in-law.'

'What's with the short notice?' Caz asked. 'We could all be busy. It's a Friday night after all.'

'And are you?' Florence asked.

'I'd have to check me diary.'

'Oh shurrup, Caz,' Janice said. 'You know you only go down the pub on a Friday night. We're all in, right, girls?'

'Right!'

The excited chatter was still bouncing around the table when their meals were presented. All modelling talk was suspended as attempts were made with chopsticks to skewer rice, chicken and vegetables with little success.

'Pretend you're knitting with one hand,' Peggy piped up, dropping the piece of lemon chicken she was demonstrating on her lap. 'Bugger.'

'Eee, I'll be putting me hand up for the swimsuit section at this rate,' Janice said. 'All I've managed to get in me gob so far is one of those red things there.'

'Capsicum,' Gina supplied.

'Bai,' Shaz raised her arm to wave out and Sabrina's eyes to water. 'Could I have a fork, please?'

'Me too, ta very much,' ten people chorused around the table.

The food disappeared at a rate of knots once they'd been supplied with the pronged utensils.

'Will there be hair and makeup on hand?' Shaz asked, putting her fork down.

'What about one of them dressers too? You know to help us change into our outfits,' Janice enquired.

Florence gave an enigmatic smile and said, 'Leave it with me, ladies.'

Sabrina frowned, wondering what she had up her sleeve because Esmerelda hadn't mentioned anything about hair and makeup. She'd assumed they'd be doing their own and she certainly hadn't said a word about professional dressers. Esmerelda's Emporium wasn't exactly in the league of the big fashion houses. It would be an intimate soiree of her best clients, not Paris fashion week.

Florence caught her expression and nudged her with her boot under the table. 'I've gorra plan,' she whispered with a wink.

Chapter Four

The Bootle Tootlers piled out of the Golden Dragon, unwrapping the free mints from the dish by the till.

'How much does it cost to get your legs waxed then?' Patsy asked as she stood on the pavement outside the restaurant, lifting her slacks' hem to peer at her shins.

Peggy, who'd joked about the cobwebs in Patsy's purse when she'd opened it to pay her share for dinner, replied primly, 'Our mam always said, "A penny saved is a penny earned."'

In a miniskirt with smooth, albeit orange-streaked legs, Gina filled Patsy in.

'Eee, I can't believe I'm going to be a model. Wait until I get home and tell our George.' Janice jiggled with the excitement of it.

'It might be your lucky night when he hears that, eh, Janice?'

Ribald cackles sounded outside the Golden Dragon, where the Tootlers were in the process of saying their goodnights.

Shaz stretched and yawned, nearly knocking poor Gina out, who only came to the other woman's armpit.

'Don't forget dress rehearsal this Sunday at Esmerelda's Emporium on Bold Street at—'

'Two o'clock,' the Tootlers chimed.

Florence grinned and linked her arm through Sabrina's once more. 'Right, see you then. It's time for us to luv you and leave you.'

'Youse two behave yourselves,' Janice threw after them.

The others called out, 'See ya Sunday, ta-ra!'

Florence and Sabrina agreed it was good to walk their meal off as they set off in the direction of Wood Street. Since she'd been jogging, Sabrina could once more slip her little finger down the waistband of her Calvin Kleins. The bi-weekly jogging sessions were perjury while puffing and panting around North Park, but she was beginning to reap the rewards now.

Once the Tootlers were out of earshot, Sabrina remembered her friend's cryptic comment before their meal had been served.

'What's this plan you were on about then, Florence Teesdale?'

'I've come up with an angle for getting our hair and makeup done for the show free of charge.'

'What angle?' Sabrina turned to her best mate in the nick of time to haul her upright before she went over on her ankle.

'Think about it, Sabs. Publicity.'

'But Esmerelda said it was going to be small, for her top clients only.'

'Sabs, I don't know how you manage to sell anything. You need to put a spin on it.'

'I don't have to sell as such. Me customers already know what they want. It's more advice and direction—'

'Shurrup for a minute and listen would you.'

Sabrina buttoned her lips.

'If we were to have a word in the ear of management at Lewis's or Blacklers—'

'Or George Henry Lee's,' Sabrina butted in, getting in the swing of things.

'You're getting the gist of it now, girl. We could convince them to let us borrow some of their make-up counter girls by telling them they'll get a mention in the local press.'

'Is there going to be a photographer there then?'

'Dunno, but Esmerelda's bound to want a picture in the paper. It's free advertising. So, all we have to do is ring the paper and tee it up. Bossy Bev managed to get the Bootle Tootlers in the newspaper. I don't see why we can't too. A fashion show's far more glam than a jog around the park.'

'And,' Sabrina was feeling excited, 'we could go around a few of the upmarket hair salons too and ask if any of their juniors would like a spot of practice as well as getting a mention in the papers.'

'Exactly! But not Top Do with Sue on Church Street. I cried for a week after that butcher's job her apprentice did on me.'

'That was years ago, Flo.'

'Sixteen is a critical year in a girl's life, Sabs. It scarred me. I looked like Friar Tuck in flares at the school disco.'

Sabrina kept a straight face as she affirmed loyally, 'Ahright then, not Top Do with Sue's.' Flo, with her rounded face, had not worn the 'Purdy' pageboy style she'd requested well. Technically it wasn't the poor girl who'd cut her hair's fault because she'd only done what her client instructed her to do, but Flo had needed someone to blame, and Sabrina was her best mate after all. She recalled Mrs Teesdale threatening to smash every mirror in the house if Florence didn't stop bursting into tears every time she caught sight of herself. Dark days indeed. 'What about dressers?' she asked, moving things along.

'Aunt Evie, of course. Who better? Bossy Bev should have to pull her weight too.'

Sabrina smirked.

Florence, realising what she'd said, added, 'For all her calorie counting, she's not exactly fading away, is she. But, given the publicity it will give the Bootle branch of Weight Watchers, she can flamin' well help out.'

'She should,' Sabrina agreed.

'It's exciting!' Florence said as they reached Wood Street. 'Us, models!'

'I know. Who'd have thought it?'

As they neared The Swan, they could hear a thudding beat. A row of motorbikes was lined up outside the pub.

Happiness at the thought of seeing Adam in a few minutes rippled through Sabrina, and she quickened her pace, hoping he was already at the pub.

'Oi, slow down,' Florence said as she was dragged along.

'You won't be able to dawdle down the catwalk, Flo.'

'Right-ho, if you know so much about it, show me how it's done,' Florence teased.

Sabrina, never one to back away from a challenge, pulled her arm free from Florence's, checked the coast was clear and put her hands on her hips. 'Right, watch and learn, girl.' She wiggled her hips and placed one booted foot in front of the other as she strutted over the cobbles.

Florence was bent double. 'Oh my God, girl, I'm wetting meself here. What was that? You reminded me of something off *Wildlife on One*,' she gasped.

'Like a panther, you mean? Cos that's what I was aiming for.' Sabrina swung around with her hands still on her hips as she grinned at her pal.

'No.' Florence shook her head as she straightened. 'More an ostrich.'

'Ta very much. G'won, then let's see you strut your stuff.'

Florence took a deep breath and licked her lips before she too placed her hands on her hips and exaggeratedly wiggled her way towards her friend.

This time it was Sabrina who was convulsing until, as though in slow motion, Florence caught her heel on the cobbles and swayed precariously with her arms windmilling before she hit the stones with a thud.

Sabrina gathered herself, rushing to Florence's aid and, bending over her friend saw her shoulders were shaking. Her stomach dropped. 'Do you think you've broken something, Flo?' She reached for her hand. Florence grasped it and righted herself. Sabrina realised she wasn't crying; she was shaking with laughter. 'You had me worried there.'

'Sorry,' Flo managed through her giggles. 'But what are we like?'

Sabrina began to laugh too.

'We're going to need some practice between now and June.'

'Lots and lots of practice,' Sabrina affirmed. 'And, Flo?'

'Yeah?'

'I think it might pay you not to wear those boots.'

Chapter Five

'I had one of them time-wanderers in today,' Mickey The Swan inn's barman said, in the same manner, he might have dropped, 'I've had a run on the pork scratchings this evening.' He didn't look up from the task of pint pulling. The second glass was already lined up, ready and waiting to be poured. Two of the same. One for Sabrina, one for Florence.

Mickey knew their orders without asking as he did all the pub's regulars. His head shone under the lights as though he'd polished it with baby oil, something Sabrina and Florence had speculated over in the past but would never be so rude as to ask about. The gold tooth he joked was a nugget for his retirement, gleamed. But it was the beard that seemed to have sprouted overnight that was distracting Sabrina.

The new growth decorating his jawline had a decidedly ginger tone to it, and she was unaware she was squinting as she did her best to visualise the bald barman as a younger man with a thatch of red hair. It was proving impossible though, no matter how hard she squinted. Wait until she told Flo Mickey was a redhead, she thought, glancing over at her friend who was twiddling her spiked hair as she waited at a table near the jukebox. Disappointingly there was no sign of Adam and the others, but it wasn't late. He'd be here soon.

'He was dressed like one of them mod fella's from the sixties. You know with the army parka and the long hair covering their ears like a girl's?' Mickey was saying.

'Who was?' Sabrina dragged her gaze from Mickey's dome.

'The time-wanderer who looked like he'd stepped out of the sixties,' Mickey repeated.

He had her full attention now as he slid Sabrina's pint towards her and picked up the empty glass, angling it under the tap just so. 'I thought he looked a proper meff when he walked in and ordered a pint. I shoulda known something was up when he asked if it was happy hour what with the beer being so cheap and ordered another two bevvies.'

Sabrina raised her eyebrows.

'So he was half-bladdered by the time he'd drained them and began demanding to know why Oasis wasn't on the jukebox.'

'Never heard of them.' Sabrina frowned because she prided herself on keeping track of the music chart's top twenty.

'That's what I said to him, and he looked at me like I were gormless and said, 'But, it's nineteen ninety-six, man, the Gallagher brothers, Oasis? "Wonderwall", mate. They're the biggest band in the world.'

Sabrina glanced to her left and right because if anyone were earwigging on their conversation, they'd think they were mad. A fella at the end of the bar swirled the contents of his tumbler then stared at the amber liquid. The intensity of his gaze suggested it contained the answers as to whether there was life on Mars or life after death. But fortunately, he was too far away to hear their conversation. 'Nineteen ninety-six?' She repeated what Mickey had said.

'Nineteen ninety-six,' he confirmed. 'So, I asked him, I did, "what else is going on in nineteen ninety-six?" and he said he'd like to know where I get my wabs from because it must be good. I told him I hadn't smoked weed since my lost year in the seventies.'

The conversation wasn't what Sabrina had bargained on when she'd barrelled through the door of the pub and told Flo she'd get the first round in. Not when she'd intended to put all thoughts of traversing time out of her head for good.

Mickey put the second pint down on the bar top and leaned towards her conspiratorially. 'You won't believe it, but according to him in nineteen ninety-six, mad cow disease is rife here, and Charlie and Di are getting divorced.'

'No!' The mad cow thing had gone over her head, but she was taken aback by the news of a royal split. 'But they're in Australia. I saw it on the news. They look so happy, and they've William to be thinking of too.'

'I'm only repeating what he said.'

The prickling on her arms signalled goosebumps. It had only been a few weeks since, with the help of Adam, she'd found Fern, and in searching for her, she'd wound up in the nineteen twenties, the sixties and forties. The risk she wouldn't be able to return to her own time was one she'd been prepared to take to find out the truth. But from now on, she planned on staying right where she was. And, if that meant taking a wide berth around Hudson's Book Shop for the rest of her days, then so be it.

Mickey didn't know about her journeys back in time. Nobody did apart from Aunt Evie, Adam who'd come with her last time, and Flo, asides from those whom she'd met on her travels. The news that someone else had inadvertently wandered back from the future made her feel strange. She knew how disorientating it was even though she'd been prepared for it! But, of course, the poor lad Mickey was on about wouldn't have known what was going on. She hoped he'd managed to step back to his own time.

'What happened after that then?' she asked, both hands wrapped around the pint glasses, ready to join Florence but wanting to hear the outcome.

Mickey shrugged. 'He said he wasn't hanging about in a pub stuck in a time warp and left. I don't know where he went. I remember you asking me whether I'd ever heard anything strange about people from another time a while back. So that's why I mentioned it. It's the first time anything like that's happened in ages.'

Sabrina gave Mickey a weak smile. She had asked, but those initial enquiries seemed a lifetime ago. 'Thanks, Mickey,' she said, receiving a nod and wink in return. She wondered how Florence would take this news of Diana's split from Charles. She needed to go and commiserate with her.

The floor, as she carried the lagers over, was tacky beneath her feet, and it was as though a thick fog had rolled in as she made her way through the cigarette smoke being exhaled by a group of hard doers putting the world to rights over the music. She emerged from the fug in time to see a lad wiggling his eyebrows at her. He had his sleeves rolled up to show off the tattoos swirling up his arms. Sabrina pretended she hadn't noticed him and focused on not sloshing a drop from either glass as she headed for the table where Flo was sitting.

'You were ages, girl. I thought I was going to die of thirst.' Florence dimpled up at her friend as she placed the drinks down on the beer mats. Then she took a long swallow of her drink to back up her sentiment. 'That's better. It doesn't half make you thirsty the Chinese. I factored the calories for tonight's dinner and a couple of pints into my meal plan for the week,' she said, indicating the golden fizzy liquid.

'Did you?' Sabrina didn't think she wanted to know how many calories were in a pint of lager.

'Did I heck,' Florence giggled. 'But we jogged on Tuesday and Thursday, so that's gorra give me some extra points. So what were you and Mickey gassing about?'

Sabrina relayed the tale of the disgruntled punter and then said, 'You'd better have another swig on that before I tell you what else this lad told Mickey,' Sabrina said.

Concern flickered across Florence's face. 'If you say so.' The glass hovered halfway to her lips. 'But, Sabs, you promised you were done with all of that time stuff since you found Fern.'

'And I am, Flo. I don't go anywhere near Hudson's these days. I cross the road and everything. Anyway,' she lowered her voice, 'It's not about me. It's about the royals, but it's not good news, so are you sure you want me to tell you?'

'The royals?' Florence shifted forward in her seat as David Lee Roth's voice sounded from the jukebox. The music would begin blaring out as the night wore on, but at present, it wasn't so loud that Florence hadn't heard what Sabrina said. A woman with hair an Afghan hound would have been envious of wandered past having finished making her music selection.

'Good choice, queen, I luv a bit of Van Halen, me.' one of the hard doers called out.

'Charles and Di,' Sabrina confirmed.

Florence leant so far forward in her seat she was in danger of face-planting the table, 'G'won then put me out of my misery.'

Sabrina relayed the news of the couple's future divorce, and when she'd finished, Florence had slumped back in her chair.

'I wish I hadn't asked you to tell me now.' She fiddled with the beer mat, processing what she'd been told. 'It can't be true.'

'Ah, sorry, girl, but that's what he said, Flo, and think about it. It can't have been easy for them living in a fishbowl like that. It's bound to take its toll on a marriage,' Sabrina said as if she had first-hand experience of being in the public eye.

'I s'pose you're right, but I'm heartbroken. I mean, what hope is there for the rest of us if they couldn't make it?'

They both gazed glumly at their pints, but Flo, who never stayed down long, perked up as she spied Adam, Tim, Tony and a couple of other fellas breezing in the door and heading straight for the bar. 'The lads are here,' she said before rummaging in her handbag for her jar of Vaseline, which would give her lips a kissable gloss.

Sabrina twisted towards the bar and the smile that took on a life of its own whenever she saw Adam spread across her face.

He waved over and mimed having a drink. Sabrina gestured to her pint glass and shook her head.

'I can't get used to him with that short back and sides cut,' Florence said. 'Not that it doesn't suit him. It's just it's so—'

'Nineteen forties,' Sabrina finished for her. He'd had his hair cut to fit in when they'd found themselves in a Liverpool they didn't recognise. 'Tony, Tim and the lads gave him a hard time about it too when we first got back.' It was still hard to believe she and Adam had been part of the VE Day celebrations.

'What did he tell them?' Flo asked, passing the jar over, knowing he couldn't very well say he'd been trying to fit in with all the other young men who were trickling home from their wartime service.

Sabrina dabbed the Vaseline on and smacked her lips together. 'He said his arl man had made noises about him needing to smarten his act up if he wanted to stay in the property game which he had been going on about for ages, so it wasn't a lie.'

Florence nodded and then winced as Tony leaned over the bar to give Mickey his order. 'Honestly, Sabs, they can't be comfortable.' She gestured towards the jukebox from which David Lee Roth was still wailing. 'He's another one who's fond of the tight trousers. I reckon he sticks a sock down his.'

Sabrina spluttered, sending droplets of ale flying. 'Look what you made me do!' She looked about to see if anyone had noticed. 'It was true, though. Tony did insist on wearing jeans a size too small, and he could have sprayed on the denim he'd squeezed into tonight.

'I reckon he gets his sister to sew him into them each time he heads out and unpick them when he rolls home,' Florence said, only half-joking. 'Otherwise, how does he get his legs in and out of them?'

She had a point, Sabrina thought, pondering the question.

'Now look at Tim. There's a man who wears his jeans well.' Florence all but drooled as she ogled him, casually resting an elbow on the bar as he waited for his drink. 'I don't need to see the red tag to know he's wearing Levi's.'

Sabrina shook her head because Linda was hanging off him, dressed inappropriately, given she'd been riding pillion on his motorbike.

'State of her,' Florence muttered. 'All fur coat and no knickers. How come she never has helmet hair.'

She was right. Linda's hair was big, Sabrina thought, subconsciously fluffing hers, and watching as they mentally swept the pub to see who was checking them out. They did make a good looking couple, a sentiment she'd keep to herself. Several lads were eyeing Linda's long legs appreciatively. The length of her legs was another source of consternation for Florence. As for Tim, with his dirty blond hair, worn too long, and self-assured strut, he had a Rod Stewart air about him and the same magnetic pull when it came to women. Present company included. 'Shut your gob, Flo,' she ordered, moving down the row of jean-clad bums to one she knew and loved. 'And he doesn't wear them as well as my Adam,' she said smugly.

The group, all clutching motorcycle helmets and wearing their leather jackets despite the temperate evening, milled about the bar a few minutes longer before making their way over to join them.

'Hiya, girls,' Tony greeted, squeezing in next to Florence, much to her chagrin. She'd been hoping Tim would sit next to her. She wasn't rude enough to say anything though, and so she sat with a sulky expression on her face while he began chatting.

Sabrina nudged her with her foot under the table.

Adam put his pint down and dragged a seat over before leaning down to kiss Sabrina. Before their lips met, her last thought was that she was glad she'd sucked on a mint after her Chinese. He tasted faintly of crisps and beer and smelled of Kouros. She hoped she didn't whiff of eau de garlic.

'Oi, get a room,' one of the other lads called over, and they broke apart grinning. Adam sat down next to her.

'Did youse have a nice meal out?'

'It was luvly, ta.' Sabrina said.

Florence filled him and Tony in on the banter and excitement over the news the Bootle Tootlers were to be stars of the catwalk.

'I've been saying to me clients me girl's a model,' Adam said, and Sabrina laughed.

Tony stared at Florence longingly, but she was oblivious.

Linda, who'd picked up the odd word like modelling and catwalk, leaned across Tim, 'What's all this about then?'

Florence's mouth clamped shut, leaving it to Sabrina to explain. Tim spoke up when she'd explained about the upcoming gig at Esmerelda's.

'What do you say, Florence. Room for one more?' He winked at her. 'Make me girl happy, and I'll take you for a spin on me bike if you like?'

It was too much for Florence. The thought of wrapping her arms and legs around Tim saw her open her mouth and let the words, 'I suppose we could use one more,' escape.

Linda beamed, 'I've modelled before. So I can show youse how it's done.' She exhaled a puff of smoke and looked pleased with herself.

'There's a dress rehearsal at Esmerelda's Emporium this Sunday, and the show's in a fortnight.' Sabrina said before shooting the scowling Florence a look that said, it's your own fault before turning her attention to Adam. 'How's the Triumph?'

'She's running like a dream, thanks to Tim.' He raised his glass in Tim's direction. 'Cheers, man.'

Tim raised his by way of return before cocking his head to one side to catch Linda's words.

'So, you're all set for the Isle of Man then?' Sabrina might have mixed feelings about the racing, but she knew how much Adam was looking forward to it.

'Almost,' Adam said, 'Me and Tony wondered if the two of youse want to come with us for the weekend, cheer us on like for Mad Sunday. Tim's bringing Linda.'

Sabrina pictured herself waving a flag as Adam zoomed past, leaving the other competitors for dust. She'd never been far from Liverpool, and yes, alright, so the Isle of Man was hardly miles away but technically, it was overseas. She looked to Florence, who was already nodding. 'We'd love to come, wouldn't we, Sabs?'

'Yeah, course we would.'

'Just as friends, mind,' Florence spelt out to Tony to avoid confusion about sleeping arrangements.

'Yeah, course.'

'Where will we stay?' Sabrina asked. She imagined herself in a thatched cottage B&B tucking into a full English breakfast.

'We're camping.' Adam informed them.

'Camping?' Sabrina and Florence chimed. Neither had much experience camping aside from school camps and the disastrous time they'd gone to a local campground with the Brownies. They'd had to abandon their tents in the middle of the night on account of the torrential rain and kip down in the main building until morning.

'But I don't have a tent,' Florence stated.

'There's room in mine,' Tony offered up hopefully. Florence fixed him with a look. 'How about an old pup tent then? I've got one you can borrow,' he added hastily, basking in the grateful smile he received.

This time the girls grinned at one another. They were off to the Isle of Man!

Chapter Six

The butt of Evelyn's cigarette from her weekly ten Woodbine allowance was ground out in the ashtray on the side table next to her sagging armchair. A soft breeze was blowing in through the window overlooking Bold Street, airing the remnants of her savoured ciggy out and she was so used to the sounds drifting up from the street below she barely registered them. The rumble of cars, odd trucks and horns, snatches of conversations. Evelyn liked the busyness of all that life surrounding her and Sabrina's little flat above the shop.

The television was on, but she'd turned the sound down when the news had delivered nothing uplifting. Now it flickered in the corner of the room. The darting movements of characters on-screen saw her glance over occasionally from where she'd moved to sit at the table. She debated whether to cook the salmon or leave it for a while, deciding on the latter because she wasn't hungry; her mind was too occupied with other things.

In front of her was a lined writing pad. Evelyn wasn't much of a letter writer. She'd bought the writing paper to keep in touch with a cousin who resided in Canada on her late mam's side. Cousin Hazel, with whom she'd promised to correspond after they'd fleetingly connected. Hazel had kept her word and written to her. The letter that had landed on the doormat downstairs one morning had been full of her life in the town where she lived. A foreign-sounding place with its moose and black bear residents appearing in her garden from time to time.

Frustratingly, Evelyn had misplaced the letter soon after it arrived. She suspected it had been swept up with the old newspaper and put out with the rubbish. So despite her good intentions to write back, she couldn't. The envelope had cousin Hazel's address stamped on it. She didn't know why she hadn't thought to jot it down at the time of her impromptu visit. Perhaps it was because she'd been grappling with the contents of another letter. A letter Hazel had presented to her written by her mam when Evelyn was still a child to the family she'd never talked about.

What was the name of the town Hazel was from? Evelyn wracked her brains, but all she could come up with was it was a few hours' from Ontario.

At first, she'd hoped her cousin would write again, but as time ticked by with no other word, she'd come to think that perhaps too much water had gone under the bridge to forge familial bonds at their time of life. So eventually, she forgot all about writing to her long lost cousin, and the pad had remained untouched under a pile of old Christmas cards shoved away in the sideboard drawer until now.

Evelyn picked up the pen and tapped the pad absentmindedly as her thoughts turned to Hazel and her visit. Sabrina wasn't the only one who'd had a mystery to solve when it came to her family, and Hazel had provided Evelyn with answers to the questions her mother had refused to answer. Their brief encounter flickered through her mind like the tele was doing in the corner of the room.

It was late on a Wednesday afternoon two, or was it three years ago now when her Canadian cousin breezed through the door of Brides of Bold Street? Evelyn cast her mind back to her first impression of Hazel.

There she'd stood in front of the counter downstairs. A bedraggled, bespectacled woman who was similar in age to herself. Her hair was silvered and barely visible, tucked away under a navy blue rain hat. She wore a matching raincoat zipped up to her chin. A pair of sodden walking shoes peeked out of the bottom of it.

Evelyn had chosen to ignore the puddle forming at the woman's feet as she sized her up, curious as to what she wanted. 'And, how may we help you today, madam?' she'd asked.

She closed her eyes briefly as the conversation they'd exchanged replayed itself.

'My name is Hazel Tremblay née Shaw, and I'm seeking an Evelyn Flooks,' said Hazel, her accent inflected with tricky vowels which saw both Sabrina and Evelyn tilt their heads to one side to listen closely.

'I'm she.' Evelyn stared at her with unabashed curiosity.

'Evelyn Flooks, as I live and breathe!' Hazel clapped her hands. 'What a pleasure it is to meet you. Although I can't say I see much of a resemblance.' She met Evelyn's steady gaze with an expectant expression as she continued to drip.

Who was this Hazel woman acting so overtly familiarly? Evelyn thought, suddenly wary as something about her eyes kept drawing her back to them. They were tantalisingly familiar, yet they'd never met.

'I'm your cousin, Evelyn, and it is delightful to meet you.'

Sabrina's mouth fell open, and Evelyn, once she'd recovered from her surprise, nudged her to shut it. Hazel hadn't travelled from wherever it was she came from to see her masticated orange Opal Fruit.

She shook hands with the stranger and introduced her to Sabrina when she'd recovered herself.

It had been near closing time, and as such, Evelyn extended an invitation for Hazel to join them upstairs for tea. 'It won't be anything fancy, mind,' she warned as she turned the open sign to closed. 'Meat and three veg.'

'Fancy food inflames my gout,' Hazel said, discarding her raincoat, which Sabrina left to dry on a hook in the workroom.

At that moment, Evelyn had been reminded of a peacock suddenly spreading his tail feathers because, beneath the swathes of waterproof navy fabric, Hazel wore a mustard wool jerkin overtop of a long-sleeved red and yellow check shirt. Her slacks were also red. A wallflower she was not.

Sabrina blinked at the burst of colour and whispered, 'She's related to you ahright, Aunt Evie,' before fetching a towel to mop up the water in the shop. If she didn't do it now, she might forget, and the last thing they wanted was a bride hopping down the aisle with a broken leg or the like because she'd slipped over in Brides of Bold Street.

Evelyn ushered their guest upstairs and plied her with sherry leaving her to flick through an album of newspaper clippings featuring the bridal shop over the years as she and Sabrina set about grilling chops and boiling veg.

Over dinner, Hazel, whose cheeks were reddened from her third tot of sherry, began sharing her story. In between bites, she announced, 'I was widowed several years ago now.'

'Sorry for your loss,' Evelyn and Sabrina simultaneously piped up.

'Don't be.' Hazel flapped the hand that wasn't holding the fork with a piece of potato speared on it. 'They say you marry your father and my father was a prize asshole.'

Sabrina pushed her chair back and got up to fetch a glass of water for Evelyn, who'd begun spluttering.

Hazel carried on, oblivious to Evelyn's choking. 'Theodore and I never had children, and when he died, I realised that was it. I was all alone in the world. Except I wasn't, was I?' She looked at Evelyn, who gave her a watery smile as she blinked back the tears that had formed from the sudden coughing fit.

'Are you alright, dear?'

Evelyn had another sip of the water and managed a nod.

'I've lost my train of thought. Where was I?'

Sabrina, who was fascinated with her unusual manner of speaking, filled her in, 'You were saying you thought you were all alone in the world, only you weren't.'

'Yes, thank you, my dear. I'm getting ahead of myself though. Where to start?'

'The beginning?' Sabrina offered.

'Yes, the beginning. A sensible idea indeed.' She looked at her fork then, as though surprised to see it in her hand and popped the potato in her mouth.

Once she'd chewed and swallowed, she spoke. 'I was my parents' only child and a disappointment from the get-go, especially to my father. He wanted a boy, you see, and Mother's inability to produce any more children was a failure he never let her forget. The consumption took my, sorry, our grandparents within weeks of one another, and we emigrated to Canada shortly after.'

Evelyn pulled the fork from her mouth, the meat she'd been about to chew on a foreign lump in her mouth as she listened.

'Our grandfather was in shipping, and it would seem disappointment was a generational thing in the family, Evelyn, because my father's lack of interest in the business was a source of constant friction between them. Of course, Father sold the business, the house and anything else that wasn't nailed down before our grandparents were cold in their graves. Then, out of the blue, he announced we were relocating to Canada, where the air was clean. He'd been offered an opportunity there to triple his inheritance by investing in the timber trade.'

Evelyn thought back to the poverty of her childhood and felt a frisson of discord with this matter-of-fact woman chatting amicably at her table. She'd never known what it was to go to bed with an empty stomach. Hazel, gnawing the remains of her lamb chop had no clue to Evelyn's thoughts.

'As I said,' she went on when she'd stripped the chop to the bone. 'When Theodore headed upstairs or downstairs, depending on who's doing the judging, I decided I wanted to find out more about my family back in Britain. I started by digging out my father's papers long since boxed up and stored away. I wasn't totally in the dark, you understand. I knew my mother had a brother she kept in touch with. George, or Georgie Porgie as she referred to him. He's married to a woman with the god awful name of Bertha, and they've two boys, long since grown-up, now with families of their own. Tomorrow, I've been invited to lunch with them at their home in Chester. As for my father, well, I'd always assumed he was an only child, but then I found a letter amongst his paperwork. It turns out he had a sister.'

'Lizzie, my mother,' Evelyn supplied while Sabrina's head whipped between the two women trying to keep up.

'Lizzie.' Hazel confirmed with a nod.

Evelyn abandoned her knife and fork. Her heart began to flutter as she asked, 'Do you have that letter with you?'

'Of course. It explains why your mother was estranged from the family. Excuse me a moment.' Hazel left the table and retrieved her bag where she'd left it on the floor beside the sofa.

Sabrina and Evelyn held their breaths, waiting for her to lay her hands on it.

'Now, where is it?' Hazel glanced up apologetically. 'All these compartments seemed like a good idea when I bought this bag to bring on my trip.' A zipper sounded, and by the time she held an envelope aloft jubilantly, Sabrina and Evelyn were turning puce from lack of oxygen. There was an audible hiss and gasp as they began gulping air, and Hazel settled herself back at the table, keen to polish off what was left on her plate. She passed the envelope across the table to Evelyn.

Evelyn tried not to snatch, and as she turned it over in her hands, she noticed a tea stain in the corner. The envelope was addressed only to Edwin Shaw, and there was no postmark. But, on the back, 46 Potter Street was given as the return address. The handwriting was her mams, and she itched to hold it to her nose to breathe in any remaining traces of her.

It made Evelyn feel peculiar to think this letter her mam had written had been squirrelled away with the papers of a dead uncle whom she hadn't known existed until a few moments ago. A deceased uncle in Canada of all places. There'd been a side to their mam she and her three sisters had never known. Now that she held the answers as to what her life had been like before she'd met their father, Evelyn was suddenly hesitant.

'Are you just going to look at it,' Hazel paused mid-conversation to ask bluntly.

However, it galvanised Evelyn, and she slipped the envelope open with her finger and carefully pulled out the letter it contained. The paper was dry to the touch and yellowed by age, and as she unfolded it, she half expected it to crumble to dust.

'What does it say, Aunt Evie?'

'Give me a chance to read it, Sabrina,' Evelyn tutted.

Hazel distracted her. 'And how is it you came to live with your aunt, Sabrina?'

Sabrina left Evelyn to devour the contents of the letter in peace as she trotted out the story she'd told so many times it almost felt true. 'Aunt Evie's cousin was my mam, and she died when I was only three. My dad wasn't up to the task of raising me, so I came to live here with Aunt Evie.'

Evelyn held the letter to her chest for a heartbeat before folding it up and slipping it back in the envelope. 'May I keep it?'

'That was my intention by delivering it to you,' Hazel said. 'And my father wouldn't have helped your mother, you know. He was a miserly man. I visited the house where I spent my formative years this morning. A grand Georgian affair indeed. But, no, Evelyn, I'm afraid it would have been a case of you made your bed now you can lie in it where my father was concerned.'

'Where did you live?' Evelyn asked.

'We lived on Clarence Street. Do you know it?'

There weren't many streets in the inner city, Evelyn didn't know, and Clarence Street in the Georgian quarter wasn't all that far from the decrepit terrace house on Potter Street where she'd grown up. The streets might not have been far apart, but the way the people who inhabited them lived was an ocean apart. She nodded, recalling how the rich had rubbed shoulders alongside the poor in those days.

'But what did it say,' Sabrina frowned.

'My mother wrote to her brother asking for help, is all, Sabrina. We knew hard times when I was young. She did her best to keep our heads above water though.'

Sabrina nodded. She'd gleaned enough from her aunt over the years to know she'd had an unhappy time of it growing up because her dad had liked the drink.

The letter had been short and straight to the point. Lizzie Flooks had written to her elder brother asking for help. She was sorry for not having listened to her father, and she now realised she'd made a terrible mistake marrying Jack Flooks. Marry him though she had and for all that had happened since she wouldn't be without her children. It was because of her children she was desperate to leave him. He was a drunkard who beat them all and gambled his wages away. She wanted to make a fresh start somewhere he wouldn't find them and open a dressmaking business to support their new life. But she couldn't do so without a small sum of money to set them up. Please would he talk to their father, she'd implored.

Her mam had been such a proud woman, Evelyn thought it must have cost her dearly to write that letter. But then, a final piece of the puzzle fell into place as she realised Lizzie had been disowned for her choice of husband. Of course, Lizzie Flooks wasn't the first woman to fall for sweet nothings and a handsome face. Oh, but what a price she'd paid for not scratching deeper beneath Jack Flooks' shiny veneer.

Of an evening when she was young when she was working alongside her mam, Evelyn had tried to glean snippets from her. She'd wanted to know what her life was like before she'd married, but it was like pulling teeth because Lizzie wouldn't be drawn on it.

She'd always suspected her mam came from money, not just because she'd heard her dad nipping away at her on those nights when he'd staggered down their street singing.

'Do you think you're better than me, then do you, Lizzie, with that plum in yer mouth?' he'd snap and snarl.

No, it was because her mam had had a way about her that was softer and more genteel than the other women she lived and worked alongside in Potter Street. Her speech, too, had echoed of having posher roots than the pocket of Liverpool near Canning Dock they inhabited.

Evelyn might not have been spoken highly of by her school teachers when she was a child, but that didn't mean she was silly. Far from it. She'd watched and learned from her mam, honing her machinist skills and filing the rough edges of her speech down until she too would have sounded perfectly at home in the big houses her elder sister, Violet, had once set her sights on.

She'd known, you see, that it wasn't just her mam's exemplary dressmaking skills that had drawn her customers to their neck of the woods but titillation. It was the reason they'd abandoned the city department stores they usually haunted. Department stores with scores of seamstresses beavering away in workrooms hidden from sight. They'd sensed it. Evelyn deduced that beneath Lizzie's careworn exterior lurked a kindred spirit. Someone like themselves, only someone who'd fallen far.

Evelyn didn't need to be a fly on the wall at their afternoon salons to know that Lizzie Flooks would be gleefully brought up and eyebrows raised over china teacups and cucumber sandwiches. There would be gasps at their hostess having slummed it over to Potter Street to have her dresses made. It would be a talking point that gave the wearer of her mam's frocks a risqué glamour.

Evelyn had never wanted to move in their circles, unlike Violet, who yearned to. She didn't want to be someone's wife whose place was in the home. Instead, she'd wanted to be a businesswoman. A woman who was answerable to no one except herself. Just as her mam had wanted to be, only, unlike her mam, that's what she'd become.

A horn's sudden tooting from the road below startled Evelyn back to the here and now. She blinked to clear the memories away and picked up the pen. She found herself back in the house on Potter Street as she began to write.

Chapter Seven

Evelyn, Liverpool, 1927

Evelyn rubbed at her gritty eyes, wishing she didn't have to get up. It was still dark, but the knocker upper's four taps had sounded on the windowpane before he'd carried on down the wall-to-wall brick houses stretching along their side of the street. His bamboo pole with the brass iron at the end was responsible for waking the residents of Potter Street and the surrounding neighbourhood to ensure they got to where they had to go on time.

Evelyn yawned. She'd have liked nothing more than to pull the blankets up under her chin and allow herself the luxury of another hour or two's sleep. There was no chance of that, though. On the wall side of the lumpy old mattress, Beatrice stirred but didn't wake. She was a heavy sleeper, was Bea, and it would take a sharp nudge to rouse her. It was her job to wake their mam and dad. Evelyn didn't envy her sister the task, leastwise where their dad was concerned. She didn't need to enter her parents' room to know it would reek of ale and piss, he was prone to wetting himself, but mercifully last night had been a whistling night. Still, he never woke up smiling. He had to report at the docks for seven which meant he didn't hang about of a morning. Small mercies and all that.

On her right and closest to the door, Violet stirred. She was taking up more than her fair share of the bed as usual. Vi would help Bea get ready for her day at school while Evelyn put the kettle on and set about making the porridge downstairs. 'One more minute, Evelyn Flooks,' she whispered out loud, her breath white on the frigid air. Then, she'd get them all up and at it.

Her eyes wouldn't feel as if they'd sand in them if she hadn't lain awake waiting for her father to come home last night. She'd listened to the steady thrum of the sewing machine below, wishing it would lull her to sleep like it did her sisters. As usual, though, she'd had her ear cocked, the tension only seeping from her when she heard the whistling grow closer. She'd succumbed to sleep not long after hearing the front door bang. Her dad's voice had wafted up the stairs as he cheerily greeted her mam.

Evelyn could picture the scene playing out below. Her mam would be swatting her husband's advances away half-heartedly, insisting she had to keep working. She'd know the sewing had been abandoned by the creaking stairs and soft laughter that followed.

Evelyn loved her mam, but she'd never understood how she could let her father with his beery breath near her. How could she accept his treatment of them so meekly? People said Jack Flooks was a handsome devil, and perhaps it was this her mam had fallen for. She didn't know about handsome, not these days with the spidery veins on his cheeks and bloodshot eyes; they'd got the devil part right, though, she'd think. The knowledge her mam still loved him despite the cruel words, slaps and punches he'd doled out over the years made her blood boil. Why couldn't she see that he'd never change? The drink would always come first. He'd never stop frittering away any money that crossed his palm at the bookies, either. A leopard couldn't change its spots, and neither could he.

Her eyes were growing accustomed to the faint light now, and she fixed on a dark patch she could see over the top of Beatrice's head. Damp was bleeding through the paper.

Violet flung an arm across her. Evelyn thought it would be strange not having her elder sister hogging the bed. She'd be gone next week when she started her new live-in position. Evelyn knew for all her impossible ways she would miss her. Violet was a splash of colour in all their lives.

Nellie was in the middle, down the bottom end of the bed, and most nights, she'd slide her cold feet up against Evelyn's back to warm them. She'd been a late baby, having arrived when Beatrice was eight. So Evelyn thought it likely she'd been conceived on a whistling night as they all had, for that matter. Nellie also had an irritating habit of kicking out in her sleep, and her three older sisters had often been jolted awake by her as she thrashed about. None of them complained though, because Nellie was the sweetest of them all with her unfailingly happy temperament.

The sisters doted on her, and the women in their neighbourhood often commented that the littlest Flooks girl had four mothers, not one. It was true enough, Evelyn thought with a surge of love for her sister even though she was digging her toes into her back!

Evelyn fancied it was when she slept that Nellie acknowledged the miserable existence of a life governed by their father's unpredictability. A man who could be sunshine and smiles one day and a fisty brute the next. The uncertainty made Nellie fidget, so how could she get annoyed with her knowing that?

Beatrice stirred again, muttering something in her sleep. Carping on to someone in her dream, Evelyn thought, nudging her with her elbow. Bea smacked her lips together. Like Evelyn, Bea took after their mam. Unlike them, though, her nose was permanently curled like she was in the proximity of a midden.

Evelyn's friend, Lucy, catching sight of Beatrice when she called one morning so they could walk to the tram stop together, had asked what the matter was with her. 'She's a face on her like sour vinegar,' she'd added, giggling. Evelyn had joined in with Lucy's laughter because it was true, but at the same time, it made her feel she'd been disloyal. Mam always said that family was everything. Mind there wasn't much about Bea that invoked loyalty. Beatrice and Violet were peas in a pod insomuch as they looked out for themselves.

Evelyn pulled herself upright, pushing the pile of scratchy blankets down. Violet tried to pull them back, but Evelyn was having none of it. Instead, she leaned over and swept the hair covering her sister's face away, saying, 'Wake up, Vi,' loudly right in her ear. Then she did the same to Bea.

It had the desired effect as it always did, and she clambered over Violet to dress hastily. The quicker you put your clothes on, the less chance there was of the cold chilling you right to the bone. She opened the thin curtains, seeing the frost etched on the inside of the window. Once she was dressed, she padded down the stairs and headed straight for the scullery where, splashing her face with cold water from the tap over the sink, she gasped. She'd sort her hair out after breakfast, knowing it would be a fight for the mirror to do so.

Wide awake now, Evelyn lit the oil lamp and the range in the kitchen. If she'd been so inclined, she could have performed her morning tasks with her eyes shut, and the same could be said for her monotonous work at the button factory.

It had been two years since she'd left school at fourteen and begun toiling at the factory. What a bewildering experience it had been to finish her classes on Friday and start work on Monday. One minute she'd been book learning and playing hopscotch in the street, the next operating the power press in a noisy factory coming home in the dark. She'd had to close her ears to the older girls' stories of fingers being amputated in the machinery through lack of concentration and make a concerted effort to stay focused on the task at hand.

Her mam worried about her working on such equipment given her tendency to daydream, but work was scarce, and beggars couldn't be choosers. Besides, Evelyn was happy to part with her earnings each week because the extra money she brought in along with Violet's wages from her job as a lady's maid to Rose Birch when Mam managed to wrangle it from her made a difference. There was money for the rent, and they could have meat in their stew, not just bones begged from the butcher.

However, it rankled to see her father enjoying a hearty stew despite squandering his wages when he should have brought them home to Mam. On the nights when he was brassic, he resorted to a tab. He'd been known to beg a few coppers outside the pub for beer too.

Mam kept the little she and Vi brought in and her own earnings from sewing stuffed inside a tin, safely hidden from him beneath a loose floorboard in the parlour.

Still and all, the nights of going to bed with an empty tummy had softened to a distant memory these days, and Nellie was too young to remember crying herself to sleep when her stomach hurt with being hungry.

Evelyn hated the pity she saw in the people they lived alongside's eyes. They had the measure of Jack Flooks, knowing the charming fella with the dancing blue eyes and coal-black hair was a Jekyll and Hyde when it came to his family. People minded their own business, though, and those that did try to help hadn't been thanked for it. Her mam wasn't well-liked along their street either because she didn't join in with the other women's gossip and chatter. A cold fish was how Evelyn had overheard that old shawlie three doors down, Ma Kenny, with the clay pipe permanently jammed in her gob, describe her.

All four of the Flooks girls knew if their mam hadn't taken in mending and sewing, life in their little house would have been a lot harder.

So, yes, it was worth trudging off to the button factory five days a week if it meant there was mutton in their scouse and they didn't have to eat the 'fades' from the greengrocers. She didn't plan on working in a factory until her dying day though.

She and Mam had a plan. One day, they'd open a dressmaker's. Their very own business and the days of the button factory and Mam toiling in the parlour would be a memory. They'd do it too. She knew this as surely as she knew that in three minutes, the kettle would begin to sing and that Nellie would come clattering down the stairs in search of her breakfast. All she had to do was figure out how.

Evelyn moved across to the sideboard to retrieve the cork mat for the teapot. She wondered how her mam had got on with Mrs Griffin's dress the night before, and once she'd laid the rest of the breakfast things out, she carried the oil lamp through to the parlour setting it down on the wing of the sewing machine cabinet. Then, pulling the curtains open, she was in time to see the hazy outline of a horse and cart through the mist clip-clopping past on the carter's way to the docks.

The dress was draped over the back of Mam's chair, and she felt excitement swell as she touched it reverently. The apricot fabric was as sheer and wispy as the spiderweb in the corner of their bedroom. What would it be like to float about a dance floor in clouds of chiffon? She wondered, gingerly picking it up and holding it next to her. She spun about, coming to a halt mid-twirl remembering the curtains were open.

Packing up her notions of dancing at balls, she inspected her mam's work. It was nearly finished now and Mrs Griffin's gown, to be worn at this Saturday's first-anniversary tea dance at the Grafton Ballroom was, quite simply, the most glamorous garment Evelyn had ever laid eyes on.

It was both current and straightforward in design, and the whimsical apricot material was offset by a bold orange bow to be tied around the hips and left to drape slightly longer than the dress. Beneath the gauzy overlay was a metallic gold and orange slip, bold enough to shine through the chiffon. Evelyn was to add the finishing touches by hand, sewing rows upon rows of gold beading around the neckline. She'd two nights in which to finish it before it was collected on Saturday morning for the ball that evening.

It was the first time Mam had been commissioned to make evening wear such as this, and it was quite the feather in her cap. Evelyn had watched entranced each evening as her mam fed the fussy fabrics through the Singer as though she worked with such fine materials all the time. She'd caught the wistful expression on her face too but hadn't understood what it meant.

They had Dot Clancy, who'd left school a few years before Evelyn, to thank for the recommendation. Her employer, Mrs Griffin's regular dressmaker, had taken ill in the days before she was due to begin making her client's gown, and Dot had remembered Lizzy Flooks. Bessie, Dot's older sister, who was married with two little ones permanently attached to a leg or her hip, had worn a dress to church that all the women in the congregation had much admired. Mrs Flooks of Potter Street had made it. All of this was imparted in an excited twitter by Dot as she stood resembling a magpie in her black and white uniform chirping away at their front door.

Lizzie had been taken aback by the unexpected visit from Mrs Griffith's lady's maid, whose expression was earnest beneath her mob cap.

Mrs Murphy, next door, had been taking an inordinately long time donkey stoning her front step as she too tried to keep up with the maid's excited chatter.

'Mrs Griffin's hesitant about trusting a woman working out of her front room. A woman who's not a formally qualified dressmaker as such. So I told her, I did, Mrs Flooks, that her chances of finding a city dressmaker who wasn't already otherwise engaged in the sewing of a ball dress this late in the day were slim.' Dot paused to draw breath before telling Lizzie she'd quelled her mistress's histrionics by assuring her she was certain Mrs Flooks was up to the task. 'You won't let me down, will you, Mrs Flooks?' She'd thrust the carpetbag she'd been holding at her. 'Everything you need's in here.'

Lizzy, who was snowed under as it was with her mending, hadn't hesitated to take it. She knew not to look a gift horse in the mouth, and she'd assured Dot she would indeed have it ready for collection next Saturday morning, even if it meant working through the night between now and then.

'Cinderella shall go to the ball,' Vi had whispered to Evelyn as they'd eavesdropped on the exchange from the parlour. There'd been envy in her tone.

Later that night, when the two younger sisters had been banished to their bedroom so Lizzy could spread the tissue paper pattern carefully out on the floor, she'd told Evelyn she should observe. 'It's important I exceed Mrs Griffin's expectations, Evie,' she'd said.

'Why Mam?'

'Because the likes of us always have to prove our worth to the likes of them. I know.'

'How?'

'Never you mind.'

Evie wanted to stamp her foot at that, but she wanted to learn how to sew more, so she'd had to content herself with a sulky expression as her mam began to cut the pattern pieces out. 'Who taught you to sew, Mam?' she'd asked, deciding she couldn't be bothered sulking. She wondered why she'd never thought to ask before.

'I watched and learned from a seamstress. She told me I'd a gift for it. You have the same gift, Evie.'

'But Dot Clancy said you weren't a qualified dressmaker?' Had her mam apprenticed as a seamstress before she married their dad? She'd never mentioned having done so.

'A gift's not a qualification that can be earned. I learned by watching same as you will.'

'Did Dad buy you the machine?' Evelyn persisted with her questions.

Lizzie shook her head, leaving the mystery of how she'd acquired it unsolved.

'Listen to me, Evelyn. There's not much I can give you other than advice, but if we do Mrs Griffin proud, she'll recommend me to her friends. If she does, then word will spread, and I'll have more work than I can manage on my own.'

'But what's the good of that?'

'Think, Evie.' Lizzie tapped the side of her head. 'Haven't I always wanted to open a dressmaker's?'

Evelyn nodded. For as long as she could remember, Mam had been making noises about this. Hope shone out of her face when she talked about it.

'You'd be able to finish up at the button factory and work alongside me. It won't be easy, but if we're careful, we can put a little aside each week, and before you know it, we'll have enough put by for a deposit for premises to work from.'

'A dressmaker's.'

'Flooks dressmakers.'

'Flooks Ladies Wear.'

'Flooks Fashions'

Their voices were breathy with the excitement of possibilities. And, just like that, the dress had gone from being a fairy-tale gown for a ball to an escape from the drudgery of Evelyn's work at the factory and a golden ticket to becoming Evelyn Flooks, a woman in business.

Now, as Evelyn placed the nearly completed evening dress carefully back where she'd found it, she knew her future clung to those chiffon folds.

Chapter Eight

Evelyn poured hot water from the kettle into the cast iron sink, then putting it back on the stove, she rolled up her sleeves before calling out to Violet. She'd last seen her sister flicking through the well-thumbed *The School Friend* comic book Beatrice had brought home from school even though she was far too old to be reading it. Instead of wiping the table like she was supposed to, Violet had been giggling. She hadn't even looked up from the comic as Evelyn began carrying the dirty plates through to the scullery off the kitchen.

'Vi, the table won't wipe itself and nor will the dishes dry themselves,' she called out for the second time. She picked up the dishcloth, thinking Violet was a lazy mare.

When their parents were out of earshot, Violet made no secret of the fact she felt she'd been born to the wrong family. It was an accident of birth that had seen her wind up in a house so small you could barely swing a cat in it, let alone fit the six people squashed within its peeling walls.

Her small, pointy chin would jut up as she'd add, 'I belong over in Hope Street in a house like the Birches with a fireplace in every room. A house that smells of fresh flowers and cook's apple pie. Not a mouse house that reeks of soot, scouse and ale.' Ever dramatic, she'd finish with, 'And I'll have velvet-covered furnishings, not a tatty old sofa with the horsehair spilling out of it, ta very much.' Then off she'd flounce. Where she went when she banged out of the front door of an evening, neither Beatrice, Nellie, nor Evelyn knew, and Mam had given up asking.

At seventeen, Violet was a law unto herself. She was a year older than Evelyn and thought herself worldly-wise and vastly superior to her three sisters. Not that you'd know she was related to the rest of them because her hair was a lustrous brown woven with gold. It had hung down to her waist in waves until late the year before when she'd had it cut into a fashionable bob. Mam had gone mad when she'd walked in the door with all that beautiful hair gone and a 'flapper's' haircut, but Violet couldn't have given a fig.

The rest of them had been handed out plain old mouse hair. Although when they'd moan about this to their mam, she'd liken their hair to the colour of chestnuts. Evelyn wasn't so sure about that, but either way, while theirs hung curtain straight, Violet's curled becomingly to hug her jawline. She'd skin the colour of honey too instead of pasty white and eyes to match.

She was the family's beauty, and didn't she know it! She'd the sort of face that saw men turn around after her hoping for a second glimpse. Not that she'd set her sights on any of the lads from their neck of the woods.

Violet was quick to attest she would marry well and that she'd not be shackled to a dock worker who drank and gambled his earnings away like their dad. He'd never laid a finger on Violet, though, when he'd stumbled in the door reeking of drink. She'd been spared. It was as if their older sister was too shiny and pretty to mar. The same couldn't be said for her sisters, who'd all been on the receiving end of his fists, even little Nellie.

Evelyn had figured out a long time ago that it was Violet's looks that gave her a sense of entitlement.

Her sister was getting her way in a roundabout fashion because soon, she'd be living under the Birch family's posh roof. Mind you, being at the beck and call of Madam Rose as she called her probably wasn't quite what she'd had in mind.

The live-in position of lady's maid for young Rose Birch was a step up from her previously held rank of housemaid and one Miss Rose herself had instigated. She was a lonely girl being raised without a mother, and given she and Violet were the same age, she was eager for Violet's company and confidence as her maid. She was also, by all accounts, spoiled and selfish. Evelyn didn't envy Violet in the slightest. She'd not be able to hold her tongue if it were her, which was why mam had steered her away from domestic service and into factory work.

The Birch family had made their money in the days of the cotton trade, and Mr Walter Birch, a widower, spent his days golfing while his sons managed the family investments. Violet had declared to her sisters with a haughty flick of her hair that her role as lady's maid would only be temporary. Nevertheless, it had given her a foot in the door of the world she would one day be part of. 'I've already caught the eye of Samuel Birch,' she'd said, referencing the youngest eligible son. 'It's only a matter of time before we'll be wed, and I'll have a lady's maid of me own! Bea, you could come and work for me when you finish school,' she'd said, deliberately trying to get a rise from her younger sister, which admittedly didn't take much doing.

'You were down the back of the queue when brains were handed out, Violet Flooks if you think a Birch would marry the likes of you. Pretty you may be, but you'll never be one of them. You can't make a silk purse out of a sow's ear,' Bea had retorted.

'Oh, don't fight youse two,' Nellie had pleaded before tugging on Violet's skirt and staring up at the sister she adored, 'Will you come and see us on your afternoon off, Violet?'

'We'll have to see,' Violet had replied sniffily, glaring at Beatrice but then, as Nellie had burst into tears, she'd patted her head and said, 'Don't cry, Nellie. Course I'll come back to see you.'

Evelyn wasn't so sure she would. She suspected her sister wouldn't look back once she left Potter Street because Violet had a hardness to her which in all likeliness would stand her in good stead. She was a survivor was Vi. Or so Mam said.

It would break not just Nellie's heart to see her go but their mam's too. She might have made her feelings clear when it came to Violet's illusions of grandeur, having told her, 'You're headed for a fall, Violet Flooks, mark my words. It doesn't do to get ideas above your station.' But that didn't mean she didn't love her daughter. On the contrary, she loved all four of them fiercely.

Her warning had fallen on deaf ears, Evelyn thought as she swished the dish mop over the plates in the greasy water. 'Violet Flooks, get off your backside and come and help me,' she bellowed this time. A few minutes ticked by, but at last, the door opened.

Evelyn didn't bother looking up as her sister pushed past her, but if she had, she'd have seen Violet had pursed her lips unbecomingly. 'Don't snatch,' she tsked as Violet took the wet cloth from her before flouncing back through to the kitchen to see to the table.

When Violet reappeared in record time, Evelyn rolled her eyes. The cloth plopped into the water, and she shoved past Evelyn to fetch the tea towel from where it dangled on the nail.

'Hurry up with them dishes or I'll reek of meat and onions by the time you're finished.'

'Oh shurrup, Vi.' Evelyn forgot the vowels she was trying to cultivate like Mam's as she passed her a plate.

The steady whir of their mother's sewing machine sounded from the parlour, and Evelyn knew their two younger sisters would be tackling the pile of hand sewing. Most evenings, Evelyn would help out once she'd finished washing up, but she'd the beading on Mrs Griffin's dress to be seeing to tonight. As for Violet, she got off scot-free when it came to the sewing and darning, given their mam had declared her too cack-handed to help.

The sisters finished the dishes in silence, with Violet hanging the tea towel up to dry before disappearing up the stairs.

Evelyn wiped the water off the worktop into the sink and emptied it, leaving the cloth draped over the side to dry. She was finishing the sweeping under the table in the kitchen when she saw Violet flash past the open door with their mam's coat on. Evelyn forgot all about the broom in her haste to catch her. 'Where are you going in that?' she hissed down the narrow hall gesturing to the coat, not wanting their mam to stop sewing mid-seam to see what the fuss was all about. But, of course, it was a pointless question, given she already knew what her sister's answer would be.

Sure enough, Violet said, 'None of your business.' She placed the hat hanging by the back door carefully on her head then smoothed the drop-waist skirt of the buttercup yellow dress visible beneath the open coat.

Evelyn's eyes were doorstoppers. 'Is that silk?' she gasped, stepping closer to inspect the fabric. She was sure it was because she might not have paid much attention when it came to her schooling, but she knew the difference between cotton and silk right enough. 'And why have you got Mam's coat on?' she demanded for a second time, a little louder. She'd have lunged for it if she wasn't terrified of tearing it in a skirmish.

The coat was a mysterious garment, and although dated, the fine cut and quality wool serge meant this could be overlooked. It was also the sort of coat a woman might have worn when riding in a motor car and the one quality piece of clothing their mam owned. She'd never breathed a word of how she'd come by it. She wore it out on occasion, seemingly oblivious as she held her head high and hurried down the street that she was feeding the other dockers' wives with further fodder to whisper about where 'Lady Muck' was concerned. It was a miracle that their dad hadn't tried to pawn it, but then he was ignorant about women's fashion.

'Shush.' Violet held her index finger to her lips and glanced warily at the door to the parlour, but the steady hum continued. 'I can hardly wear my tatty old coat over a dress like this now, can I? Besides, Mam hardly ever leaves the house these days, and I'll freeze without it.' Her face took on a sly quality as she persuaded, 'I'll let you have a feel of me dress if you like. I might even let you borrow it some time. It's like running your hands over water.'

Evelyn forgot about the coat in her longing to touch the shimmering fabric just as Violet had known she would. She wiped her hands on the rough cotton of her skirt to be confident they were bone dry before reaching out to tentatively stroke the expensive material. It was like trailing your fingers over cool water. She was destined to spend her days working with fabrics like this and Mrs Griffin's chiffon gown and not in a dirty factory. Another thought occurred to her then, and she snatched her hand back like she'd been scalded.

'How did you afford it on your wage, Violet Flooks?' Suspicion made her eyes narrow. What exactly was she up to when she ventured out of an evening? Evelyn doubted it was friends she was after meeting with, not dressed like that. And, were those silk stockings peeking out from beneath the dress, not to mention new shoes, lambskin by the looks of them.

Violet's cheeks pinkened. 'Don't take that tone with me, Evelyn. It was a gift from Miss Rose because she's excited about me coming to live in.'

'And what about those stockings and shoes, were they gifts 'n' all?' She was lying, Evelyn thought, studying her face. She'd always been able to tell when Violet wasn't telling the truth. Her head would tilt slightly to the left as it was now.

Her sister's tawny eyes flashed challengingly, and then she turned on the heel of her new pumps and let herself out of the front door.

This time it was Evelyn who pursed her lips as the door clicked quietly shut behind her. She was going to come a cropper one of these days, was Violet. She added sneaky and selfish to her earlier sentiment of lazy when it came to her elder sister as she hesitated in the passage.

Evelyn was at a loss as to what she should do because she loved Violet, for all her faults. The sense of foreboding she couldn't shake when it came to Violet of late was making her stomach churn in a manner that saw her swallow quickly for fear she'd bring up the stew she'd not long eaten.

Evelyn wasn't a seer, not like the old gypsy woman in the camp on the waste ground over in Aintree. Her friend, Annie's mam, had been to see her, not that she'd told Annie what she'd said to her. She might not be a fortune teller, but she knew when trouble was coming alright, like the time when Dad had twisted Mam's arm back and she'd not been able to sew for a week. They'd had to live on watery soup with not a scrap of meat to be found swimming in it. Or when Mam lost the baby she'd been carrying in between Bea and Nellie. Yes, she could feel it in her water, alright. Something bad was heading Vi's way.

It was no good. She wouldn't be able to concentrate on sewing the beading onto Mrs Griffith's dress until she knew what Vi was up to. She was likely to make a mess of it for worrying, and if she had to stay up half the night to make the time up, then so be it. It was with this thought she strode determinedly to the front door pausing only to snatch her coat off the hook and pull her hat down over her pinned hair. 'I'll be back in a jiffy, Mam, don't be worrying about me now.'

Evelyn closed the door on the protests that floated forth as she hunched down into her coat and hurried down the street after Violet.

Chapter Nine

A fine mist had descended on Potter Street along with darkness since Evelyn had arrived home from the factory earlier. An Arctic wind was whistling up the street, which at times seemed to act as a tunnel for it, and she shivered despite her coat.

Violet would've caught her death if she hadn't pinched Mam's coat, she thought, squinting into the night. The houses were jammed in on either side, and the street wasn't well lit. The glow from the sporadic gas lamps was subdued at best. Overhead a half-moon drifted between shifting clouds.

At least it wasn't a pea-souper tonight, Evelyn mused, trying to make out whether the swiftly moving shadow halfway down the street belonged to Violet. When the fog rolled in off of the Mersey, mingling with the soot and smoke, finding your way down the narrow streets and winding lanes spanning out from the docks was nearly impossible.

In the distance, she could hear clanking trams and the puttering of motor vehicles. A lonely horse and cat rattled past her, but it was a ship's horn reverberating like a mournful cry that made her jump. 'Don't be silly,' Evelyn told herself, taking a deep breath.

Given there wasn't another soul on the street, it had to be Violet, and Evelyn avoided the circular puddle of light from the gas lamp outside their house. She didn't want her sister swinging around and spotting her. Violet would go mad if she knew she'd intended to follow her, and buttoning her coat up as she went, Evelyn hurried after her.

Violet was nearly at the corner that ran onto Eldonian Way now. At least she hadn't turned right when she'd left the house in the direction of the docks. They were no place for a girl to be at night. She'd heard stories told at the factory of the women who plied their trade for the sailors fresh off their boats. A girl, even one as self-assured as Violet, could get into bother were she to hang about down there.

The lighting was better once she'd turned onto Eldonian Way and the buildings reared imposingly on either side of her. It was reassuring hearing the sounds of life emanating from the courts tucked away down the rabbit warren of alleys spidering off it.

Evelyn slowed a little, trying to catch her breath now she could see her sister. The cries of babies mingled with chattering voices, bursts of laughter and the odd shout as she made her way along the gently winding thoroughfare. There was something else too. Something she couldn't put her finger on, but it was like the air itself had suddenly stopped breathing, this despite the wind. Yes, she mused, a tension of sorts like an elastic being pulled so tight it was about to snap.

'You're being fanciful,' Evelyn silently chastised. So intent was she on her thoughts and keeping Violet in her line of sight, she nearly collided with a woman wrapped in a shawl. Her hair hung loose and wild down her back as she emerged from an alley.

'Oi, watch where you're going, girlie,' she wheezed, not pausing as she hurried off in the opposite direction to Evelyn, leaving a whiff of stale tobacco in her wake.

'Sorry,' Evelyn called after her, but her voice disappeared in the wind.

Violet had turned left onto Burlington Street, where the shops with their cramped rooms above them would be bustling in the daytime. Now they were hiding behind their night-time shutters. A few people were making their way to wherever they were going, swathed in winter coats with their faces hidden by hats.

A short distance further on was The Ship's Head, a murky beacon on a cold night if ever there was one! It was a blessing there weren't the usual gang of yobs pestering passers-by for beer money outside it, she thought. Evelyn had never stepped foot inside the public house but knowing their dad drank there sometimes was enough to make her top lip curl.

Everybody knew The Ship was popular with the black squads when they came ashore. They were an unruly mob of stokers and trimmers who sweated in the bowels of the ships they sailed on, shovelling coal into the hungry furnaces day in, day out.

She hoped her dad didn't decide to come home early for some reason. If he caught sight of her or Violet out like this, they'd have some explaining to do, and she doubted he'd bother listening before he lashed out. He'd not be happy to see Violet dressed up like a dog's dinner and out on her own. She knew too it wouldn't be Violet who copped it either. Somehow it would all be her fault.

A raucous din was audible as the door to the pub swung open, expelling a man onto the pavement. Please don't let it be Dad, Evelyn whispered to herself, her breath a puff of white. She came to a halt and watched wide-eyed as Violet drew level with the man who was swaying about alarmingly.

'Ere, girl, spare a lonely old sailor a kiss, why don't yer?' he slobbered, trying to grab hold of her arm.

Violet swatted him away and shot him a disdainful glance. 'Ger away with you. I wouldn't kiss the likes of you for all the tea in China!' Then, holding her head high, she tip-tapped on her way.

He staggered after her, and Evelyn began to hurry towards him, hoping he didn't turn nasty because she'd have to intervene if he did. Although what she'd do exactly, she hadn't a clue.

'Eee, yer uppity Judy!' he shouted, flapping his hand as though dismissing her. Grousing, Evelyn couldn't make out followed, and then he turned to relieve himself against the pub's wall.

Disgusting, she thought, holding back until he'd finished. She waited until he'd weaved his way over the cobbles to the other side of the street. Then she charged after Violet and was in time to see her reach the long stretch of Vauxhall Road. Her mouth dropped open as her sister marched boldly up to a parked motor car. She tapped on the driver's window and dipped her head to speak to whoever was behind the wheel. Who on earth was she talking to? Evelyn tried to think but didn't have to think too hard because it wasn't anyone she knew. No one in her world drove a motorcar.

It was like she'd taken root as she continued to stare while Violet's tinkling giggle rippled forth. Finally, the car door swung open and a man got out. Evelyn was desperate to see his face, but she was too far away. The tip of a cigarette glowed, and she could see enough to tell he was dressed like a gentleman. He leaned in to greet her sister with a kiss, and Violet giggled as she pushed him off half-heartedly. The cigarette was flicked to the ground as the man and Violet moved around to the passenger door. He held it open for her and Violet was swallowed up as the door banged shut.

Now was her chance. Evelyn urged herself to call out to her sister, but no sound came out when she opened her mouth to do so.

The car rattled into life and pulled out into the road behind a horse and cart meandering along. A parp of irritation sounded, and the carter steered his horse over to the side of the road to let them pass. Then, it was too late. They were gone.

Evelyn was trembling. Whatever Violet was up to with that man, she knew it wasn't moral, or she wouldn't be behaving so furtively.

There was nothing for it now but to go home and she'd best come up with an explanation as to why she'd gone gallivanting off for her mam. Lizzie had long since given up on keeping a leash on Violet, accepting her airy announcements that she was off to visit her friend Helen or Mary or whoever. The words, 'Just be sure to be home before your father,' unsaid but understood nonetheless. It was different for Evelyn though. She didn't have the wildness in her Violet did. She'd have to tell Mam she'd forgotten she'd promised to call in on Ida after tea to cheer her up. 'She had a terrible telling off at the factory today for being late, Mam,' she practised out loud as she began to retrace her steps.

It wasn't in Evelyn's nature to fib nor sneak about at night either, and she uttered a cuss word about her sister. It was foreign to her lips, but she relished its badness. She'd be having words with Violet when she crawled into bed later, alright. She'd not be keeping her secrets for her from Mam because how would she live with herself if Vi came a cropper and she'd stayed silent. So, turning on her heel, she began to retrace her steps, gnawing on her bottom lip as she reached the pub once more.

Mercifully, the door stayed closed this time.

She didn't see the lad peel himself off the lamp post three doors down from the pub. Not until she was nearly upon him. Evelyn stopped short. Perhaps she'd not had a lucky escape from the rabble-rousers in The Ship's Head after all. Her heart began to bang against her chest.

Chapter Ten

'Ger out of my way!' Evelyn did her utmost to hold the lad's eye as she tried to emulate Violet's earlier cockiness with the drunk. Don't let him sense you're frightened, Evie, she told herself, glad he couldn't see her shaking hands hidden inside her coat pockets. It's like with dogs. They'd pounce if they sensed you were scared.

He doffed his bucko cap before adjusting it to a jaunty angle. 'Don't be like that, girl. I'm offering you me services, aren't I?'

Evelyn watched warily, taking a step back as he flicked the butt of his cigarette into the gutter then straightened the lapels of his tight-fitting, button jacket. A wide leather belt held up a pair of bell-bottom trousers, and on his feet were a sturdy pair of hobnail boots. Her eyes, however, were transfixed by that belt, knowing it was a weapon. She also knew some of the street thugs didn't discriminate when it came to beating innocent men or women if they so much as glanced at them the wrong way. He had to be part of a gang; he was too nattily dressed in his tailored suit to be a seaman, and no respectable person would be hanging about like so.

Her mam's face when the policeman knocked on the door in the morning to tell her her daughter had been fished out the Mersey flashed before her, and she swallowed hard. It took all her strength to quash those thoughts that wouldn't help her and maintain a dismissive façade. What did he want with her? She could ask him outright, she mulled but decided that no, it would only encourage him. 'Well, I don't need anybody's services, ta very much,' she retorted, fear ridding any hint of her upper-class vowels. 'Now, on yer bike.' She attempted to move past him.

He continued to stand in her way. 'Listen, it ain't safe for a girl to be wandering about 'ere in the dark, not with things about to kick off in there tonight.' He inclined his head towards The Ship's Head. 'I'll see you out of harm's way.'

Evelyn took in his steady stance. His speech wasn't slurred either, and he didn't reek of ale. That was something, she thought. It was easier to reason with a sober man than a drunk one.

'So,' he spoke slowly now. 'Like I said, I'll be escorting you on yer way.' He held out his arm, 'Now, shall we?'

'You will not,' Evelyn retorted, sparks of anger replacing her fear. 'Now get out of my way or I'll, I'll—'

'I ain't asking, girl, I'm telling.' He took her by the elbow and began to hustle her down the street.

'I'll scream,' Evelyn threatened as she cast about for help.

'Ain't no one to care if you do. They're otherwise engaged.'

At this, Evelyn desperately tried to wriggle free so that she could make a run for it.

'Oi, settle down. I ain't gonna hurt yer.' He loosened his grip on her arm. 'I've got sisters 'n' all, ain't I? Even if I don't see 'em anymore, I wouldn't like to think of them wandering on their own at night when the River Rats is about like they are tonight. Lord only knows what could 'appen to a girl.'

Evelyn felt as though the air was being squeezed from her lungs. She'd been stupid to head out after Violet. Mam was right; Violet was a survivor because whatever her sister was up to with that gentleman friend of hers, Vi would be alright. She'd come up smelling of roses like she always did, but as for her, well, she didn't want to let her mind go there.

They turned the corner leaving the pub behind, and Evelyn tried to understand what was happening. The River Rats were bad news. Everybody knew that. However, they were farther from home tonight if they were drinking in The Ship. Their usual stomping ground was down by the docks where they lay in wait for the sailors who ventured off the ships in search of beer.

'Don't look like that! I ain't one of 'em. I'm a Lime Street Boy,' the lad stated proudly. 'We don't go round pounding the living daylights outta people for no reason. We're a proper crew, organised like.'

'That's not what I've 'eard,' Evelyn challenged him. What did she have to lose after all? She risked a glance at his face. He was clean-shaven despite his swarthy colouring, baby faced almost and only looked to be a year or so older than herself. His eyes were nearly black and glittered with a pent up excitement. The hair sticking out of his cap was even darker than his eyes. It was shiny like a lump of coal. He didn't look like a ruffian despite his clobber. She tried to find some comfort in that.

'And what have you 'eard then?'

Was that amusement she saw flicker across his face? Evelyn wondered, unsure if she should answer him but not wanting to rile him either; she settled on, 'Things, is all. And what did you mean when you said it wor about to kick off in the pub?'

'Just that, girl. The River Rats 'ave gone too far this time. There's wrongs that 'ave gorra be put right, and you don't want to be out on these streets when that happens.'

For a moment, the rogue notion that her dad might get a taste of his own medicine interrupted Evelyn's racing thoughts as she tried to think on her feet. Finally, she decided to deploy another tack and softened her voice. 'Listen, I think we got off on the wrong foot. It's very kind of you to offer to see me on me way but I'll be safe as houses on me own. Your, erm, pals might need your help, mightn't they? How would you explain to them you were too busy strolling with a young lady to help them out?'

'C'mon,' he growled, unswayed. 'Keep walking.'

The unmistakable noise of splintering glass followed by angry shouts sounded behind them. Evelyn's muscle's tensed and the hairs on the back of her neck stood on end as she became aware of footsteps running towards them. She was nearly hyperventilating as he pulled her into the shadows. The man whose face she caught a glimpse of as he pounded past had the same wild-eyed look her dad would get before lashing out.

They carried on, only this time Evelyn didn't resist in her eagerness to put distance between herself and whatever trouble was unfolding outside The Ship.

What's yer name?' the lad asked as they neared the alley the man had disappeared down.

'Evelyn. I'm Evelyn Flooks,' she answered automatically and then added the fib, 'and me dad's a bobby.'

'Ray Taylor and I'm pleased to make your acquaintance Miss Flooks whose dad's a bobby. Only wish it were under more auspicious circumstances, but you'll be ahright with me, girl.'

Evelyn's eyes were like organ stoppers as a sudden commotion erupted from the depths of the alley. He hurried her past. 'You don't want to be anywhere near there when that mob charges.'

They were nearing Potter Street now, and Evelyn twisted her head back in time to see men swarming from the alley with lumps of wood in their hands. The solid arm that had hold of hers no longer felt threatening. She was grateful for this Ray Taylor, Lime Street Boy or no Lime Street Boy, and when he said, 'C'mon, best we run for it.' She did.

The telephone was ringing Evelyn realised, being dragged from her recollections. She put the pen down, oblivious to how much time had elapsed in the interim and hauled herself up from her seat. As she padded over to answer it, she remembered the salmon planned for her dinner, and her stomach growled accordingly. The phone was winding into its sixth ring as she picked up the receiver, 'Hello, Evelyn Flooks speaking.' Her peckishness made her tone terse.

'And what's got your knickers in a knot, Evie?' Ida chirped down the line. She didn't wait for a reply.

'Can you believe what that Margo was after doing tonight?'

'Worra you on about?' Evelyn's brain felt foggy.

'Margo, of course, you know, Penelope Cook. *The Good Life*. We never miss it. You've not had a funny turn or something have you because you sound more like me than posh Margo?'

'No, I have not ta very much. I've not had my dinner is all, and I didn't manage to catch the programme this evening, I'm afraid. I was otherwise engaged.'

'What doing?' There was a note of disbelief in Ida's tone.

Evelyn should have known her reply wouldn't wash with her old friend because she'd have said the same thing if the shoe were on the other foot. They were birds of a feather, not to mention creatures of habit. You could set the clocks by their daily routines.

'If you must know, I've been writing.'

'Writing what?'

'An account of my early years on Potter Street.'

'You what?'

'Ida, close your gob,' Evelyn bossed, well able to picture the look on her friend's face. Then she regrouped and explained. 'I'm writing it all down, aren't I? What happened with mam and me sisters, how I met Ray, Dad, all of it, including how I came to get my foot in the door here on Bold Street.'

'You're after airing your dirty laundry you mean.'

'I wouldn't have put it quite like that, Ida, but I need to tell our Sabrina what went on between Ray and me. The time's never right to talk to her though, and I thought it might be easier to put it in writing for her. That way, she can read it on her own and digest it all.'

'You don't have to breathe a word of it.' Ida was straight to the point. 'The past belongs right there, in the past, in my opinion.'

'Be that as it may, Ida, I don't want her thinking ill of me after I've popped my clogs. Can you imagine worra shock it would be to her when old Mr Holmes reads me will?'

'She'd get over it, Evie, and if I know you, you won't be shuffling off this mortal coil anytime soon.'

Evelyn twirled the phone cord. 'I've no plans to meet my maker just yet, you're right there, but I don't think she would get over it, Ida. Not when I've drummed it into her that honesty is the best policy.'

There was a snorting sound down the line, and Evelyn held the phone away from her ear. 'Ahright, ahright. I might have told her to tell the odd white lie, but it's not like we had any choice.' Ida was the only one apart from Flo and Adam who knew how Sabrina had come to live with her.

'I don't think she'll thank you for it is all, Evie, and neither will Ray for that matter.'

'It's because of him I've not breathed a word before, but now she's so cosy with his lad. Well, she'd feel betrayed if she finds out from someone else.'

'And what if Sabrina tells her Adam? Have you thought of that? Is that fair on Ray after what he did for you?'

Evelyn remained stubbornly silent.

Ida sighed, she knew her friend better than she knew herself at times, and when she'd made her mind up to do something, there was no stopping her. 'Be it on your head then, Evie.'

Evelyn didn't want a sermon, she wanted her salmon, and as such, she finished the call as tersely as she'd begun it.

Part Two

Chapter Eleven

Sabrina gazed dreamily down at the plopping porridge as she recalled the lingering goodnight kiss she'd shared with Adam There was a familiar quickening in her loins at the memory.

'Quickening in her loins' was pinched from one of Mrs Teesdale's bodice rippers. She and Flo had sneakily giggled over it, flipping through the pages to read out the naughty bits when they were around the same age the twins were now. They'd never forgotten it and still asked one another upon meeting a new fella, 'did he make your loins quicken then, girl?' It usually elicited a snort of laughter.

Sabrina grinned to herself, but her expression swiftly switched to a frown. All this quickening of the loins was frustrating because the goodnights were getting harder and harder. She didn't want to have to say goodnight at all, but it wasn't as if she could haul Adam upstairs to the flat to spend the night with her. Aunt Evie would have a fit for one thing, and for another, she'd hardly be able to relax knowing her aunt was snoring in the bedroom next door, falsies in the glass of water on the bedside table. The very thought of trying to be amorous under those circumstances made her pull a face!

Sabrina switched the element off. Adam lived at home too. She refused to sneak out of the house that seemed too big for just him and his dad come morning. Skulking around was not her style. Adam had tried to convince her his dad wouldn't be bothered if she stayed over, but she wasn't having it. Ray might not care, but she flipping well did! How was she supposed to look him in the eye when he called into the shop to see Aunt Evie knowing he knew she was copping off with his son? No, it wasn't happening.

It wasn't even as if they could park up somewhere secluded and clamber over into the backseat of his car because he rode a flamin' motorcycle, she thought, pouring the porridge into the two waiting bowls. Instead, they'd had to make do with snatched occasions when she'd been assured there was no chance of Ray coming home out of the blue and catching them out.

Sabrina went through her Goldilocks' routine, knowing how both Aunt Evie and Fred liked their porridge. What would it be like to wake up beside Adam every morning? she daydreamed, pouring the heaped spoonful of sugar over Fred's. To open her eyes and see his lashes shadowing his cheeks as he slept. A warm glow settled over her as she mentally reached up to trace her index finger down his cheek and along his jawline, feeling the bristly morning stubble beneath her fingertips.

She'd told Adam she didn't want to move in with him when he'd mentioned them getting a flat together. Loads of girls lived with their fellas these days, but she'd no interest in 'trying before buying' as Flo had worded it. She was old-fashioned, and when she set up home with Adam, she wanted to be his wife.

Sabrina teetered on the edge of a wedding day fantasy, but before she could picture herself gliding down the aisle, she remembered their conversation the night before. A happy jolt shot through her because she *would* get to wake up next to him soon, on the Isle of Man! They'd have plenty of time to be together then. At least, she hoped they would. Surely it couldn't all be about motorbikes? Could it?

'Aunt Evie,' Sabrina called out, pulling herself back to the here and now as she put her aunt's bowl down on the table along with the rest of the breakfast things. 'Don't let your porridge get cold.'

'And what about your own?' came the huffy reply.

She must be getting dressed, Sabrina deduced, retrieving Fred's breakfast. He hadn't been in his usual spot for a few days now. The doorway outside the empty shop which had once been home to the

Christian book shop had been empty aside from a few cans of lager rolling about on the wind.

'I left it in the pot like I always do, Aunt Evie.' She rolled her eyes. Her aunt knew full well she'd warm it up once she'd been to check on Fred.

'A waste of time and a thankless task if ever there was, waiting on that vagabond,' Evelyn sniped from her bedroom as Sabrina made her way carefully to the door.

She heard the sound of a zipper sliding into place as she gingerly balanced the bowl in one hand and opened the door to the stairwell with the other, ready to make her escape.

Aunt Evie didn't talk about her childhood much, but Sabrina knew from the snippets she let slip now and again it hadn't been a happy one. Her father had been a drunk who'd made his family's life a misery. As such, she'd no sympathy for Fred. She didn't see his drinking as a sickness but rather an affliction.

It's only a bowl of porridge, Aunt Evie, Sabrina would retort if she wasn't quick enough to make it down the stairs before she started in.

It was a simple thing, but it made her feel better to know that if nothing other than the gut rot he drank passed Fred's lips for the rest of the day, at least he'd got something solid in his stomach.

She was fond of the old fella, knowing there was more to him than met the eye. Sabrina had long since fancied he'd trodden the boards at some point in his life, given his theatrical streak. It was something that had been confirmed on her foray back to nineteen forty-five when she'd come across a flyer advertising a production being staged at the Shakespeare Theatre. Her eyes had popped seeing Fred pictured as part of the cast.

One of these days, she'd get his story from him, she vowed, but to date, he'd proved evasive each time she'd tried to get him talking about his past.

As for Aunt Evie, it was a case of all bark and no bite because when Sabrina had gone on her time sabbaticals as she sometimes thought of them, who was it who'd taken him his breakfast? Aunt Evie, that was who.

She pulled the door to, leaving her aunt to witter on, as flicking the light on, she trooped down the stairs passing by the silent workroom. The place was in order, she saw, pausing momentarily to give it a mental sweep.

The rays of sunlight dancing on the front windowpanes reminded her she'd need to give the windows a going over before they opened for the morning. The light streaming through them was making the mannequins posed in their wedding finery look spectral too. She was a little later than usual bringing Fred's breakfast down but knowing him, he'd still be snoring, and it was Saturday morning after all.

Being careful not to spill a drop of the hot oats like she'd done last Saturday morning, she padded over the same route. This time a week ago, she'd had a banging head on her, and it had made for a very long morning. All their customers had been demanding, or at least it had seemed that way. This morning she'd three brides-to-be coming in for either their final or second fittings. It was going to be hectic, and she'd a feeling her ten o'clock appointment with Kim Murphy was going to confirm her gown needed bustling.

Sabrina fiddled with the lock and opened the door, stepping outside to greet the day. The sky was blue and the street quieter than Monday to Friday. She liked Saturday mornings.

A lad mooched past with his head down and his hands hidden in the pockets of his jeans. He looked crumpled like he'd had a rough night, and she puffed sanctimoniously, pleased she'd not overdone it at The Swan. Although the same couldn't be said for Flo, she thought, pulling the door to behind her. She'd be feeling sorry for herself this morning, and she winced on her pal's behalf. There'd been no stopping her, and she had tried.

Poor Flo, she wouldn't want to be in her shoes when she opened her eyes and recalled how she'd demanded Tim keep his promise and give her a ride home from the pub. Tim had played along with her thinking it was a great joke, and he'd picked up his helmet, tossing Linda's to Flo before giving his unimpressed girlfriend a wink. Then he'd swaggered out of the pub.

At least he hadn't been knocking them back like Flo, Sabrina thought, pausing to peer in the window of Esmerelda's. There was no sign of life in the emporium as yet. Her thoughts returned to the night before. Linda and Tony hadn't been best pleased at the turn the evening had taken. They'd sat at their tables nursing their drinks, looking like two kids whose pocket money had been nicked.

It was Tony, Sabrina had felt sorry for. If only her friend would take off her rose-tinted glasses where Tim was concerned, then she might see that beneath his ridiculously tight jeans, Tony was a lovely fella. He thought the world of Flo, and he'd treat her like a queen.

She'd waited until Tim cruised back into the pub minus Florence a while later before telling Adam she was ready to go. At least that way, she knew Flo had made it home safely. She just hoped she'd behaved herself and not done anything she'd regret, like throwing herself at him. Nevertheless, it had been satisfying to see Linda give Tim the cold shoulder. Served him right.

A phone call was in order before she opened up for the day, Sabrina decided, sidestepping a bold pigeon on the scrounge who wasn't going to move on her account. Not that Flo would thank her for waking her up, but she wasn't going to wait the entire morning to find out what had happened.

Shivering inside her summery jumpsuit, she wished she'd put a jacket on. The day ahead might be a scorcher, but it wasn't there yet, she thought, seeing what looked like a pile of rags in a doorway a little way down.

Fred was there! She was pleased her efforts hadn't been wasted.

'Rise and shine, Fred,' she called cheerily, and when the mound didn't move, she gave him a gentle nudge with the toe of her shoe, 'C'mon, Fred, you don't want your porridge to get cold.'

Sabrina frowned as she received no reaction, and crouching, she set the porridge down on the pavement beside her.

'Fred,' she coaxed. A woolly hat was all that was visible, and she began to peel back the layers of coats. How he slept rough like this night after night was beyond her, but at least it wasn't Baltic. She'd been petrified the last winter would kill him, but on the worst nights, he'd had the sense to take himself off to a shelter.

His eyes were closed, and he wasn't his usual ruddy colour, Sabrina realised. There was a bluish tinge around his lips too. 'Fred!' This time, she shook him, and the whisky bottle he cuddled like a baby rolled free. 'Wake up, Fred!' Her voice was shrill, and she swung her head about seeking help, but the shops were shuttered and the foot traffic too far away to hear her. She didn't want to run back to the flat to call an ambulance. Her heart was racing as she straightened, deciding Esmerelda's was her best bet.

'I'll be right back, Fred. Hold on.'

Sabrina hammered on Esmerelda's door with both fists. It was flung open what felt like minutes later but was probably only a matter of seconds by a disgruntled Esmerelda. Her cigarette in its black holder was in one hand and an eyebrow pencil in the other. She'd only managed to draw one in, and she raised it. 'Wor on earth's gor into you, Sabrina, banging on me door like that?'

Sabrina could feel her insides trembling with both adrenaline and shock. 'It's Fred, Esmerelda. Phone an ambulance. He's not waking up!'

Chapter Twelve

'Will you tell Aunt Evie where I've gone?' Sabrina called across to Esmerelda as she dipped her head and clambered in the back of the ambulance. Fred was already lying inside the vehicle on a stretcher. A paramedic was placing an oxygen mask over his face. He looked frail and spindly, minus his usual layers. She wouldn't have even known it was Fred if it wasn't for the woolly hat still pulled down on his head.

The woman and her two colleagues had leapt from the ambulance, which had arrived with siren blaring minutes after Esmerelda had made the 999 phone call. But again, time had played tricks on Sabrina as the wait had felt interminable as she crouched alongside Fred, holding his clammy hand. She'd told him in no uncertain terms he was to hold on until help got there because he wasn't allowed to go anywhere. You're going to tell me your story one of these days, Fred, she'd bossed, squeezing his hand.

The only female officer of the trio had kind brown eyes and an authoritative demeanour which had managed to quickly calm Sabrina and Esmerelda as her colleagues assessed the situation before setting to work on Fred with some kind of electric shock machine.

Sabrina, willing Fred to be alright over and over in her head, barely heard Esmerelda when she explained the machine was called a defibrillator. She knew this because her cousin Mack's heart had stopped suddenly, and the piece of equipment making poor Fred's body shudder so had managed to get it beating again.

It had worked.

Sabrina had begged to be allowed to ride in the ambulance with Fred. The officers agreed so long as she kept out of the way.

Now, Esmerelda was like Puff the Magic Dragon as she exhaled clouds of smoke, assuring Sabrina in her gravelly voice that she would go straight round to Evelyn and inform her of what had unfolded. 'Here,'—she dug into the pocket of her emerald caftan and produced a few pounds—'Take this to get yourself a brew and to telephone your aunt and me as soon as you've any news, ahright kid?'

'Thanks, Esmerelda.' Sabrina pocketed the money gratefully because her purse was back in the flat, and the only thing in her pockets was half a tube of Opal Fruits. But then there was no time to say anything further because the doors were closed on them.

'I'm Joan, luv, and you can sit over there.' The woman whose hair was pulled back into a neat brown, grey bun indicated the bench seat with her head. A blue and white NHS emblem decorated one pocket of her crisp army green shirt, an ambulance service design the other. She was immaculate despite the drama, which gave Sabrina confidence. She felt like a crumpled wreck as she sank onto the hard bench and tried to get her breathing steady as Joan finished attaching the oxygen mask. She watched as the older woman sought a vein in the crook of Fred's arm but turned away as she began to insert a tube into it.

'Will he be ahright?' Sabrina was almost frightened to hear the reply.

'We'll do our best for him, luv,' was the reply and the words, but I can't make any promises, hung unsaid on the close air.

The engine rumbled to life, and the siren screamed as they set off. The waft of booze, fags and a general unwashed odour coming off Fred was suffocating and Sabrina pulled at the neck of her jumpsuit as she began to overheat. She couldn't be sick, not here.

Not glancing up from the skilled task, Joan asked her how she knew Fred.

'I live above Bold Street Brides where I work, and Fred sleeps rough a few doors down. I bring him his breakfast, but this morning, well, he wouldn't wake up.' Sabrina sniffed. The distraction had taken her mind off her queasiness.

'Bold Street Brides, you say?'

'Yes,' Sabrina nodded, still not looking over for fear of what she might see.

'Well, now I'm sure that's where my niece had her dress made for her wedding last year. She looked like a princess.' Joan told her her niece's name, and Sabrina remembered her as a pretty girl taking her upcoming nuptials in her stride, unlike some of their more demanding brides. The distraction worked a treat, and by the time Joan had finished telling her what a lovely wedding her niece's had been, they were already pulling up alongside the ED department of the Royal.

Sabrina sat on the bench while Fred was unloaded.

'You go and report to reception, luv. Joan gave her a comforting smile, and Sabrina watched as she and the other officers trundled him inside the building. She felt bereft watching them go before taking the ambulance driver's hand. He helped her down, and thanking him, she hurried towards the main doors.

Chapter Thirteen

'He's had a heart attack, Aunt Evie,' Sabrina informed Evelyn as she made the first of three phone calls from the payphone in the foyer of the Royal Liverpool Hospital. Her free hand was pressing her ear closed to hear her aunt's reply over the din of a typical day at work in the city's busiest hospital. 'They're going to do surgery to try and open his blocked arteries. The nurse told me if I hadn't found him when I did, he wouldn't have made it.' Her words came out in a rush, and she supposed she was still in shock. A hot, sweet cup of tea would help with that, but she'd not been able to stop the trembling in her hands until the nurse had sought her out with an update and she hadn't fancied scalding herself on top of everything else.

'Humph. More than he deserves,' Evelyn huffed, and muttered on about him, having brought it all on himself. She might have sounded hard, but Sabrina wasn't fooled. She'd heard the concern in her aunt's voice when she'd answered after only two rings, and she'd pictured her snatching up the telephone in the shop desperate for an update, customer or no customer.

'Will you tell Esmerelda what's happening?' Sabrina interrupted her aunt. The antiseptic and slightly bitter tang in the air was making her throat itch, and she swallowed hard. 'She loaned me some money so I could call you with an update and get a brew while I waited.'

'Of course, I will, luv,' Evelyn replied, her voice softening. 'And what will you do now?'

Sabrina glanced over at the seats, most occupied by anxious-looking people with pale, drawn faces. One woman, in particular, was working her way through her packet of Camels at a rate of knots, and she watched as she ground out another ciggy beside a smouldering butt in the silver ashtray next to where she was sitting.

'There's not much I can do, but I'd like to stay until he's had his operation and I know he's out of the woods.' She'd made her mind up to stay positive. There was power in positive thoughts, she'd told herself. 'I want him to know I'm here and that he's not on his own. I wish I knew whether he had any family. The nurse asked me, but I had to say I didn't know. I'd call them myself if I did. It's not right him having no one.' Her voice hiccupped on her last few words.

'He's not alone, Sabrina. Hasn't he got you? And he's a luckier man for it,' Evelyn soothed.

Her fear that Fred might not make it through the surgery despite her positive vibes made anger flare. 'Even if he did have someone, they must be bleedin' hard-nosed to leave him to fend for himself on the streets like so.'

'It's not your place to sit in judgement, Sabrina. That's not how you were raised. Family's not always straightforward, and there are always two sides to every story.' Evelyn was terse as her history sprang to mind. 'You've no idea what sort of a life Fred led before he wound up sleeping rough or how he treated the people around him. Or how he was treated for that matter.'

Sabrina was chastened, and as she saw the pence mounting up on the display panel, she moved on. 'But will you be ahright in the shop on your own this morning? I know it's going to be busy.'

'Ah, you're a soft touch, Sabrina Flooks.' And where a second ago her aunt had been irked, pride had now sneaked into her tone. 'And I could run this shop with my eyes closed. So you're not to worry yourself. Stay there. You'd be worse than useless in the shop today anyway.'

It was true, Sabrina thought, hanging up a moment later, grateful to her aunt for understanding. There was no way she'd be able to give her customers the attention they deserved with her mind all over the place like it was right now. Aunt Evie could run the boutique with her eyes closed and her hands tied behind her back for that matter too!

She bit her bottom lip as, picking up the receiver once more, her index finger punched out Adam's number. Ray Taylor answered after a few short rings.

'Hiya, Mr Taylor, it's Sabrina. Is Adam about please?'

'Sabrina, you read my mind. I was thinking about Evelyn. How's she—'

Sabrina cut him off before he could finish his sentence. She didn't want to waste her precious change filling him in on Aunt Evie, not when she was desperate to talk to Adam. Besides, it wasn't even a week since he'd last called into the shop. 'I'm sorry, Mr Taylor, but would you mind putting Adam on for me? It's urgent, and I'm ringing from a public telephone.' She sensed his hesitation and imagined a mental debate about whether he should ask if everything was okay. In the end, the phone clattered down on the telephone table she knew was in the hall, and she heard him call out to Adam that she was on the phone and that it was urgent.

The sound of his steady voice as he picked the telephone up with a question, 'Sabrina? What's going on?' made her nerves stop tingling, and she relayed the dramatic turn the morning had taken without the breathiness of her previous phone call.

'I'll come down to the ozzy now.'

THE SUMMER POSY

She wanted him to more than anything, but there was nothing he could do apart from holding her hand. 'No, don't. I'm only sitting here, Adam, and besides, the lads will miss your goal keep skills if you don't show up for this morning's match.'

'Don't be daft. It's only a friendly. I'll be there as soon as I can.'

If it were at all possible to love him even more than she already did, then right at that moment, Sabrina's heart was fit to burst.

The last call she needed to make was to Florence, and hopefully, by now, her friend might be awake. She tapped out the number she knew by heart and waited while it rang out. Mr Teesdale answered, and his harried voice was explained, 'Hiya, kid. No other bugger gets off their arse to answer the flamin' phone, and I'm just on my way down to the allotment. Hang on while I give her a shout.'

In the background, Sabrina heard him holler up the stairs, and she couldn't help but smile as he told his eldest daughter she was sleeping her life away!

Florence's voice was a sorry croak as she picked up the upstairs extension in her parents' bedroom. 'I've gorrit, ta, Dad and don't shout like that. It hurts me head.'

'You'll not ger any sympathy from me, young lady,' he said before the telltale click sounded, which meant he'd hung up the downstairs phone.

'Hiya, Sabs. I'm dying here,' she rasped. It was swiftly followed by 'Ger out!' and a commotion of sorts.

'Flo, worra you doing?'

'I threw one of Mam's slippers at our kid. She was earwigging again.'

Sabrina didn't ask which of the twins was annoying her as she told her not to worry about that, adding, 'Flo, listen, would you. I can't talk long. I'm on a payphone at the ozzy.'

'Oh my God, girl, what's happened?' Florence was instantly on high alert.

'Calm down. It's not me. It's Fred.' The worry in Florence's voice was contagious, and Sabrina allowed a sob to escape. 'I thought he was dead, Flo, when I took him his breakfast this morning. It was an awful fright.'

'But he's going to be ahright?'

'I don't know. I'm waiting to hear. It was a heart attack, and Fred's in surgery now. They're trying to unblock his...' she tried to snag the word she was looking for, but her mind had gone blank.

'Arteries,' a know-it-all, familiar voice piped up.

'Shona Teesdale, hang that phone up right now or I'll come down those stairs and slap you hard.'

The two friends were silent for a beat until they knew she'd hung up. 'I'll swing for her one of these days.'

Sabrina eyed the coin display. If she hurried the conversation along, she might end the call with enough cash left for that much-needed brew. So she got straight to the point, 'What happened last night when Tim dropped you home then?'

'Aw, Sabs, you've made me head hurt again,' Florence wailed. 'I'll never be able to show me face down The Swan again.'

'It can't have been that bad.'

'Yes, it can.'

'Out with it.' Sabrina was gripping the receiver tightly, her face screwed up in anticipation of what she was about to be told. She almost didn't want to know.

'He was a proper gentleman. He walked me to the door and everything, but then I ruined it by kissing him, didn't I.' It was a statement, not a question.

Sabrina pictured the scene with her drunken pal lunging at Tim outside her house. 'Did he push you away?' It was embarrassing, yes, but hardly the crime of the century. She was already preparing her speech where she reminded her friend of the time she'd hit the dance floor at the local disco when they were teenagers, oblivious to her dress being caught up in her knickers. Flo hadn't thought she'd ever live that down, but she had. Although she still turned puce whenever Sweet's 'Ballroom Blitz' came on the radio. She could give him a quick call and apologise, saying it was down to the ale. It would be like ripping a plaster off. It would only hurt for a split second, and then it would be over and done with.

'No, it was worse. Tim kissed me back. Properly kissed me back, and,'—she lowered her voice to a whisper—'tried to cop a feel.'

Sabrina was lost. Surely that's what her friend had intended when she'd made her move? Why was she so horrified? Unless she'd had a crisis of conscience over Linda, but given the state she'd been in, that wasn't likely. Florence hadn't finished though.

'It was me who pushed him off in the end because I had to dash to the gutter.'

'You didn't—'

'I did. I threw up. Chinese and beer, ugh, I can still smell it in me hair.'

'Flo!'

'Don't say me name like that. You're making me feel worse, and I already feel sick again just thinking about it.'

'Well, I hope he didn't roar off on that bike of his leaving you there being sick.'

'Course not. He's not that much of an arlarse.'

Sabrina wasn't so sure. She hadn't forgotten how he'd laughed his head off when Florence had gone head over heels on the Bootle Tootler's maiden jog. It had been Tony who'd come to her rescue.

'For your information, he helped me find me key and unlocked the front door because I'd no show of making it fit in the lock. Then he went and ruined it all by pinching me bum and saying that what had happened could be our secret.'

'You being sick?'

'No, you div, the kissing and the grope. He said, Linda doesn't need to know, and we could meet up on the quiet if I were up for it.'

'See! A complete arlarse, girl. Don't even think about taking him up on that, Florence Teesdale.' Sabrina might not be fond of Linda, but a code among females had to be adhered to.

'I know, and don't shout, me head hurts.'

The phone made a pip-pipping noise. 'I'm about to run out of money, Flo, I've gorra go, but I'll call around later when I know how things are with Fred, ahright?' The phone had already disconnected.

Chapter Fourteen

Adam was a sight for sore eyes as he strode in through the doors of the Royal. The shirt he wore beneath his leather jacket was crumpled and hanging out of the back of his jeans. He was carrying two helmets and had obviously dressed in a hurry, Sabrina thought, moving to greet him.

The shirt looked very much like the one he'd been wearing at the pub the night before. Not that she cared, and seeing him open his arms wide as he saw her, she stepped towards him and sank into the space in between. Her cheek rested against his shirt, and his chest was warm and solid, steadying. She inhaled deeply. The shirt reeked of ale and ciggies, but there was comfort in the leather, apple, and spice scent under riding it. The subtle hints of the shampoo and aftershave he used, along with his jacket, were so uniquely him. She stayed cocooned with his arms closed tightly around her, listening to his heartbeat.

'People don't see Fred,' she mumbled into his chest after a moment or two.

'What was that?' His breath ruffled her hair, and she disentangled herself from the embrace to look up at him.

'I said people don't see Fred. All they see is an old drunk who sleeps rough, but they don't see Fred, and there's so much more to him than that.'

Adam stroked her hair, 'You care about the arl fella, don't you?'

Sabrina nodded, thinking about all the times she'd taken him breakfast or some other treat going spare, lingering to seek his advice. Fred was a wise man.

'I think he knows that, Sabrina.'

Her expression was hopeful, 'Do you think so?'

'I do. There's not many who'd bother looking out for him the way you do.'

'I don't do much. Just take him some breakfast. I wish I could do more because he's my friend. You look out for your friends.'

'Well, it's more than most would do, friend or not, and I luv you for it.' Not for the first time, Adam wished his mam was still alive because she'd have loved Sabrina too.

'He helps me too because I can talk to him. He's like one of them agony aunts where you write in with your problems. He's a listener is Fred.'

Adam cupped her face with his palms and then kissed her forehead. 'I understand.' A siren's scream sounded, and he moved her away from the entrance.

Her eyes filled. 'And I can't stand the thought of him waking up here thinking not a soul in the world cares for him.'

Adam echoed her aunt Evie's sentiment. 'But he won't, will he? Because you'll be here, and so will I.'

Sabrina blinked the tears away. Her emotions were snowballing in on her. She'd had to say goodbye to her mam, and she wasn't ready to say goodbye to Fred too.

Adam tugged at her hand. 'C'mon, have you had a brew yet?'

'No, and I'm gasping.' Aunt Evie always said, no matter what was happening in the world, there was always time for a cup of tea, Sabrina thought, following his lead.

'Me too. I'd not long got out of bed when you rang, and I came right away.' Adam weaved his way around with his hand wrapped around Sabrina's to the cafeteria, and once she was seated, he joined the line waiting to order.

Sabrina twiddled the salt shaker while she waited, unable to keep her hands still. The conversations ebbed and flowed around her, along with the scraping of chairs as people came and went. Hospitals were like airports with all the comings and goings. Not that she'd had much experience with the latter.

The closest she'd got to going overseas was her upcoming trip to the Isle of Man. Her stomach grumbled, reminding her she'd not had any breakfast, but the peculiar, meaty smell of hospital food clung to the air and she didn't think she could eat a bite.

Her hand slipped and the salt shaker toppled over. She tried to snatch it back up, but it was too late and the lid, which wasn't screwed on properly, rolled off. By the time she'd righted the glass canister, a small hill of salt had spilt forth.

'You'll have to toss a pinch of that over your shoulder now, queen.' A dapper gent twinkled at her as he paused to lean on his walking stick.

Sabrina gave him a weak smile. She wasn't running any risks, and he watched as she scooped up a pinch of salt between her thumb and forefinger. Then, checking the surly waitress clearing tables wasn't looking her way, she flicked it over her shoulder.

The man gave her a wink before ambling on his way, satisfied all was right with the world.

After that, Sabrina left the salt cellar alone, turning her mind to Fred. What had happened to him that had seen him go from taking a turn on stage at the Shakespeare to sleeping rough in the doorway of the old Christian book shop? It was a mystery, and she was good at solving mysteries. Hadn't she found her mam?

Yes, she resolved, putting a paper napkin over the salt hill and trying to scoop it up. Once he was allowed visitors, she'd be right there by his bedside with a box of Thornton's choccies. But he'd not be allowed a single one until he told her the truth of his life either. This time she'd not let him get away with changing the subject or launching into song when she broached the topic of his old life.

'My mam used to say you'll stay like that if the wind changes whenever I'd pull a face,' Adam said, putting the tray down in front of her.

Sabrina didn't know what he was talking about because she wasn't pulling a face.

'The frown on you.'

'Oh.' She made an effort to unfurrow her brow.

'That's better.' Adam glanced up from the task of pouring the tea. He settled opposite her sliding a dry looking scone towards her. 'I didn't think you'd have eaten. It's buttered,' he offered up half-apologetically.

'Ta, I haven't.' She eyed the scone, deciding she'd have to attempt it now he'd gone and bought it. First things first though. She added a heaped teaspoon of sugar to her tea, stirring it in briskly.

Adam raised an eyebrow, knowing she didn't usually take sugar.

'I need it today.' Sabrina raised the teacup to her lips. The hot, sweet liquid had the soothing effect she'd hoped for and she picked at the scone. It was even drier than it looked despite the slather of insipid yellow in the middle of it. Mind you, she was spoiled when it came to the humble scone because she was used to scoffing down Mrs Teesdale's, and they were light and airy the way a scone should be. Still, food in her tummy would make her feel better.

She appraised Adam, who was lost in thought. She'd been so caught up in herself she hadn't noticed how pale he'd gone or the tight set of his jaw. 'Adam?' she queried, but he didn't answer. So instead of repeating herself, she reached across the table and touched his hand fleetingly. This time he raised his gaze from the contents of his teacup to meet hers. 'Are you ahright?' She looked deep into his eyes, twin black pools, trying to read them but couldn't.

He shrugged. 'It's being back in this place. It's made me feel strange. It's different being a patient when you have the nurses running after you and you're flat on your back. I don't like being the one waiting for news.'

Sabrina didn't know if she should be annoyed at the thought of the nurses fussing around her lovely Adam, but she could tell he didn't mean it like that. He'd spent time here himself a year or so back when a car had turned unexpectedly, cutting him off on his motorbike. It was an unfortunate accident that had left him with a ruptured spleen, but every cloud had a silver lining and all that because it was also here at the Royal their romance had begun. 'You were lucky to get off so lightly. It could have been worse.' She shuddered.

Adam didn't speak for a few seconds, and they both jumped at the sudden splintering of a plate as it smashed on the lino. The septic waitress Sabrina had kept a wary eye on earlier knelt to pick up the pieces. That wouldn't improve her mood, and she almost felt sorry for her. She leaned forward to hear Adam better when he finally spoke up.

'I'm thinking about me mam and how I used to sit here and eke out a pot of tea while I waited for her to finish her weekly treatments.'

'Oh, Adam,' This time, as Sabrina's hand touched his, she left it to rest there. He was a closed book for the most part when it came to his mam, who'd died when he was a teenager. The little she'd gleaned, though, was enough to know he'd thought the world of her. She felt the surge of anger towards his dad she always did when she imagined Adam as a lad bearing the weight of his mam's illness on his own. His father should have been the one coming along to support his wife. Not his son.

For whatever reason, Ray wouldn't face her illness though, and it was this that had left a rift between father and son despite their living under the same roof and working together. When Sabrina had seen them together, they spoke to one another stiffly and only when necessary. There was an undercurrent of things that needed saying, but it was a conversation neither man was prepared to start.

Sabrina would have loved to have sat them both down and got them to open up and put their hurts to bed, but it wasn't her place to interfere, and she knew Adam wouldn't thank her for it.

She recalled their conversation the day they'd gone to Blackpool. He'd confided how he'd overheard his mam telling his aunt she might be Mrs Taylor with the ring on her finger to prove it, but Ray's heart belonged to someone else. The sinking sensation she always experienced when her mind wandered back to that conversation on the pier made her put the scone down. It was like sawdust in her throat. Adam was oblivious to the guilty flush creeping up her neck as he sat lost in his memories.

She might be good at solving mysteries, but she'd yet to get to the bottom of the mystery behind Aunt Evie and Ray Taylor's relationship And, it would take more than a box of Thorntons to do so because when it came to talking about their younger days, Aunt Evie was a closed book. Her face shut down, and her lips tightened, and Sabrina knew the conversation was closed. However, one thing Aunt Evie hadn't reckoned on was her stubborn streak. Whether you believed in nurture over nature or the other way around, Sabrina was convinced it was a trait inherited from her aunt and she would get to the bottom of things.

Chapter Fifteen

Sabrina sought out Florence and, popping an Opal Fruit in her mouth, strode towards the group mingling outside Esmerelda's Emporium.

The Bootle Tootlers who'd agreed to take part in the upcoming fashion show were gathered as per Florence's Friday night instructions because, according to the clock she'd checked before leaving the flat, it was five to two. So much had happened between then and now, she thought, spying her friend bobbing about the small group like an excitable puppy.

Sabrina knew she wouldn't have been looking so perky the day before.

Her head felt woolly, which wasn't surprising given how late she'd slept that morning. Still, she was entitled to a lie-in now and again, and Sunday was a perfect day to languish in bed. Although eleven am was getting on even by her standards. She'd woken initially around eight o'clock, hearing Aunt Evie moving about as she went through the motions of getting ready for church. If she'd got up, then her aunt would have tried to coax her into going along with her. With this in mind, Sabrina had pulled the sheets back up over her shoulders and gone back to sleep.

The events of the day before had left her exhausted, and the extra hours of sleep were welcome. Eventually, though, the sun streaming in her window had got too much.

It had been late when she'd stolen back into the flat the night before, hoping not to wake Aunt Evie. Her head was lolling as she sat in front of a flickering television screen, but as the floorboards creaked, she'd snapped to attention, eager for news.

It was further proof, Sabrina had decided as she filled her aunt in on how Fred was faring, that her insides were gooey despite her crisp toffee exterior. The good news, she'd informed her, was Fred had made it through surgery and was doing well.

The redheaded nurse who'd been keeping Sabrina and Adam updated had sought them out once he'd been trundled back onto the ward. She'd said one of them could go and see him for themselves so long as they were quick. It was just as well because Sabrina would have camped out all night waiting to see him. Adam had given her a nudge and she'd followed the kindly nurse's lead, trying to look inconspicuous given visiting hours were over.

Tears had sprung at the sight of Fred with tubes hanging off him, but it had been a relief to see his pallor had lost that awful grey tinge she'd been confronted with that morning. His breathing, too, was rhythmic. She'd wished she had a jar of Vaseline on her, because his lips were dry and cracked. Still, leaning over his bedside, she thought that there were worse things than cracked lips.

'I'm here with you, Fred,' she'd murmured, picking up his hand. She gave it a gentle squeeze, reassured by the warmth of it. 'And I tell you what. You didn't half give me a fright this morning.' She could sense the nurse lurking in the hall, keeping an eye out as she stood over him. A snore erupted from a curtained-off bed further down the ward. The culprit swiftly followed it up with two parps as he broke wind.

The relief that Fred was still with her had seen a childish giggle threaten to burst forth, and Sabrina had had to bite down on her lip to stop it in its tracks. As for Fred, his eyes might have been closed, but she was sure she saw the corners of his mouth twitch. Whether it had been from his ward mate's bodily functions or knowing Sabrina was there, she didn't know, but the sound of a throat clearing in the corridor galvanised her. 'I've gorra go now, Fred, but I'll be back to see you tomorrow evening. You behave yourself now, do you hear me?' She'd given his hand a final squeeze.

THE SUMMER POSY

Adam had dropped her off on Wood Street and their kiss goodnight had been intense thanks to their having spent the day together at the hospital. Being privy to life and death playing out on a continual spin cycle would do that to a couple.

Now, Florence broke away from the Tootlers to greet her, 'Hiya, queen.' She was pleased for an excuse to move away from Janice, who'd been harping on about how she was glad it wasn't too hot. The heat, Janice said, brought chafing on, and if the mercury hovered above twenty on the evening of their modelling debut, well, she couldn't promise she wouldn't look like a cowgirl swaggering down the runway.

Sabrina appraised her friend's bold pink batwing sleeved blouse and white trousers and, on closer inspection, could see she'd gone to town with her war paint. 'You could pass for a Hot Gossip dancer with those panda eyes, girl. Very glam.' There was no sign of the previous day's hangover. She wished she'd made more of an effort with her hair and makeup now.

'Well, we models can't let the team down,' Florence said, striking a pose. 'And yesterday wasn't a complete waste of time. Mam took pity on me and cooked me a fry up. I felt like a new woman after that.'

Sabrina grinned, her mouth watering, 'Bacon, eggs, sausage—'

'And baked beans,' Florence confirmed. The Weight Watchers menu went out the window when she was feeling seedy. 'Anyway, I didn't want to mooch about at home feeling sorry for meself so, I got busy. I rang *The Echo* who said they'll send a reporter along to the show. Then, I decided to visit a few of the big department stores to see how the land lay and, guess what?'

'What?' Sabrina was suitably impressed her friend had even managed to pick up the telephone to ring the paper given the state of her when she'd spoken to her the previous morning.

'We've got Cynthia and Kimberley coming to do our makeup for the show!'

'That's brilliant, Flo! Well done,' Sabrina enthused. Then she took a good look at the ten or so other women. They were chattering excitedly and had all slapped on the makeup in honour of the day's rehearsal. Patsy had been exceedingly heavy-handed and might have carried off her super-tanned look if it weren't for the tideline along her jaw. They'd all made a big effort except for her, and she shouldn't criticise, but they were going to need some help in the makeup department. 'So, that leaves hair?'

'No.' Florence shook her head, grinning like a Cheshire cat. 'I've already told the others. Not only are we sorted in the makeup department, but we have John-Paul and Penny from Sassy Scissors coming to sort our hair out. The girls are dead excited.'

Sabrina clapped her hands delightedly and gave a little squeal. It was all coming together. 'So am I!' She grabbed her friend and hugged her. Then, releasing her, asked, 'You're all recovered then?'

Florence nodded, 'I still feel sick each time I think about it though.'

'Think about what?' Gina, who had a nosy streak and two streaks of pink blusher on her cheeks that made her resemble a Native American warrior, asked.

'Mind your own,' Florence batted back fast as lightning. 'How's Fred?'

'Sorry I didn't make it around to see you yesterday afternoon,' Sabrina apologised. 'I didn't leave the ozzy until late.'

Florence flapped the apology away. 'I rang Aunt Evie and she told me you were still there waiting for news which was why I took meself off into town.'

Sabrina nodded and gave her the rundown, but as she reached the part about sneaking onto his ward, she was distracted by a loud trilling.

'Yoo-hoo!'

Ten pairs of eyes swung towards the source, hurrying down Bold Street, and Florence muttered something unladylike under her breath as she spied Bossy Bev. The Bootle branch of Weight Watchers' team leader was waving at them with the same vigour as those seeing off family members as they set sail for America from the Liverpool docks over the years.

'Flamin' 'eck she's like your woman off *Hi-de-Hi*. Who told her about the rehearsal?' Florence swung around, glaring accusingly at the Tootlers. They were all but whistling as they feigned interest in the pavement. 'She'll try and run the show. I've already told her we've gor enough models and she'll be better put to use as a backstage dresser. She didn't need to come today.'

'Eee, get a load of you, backstage dresser!' Janice piped up.

Sabrina hadn't done much to help with the organising, but she could help smooth Flo's ruffled feathers, and so she took charge, 'We won't let her take over. She'll have to toe the line and do as she's told. Right girls?'

A Mexican wave of consent sounded.

'If she offers youse any free Weight Watchers baked beans to swap places you're not to be bought, do you hear me?' Florence stated, hands-on-hips.

A consensus of 'no to the beans' whipped around the group just as Bev drew level.

'Hellooo,' she chirruped, her face alight with excitement. 'What was that about beans?'

'Nothing,' Florence mumbled.

Bev fanned herself with her hand. 'I hope my makeup hasn't run; it's scorching, and I all but ran from the station because a little birdy told me there's a dress rehearsal happening here today, and I thought I was going to be late.'

Sabrina found it difficult to tear her eyes away from Bev's hair. Florence had told her it was big on any given day, but in honour of today's practice, she'd teased it out to even greater heights.

'A flamin' cyclone could whip down Bold Street and not a hair on her head would move,' Florence whispered out of the corner of her mouth, and Sabrina giggled.

Bev shot them both a look before clapping her hands together like a camp leader. 'What a coup, Florence. The Bootle branch of Weight Watchers in a fashion show. Think of the publicity! I wonder if we could have a display on the big night? What do you think?'

'A big no to that. It's Esmerelda's gig,' Florence informed her curtly, 'You're here to help us get dressed in our clobber, I take it?'

Before Bossy Bev could reply, the doorway in which they were clustered was flung open, and there a shimmering vision in a gold lamé caftan and matching turban, was the woman herself. Her cigarette was angled just so in its black holder with grey-blue smoke spiralling forth. She blocked the entrance as she appraised the motley crew clustered in front of her shop with narrow kohl-rimmed eyes.

The Bootle Tootlers and even Bossy Bev were rendered speechless as they took in the golden apparition before them.

'Esmerelda,' Florence beamed. 'Meet your models. The Bootle Tootlers!'

'And me, Linda.' Linda had appeared seemingly from thin air in all her crimped glory. 'I've modelled before if any of youse need any tips.'

Florence's face went pink seeing Tim's girlfriend and she scowled. She'd forgotten about that part of the evening.

'You did promise she could join in,' Sabrina whispered.

'Don't bloody remind me.'

Esmerelda was currently the star of the show; however, Linda and the women watched awestruck as the glowing tip of the cigarette burnt to the butt as Esmerelda sucked pensively on the black holder. Finally, she exhaled skywards and then stepped aside to allow them to pass.

This lot wasn't quite what she'd had in mind, but beggars couldn't be choosers.

Chapter Sixteen

'That went well,' Sabrina said to Florence as they exited the emporium stuffing the coins she'd tried to reimburse Esmerelda with back in her pocket. Although she downplayed it, Sabrina could tell she was relieved Fred had made it through surgery.

They were the last to leave and Esmerelda had locked the door behind them. What an afternoon it had been! Sabrina thought as they linked arms. It had passed in a blur, and her fuzzy head had long since cleared, lifting her mood right along with it. She knew she wasn't the only one on a natural high either. They'd all been rough diamonds, to begin with, but by the end of the afternoon and under Esmerelda's guidance, they'd begun to sparkle. She was a hard taskmaster with a vision.

'I think Esmerelda must have been a ballet teacher in another life,' Florence stated. 'Didn't she remind you of Miss Anderson?'

'A chain-smoking version, in gold lamé but the way she wielded that cane, tapping out the orders, and taking us through our paces, she did.' Both of them drifted off thinking back to the ballet lessons they'd briefly attended as children. Neither had shown any burgeoning talent and had been more like a pair of baby elephants thumping around the studio. Their dance careers had lasted all of two terms before they'd lost interest and begged to join the Brownies instead.

Florence made Sabrina jump by suddenly shouting, 'Oi, Janice, don't forget to practise!' The older woman was a little farther up the street, laughing with Gina over something. The rest of the Tootlers and Bev had dispersed.

At Florence's voice, Janice came to a halt and swung around to salute her. Florence grinned and turned to Sabrina, 'Oh my God, girl, I sounded just like Bossy Bev then, didn't I? That's scary, that is. But honestly, Janice looked like she was staggering in them heels she brought along, not gliding.'

Sabrina laughed. It was true. Janice, a meter maid, spent her days wearing sensible strolling shoes. She'd swapped them for a pair of stilettos that probably hadn't seen the light of day since the early seventies.

'What I'd like to know is how Esmerelda did it? I mean, the emporium's fit to burst with crystals, joss sticks, dragons, fairies, caftans and dresses normally. So, how did she manage to carve out floorspace down the middle of the shop floor for a runway?'

Sabrina shrugged. 'Magic? Perhaps she twiddled her nose, you know, like in *Bewitched*.'

'It wouldn't surprise me. I luved that programme. I used to try and do the nose thing when Mam wouldn't let me have a second helping of pudding. And Esmerelda does have a look of Endora. She soon showed Bev who was in charge too.'

The Bootle Weight Watchers' branch, head honcho, had indeed tried to be King Pin issuing orders from the sidelines, but in the end, it was Esmerelda who was very much in charge.

'Well, you can't argue with a woman wielding a cane,' Sabrina replied.

Esmerelda had also put Sabrina's seamstress skills to good use by enlisting her to tweak and pin where necessary. Given her love of the forgiving caftan, dress size wasn't an issue for the best part. However, she'd had to adjust Linda's dress, a modernised kimono, pinning it at the back before she slid the boxy jacket over the top, and Flo's siren red ensemble with the black leopard spot print had needed the hem pinning.

'What did you think of your outfit then?' Sabrina asked. She'd taken fright initially when Esmerelda had unhooked the dress she'd picked out for her from the rack upon which all the colourful items she wanted shown were vying for attention.

Sabrina's style wasn't outlandish, although she often wished she were a little more flamboyant, and she'd stared at the asymmetrical fitted electric blue leather dress with a mix of horror and excitement. It screamed, 'Look at me,' and she'd never been one who liked to be in the spotlight. However, she didn't want to float down the runway wearing bog-standard jeans and a blouse either. Nor did she want to argue with Esmerelda, and it was her show after all.

So, she'd dutifully squeezed into the dress, keeping both eyes shut in front of the free-standing mirror in the back room acting as their dressing room. She only opened them when Florence elbowed her and said, 'You look like you should be on *Top of the Pops*, girl.' She peeked at the image reflected at her and hadn't seen Sabrina Flooks but rather a sexy, bold young woman who, if only she could hold a tune, could've been the next big thing.

'I luved it,' Florence replied now. 'I was worried Esmerelda would put me in one of her caftans and I'd look like I'd stuck a psychedelic sheet over me head and cut a hole in it. It was a dress me dad wouldn't let me out the door in, but it was fun feeling like someone else once I got the hang of the foot in front of the other hip-swinging walk.'

'I felt like that too. I'd never wear a dress like that normally.'

'Adam's eyes will pop out of his head when he sees you in it.'

Sabrina laughed, 'So will Aunt Evie's.' She was sure her aunt would have plenty to say. She made a mental note to ask her later if she'd volunteer her services as a dresser for the show.

They were walking up the street, but Sabrina had no clue where they were going, nor, she suspected, did Flo. 'And what about those shoulder pads of yours. They were so wide and pointy you could have taken an eye out with them.'

'I was tempted to accidentally on purpose knock into Linda, but then I saw Esmerelda had chosen an acid yellow dress that looked like one of those Japanese kimono's for her. Did you see her face when she was handed it? She didn't say anything though. I reckon she was frightened of Esmerelda.'

'Flo!'

'What?'

'It wasn't her kissing someone else's fella on Friday night.'

Florence's face matched the colour of her batwing sleeved blouse. 'You're right. I'll stop being such a cow.'

'I still luv you, and the colour made her face look green.'

'And the walk on her. I thought she was going to dislocate her hips the amount she was swinging them about.'

Florence gave a quick demo of the Linda strut and they giggled before Sabrina asked, 'How do you feel about Tim now? I mean after what happened.' She'd her fingers and toes crossed inside her jellies that Flo had finally taken off her rose-tinted glasses where Tim Burns was concerned.

'Confused. He's still drop-dead gorgeous, girl.'

'But he's also an arlarse who wants his cake and to eat it too, and every time he parades into The Swan, I expect 'Da Ya Think I'm Sexy?' to come on the jukebox.'

'Well, he is sexy, and I never got that saying because it's obvious. I luv a bit of cake, me, so of course, I want to eat it too.'

'That's not what I meant, and you know it,' Sabrina gave her friend a gentle nudge.

'Sabs, I don't want to be his bit on the side. I want to be his girlfriend.'

'But he has a girlfriend, Flo, and he's got no intention of breaking things off with her to go out with you.'

Florence's bottom lip trembled and Sabrina worried she'd gone too far. 'I'm sorry, Flo, I don't want to upset you, but he said as much to you himself.'

Florence shook her head as though she'd water in her ears, and when she spoke, she'd regained her previous good humour. 'Let's not talk about Tim.'

'Shall we talk about Tony then?' Sabrina said slyly, eying her friend.

Florence ignored her. 'It's just dawned on me?'

'Wha?'

'We're still doing it. The walk. Look.'

Sabrina snorted as she realised they were strutting rather than strolling. Florence looked at her, and she at Flo and the next moment, they were bent double in fits of laughter. An older couple took a wide berth around them, and the girls laughed even harder as they heard the woman mutter something about the youth of today all being on the drugs.

'Eee, me tummy's hurting,' Florence gasped when they'd finally managed to get themselves under control.

'Mine too.'

Where are we going anyway?'

Sabrina glanced at her watch. 'It's close to visiting time at the Royal. So I'm going to head to the ozzy and see Fred. I wanted to get him a box of Thorntons finest, but seeing as they're closed, it'll have to wait.'

'I'll come with you if you like.'

Adam was working on his bike. They'd arranged to meet for a fish 'n' chip supper later, and she'd be glad of Florence's company. Hopefully, Fred was up to having visitors. 'I wonder if he's awake yet.'

'Only one way to find out. C'mon.'

Chapter Seventeen

'I don't like the smell of ozzies,' Florence stated, her nose wrinkling. She was oblivious to the effect her pink top and tight white trousers ensemble had just had on a male orderly. The poor patient stretched out on the stretcher the orderly was trundling to the lifts had nearly been tipped off when he'd come to an abrupt halt. His eyes continued to follow Florence's derriere as she sashayed down the corridor, following Sabrina's lead.

'No one does,' Sabrina stated.

Florence rubbed at her arms. 'It gets into your skin. I wonder if you get used to it if you work here?'

'I suppose you'd stop noticing it after a while.' Sabrina gestured to the ward on her right. 'This is us.'

This evening it was a different scene to the one that had greeted Sabrina the night before when the ward had been in silence apart from the sounds of patients slumbering. Instead, visitors filled the ward, awash with grapes and flowers. The only bed that didn't have someone sat alongside it Sabrina saw, doing a quick sweep, was Fred's. Well, they'd soon put that right, she thought.

His eyes were fixed in their direction, but given his glasses had somehow wound up smashed a while ago, she doubted he'd be able to make out who it was.

There was nothing wrong with her sight though, and while he might still be pale, there was an encouraging pinkish tinge to his cheeks and he didn't have half as many tubes hanging off him either.

'What's with the grapes?' Florence whispered.

'I don't know, do I? It's just what people do when they visit someone in the ozzy.'

'Well, if I'm ever in one of those beds, don't be bringing me grapes. They make me constipated.'

'Flo!' Sabrina remonstrated as her pal promptly sneezed five times in a row.

'It's the pollen,' she managed to gasp out.

Sabrina felt the heat of wary eyes boring into them and she cleared her throat. Her voice carried across the ward to the five-star beds beneath the windows bathed in the glow of early evening. 'It's the pollen setting her off,' she informed the ward before they were lynched for bringing something contagious onto it.

'I'm ahright now,' Florence said, her eyes streaming as they padded towards Fred. 'He doesn't look too bad, all things considered.'

'He looks much better than he did yesterday.'

Fred was trying to hoist his frail frame further up the bed as they drew level. 'Sabrina, my angel! What a sight for sore eyes you are,' he rasped.

'Hiya, Fred,' Sabrina beamed. 'Here, let me help you.' She began adjusting the pillows, allowing him to rest back more upright. 'It's good to see you,' she said once she was satisfied he was comfortable and then she leaned down and gave him an impromptu kiss on his forehead.

His eyes were bloodshot, which was par for the course, and he looked exhausted, but there was something different. It wasn't only the strangeness of seeing him tucked in with a starched white sheet instead of a pile of coats, and it took her a moment, but then it dawned on her. He didn't look as unkempt as he usually did. He'd had his hair washed, and he smelled fresh, having lost the sour whisky odour that usually radiated off him. 'Are they taking good care of you then?'

'I can't complain, Sabrina, although the roast beef was on the fatty side and the tea insipid. As for any other sort of beverage. Well, I'm afraid they're sorely lacking. Not so much as an ale for an ailing man.' He began to cough, and Sabrina poured him water from the jug on the unit beside his bed. He took it gratefully, and she noticed his hand was trembling as he had a sip. A sheen of sweat coated his forehead, but there was also a glint in his eyes that Sabrina had been frightened she wouldn't see again.

'Ah, thank you, my girl,' he said, his eyes fluttering shut for a second as he swallowed the water. When he opened them, he was looking beyond Sabrina to Florence. 'And pray tell, who else has come to visit me?'

'It's me, Florence, Fred,' Florence replied, bobbing her head around Sabrina. 'It's good to see you. You had us all worried.'

'Young Florence, or is it, Florence Nightingale, perchance? I'm honoured.'

Florence tittered. 'I don't think I'd make a very good nurse, Fred. I faint at the sight of blood.'

'I shall keep the charming Nurse Daly from Dublin's fair city on then. Sit, sit, both of you.' He gestured to the chair beside the bed with the hand that wasn't attached to the intravenous tube. Sabrina sat tentatively on the edge of the bed and Florence sank down on the chair beside it.

'And I am told, it is thanks to you, Sabrina, my angel sent from the heavens, that I shall live to see another sunset.' His eyes flickered towards the rainbow-like sunbeams at the far end of the room.

'I don't know about angel, Fred, I'm just glad I was there. You gave me such a fright.'

'For which I offer you one thousand apologies.'

'We've all been worried sick. Aunt Evie, Esmerelda, Adam...' Her voice trailed off as her eyes moved to the drawers next to the bed upon which sat several pamphlets.

Fred tracked her gaze. 'The do-gooders have a sixth sense it appears, as I'd no sooner opened my eyes and there they were. It would seem they are eager to save my soul and deprive me of my one true love.'

'And did you listen to what they had to say? Because things have gorra change, you know, Fred.'

Fred shrank back into the pillows, his expression that of a naughty boy being chastised by his mam, but then his eyes narrowed slyly. 'I don't suppose you have a drop of Scotland's finest on your person, do you, Sabrina, my angel?'

'No, I do not,' Sabrina stated primly.

'And would that be a no from you too young Florence Nightingale?' He angled his head towards Florence.

'I'm afraid so, Fred.'

'I feared as much.'

'But I promise I'll bring you a box of choccies from Thorntons next time I call up,' Sabrina offered lamely.

'Ah, Sabrina, my angel, I am as partial as the next man to a dollop of sweetness in my life, but I'm afraid chocolate won't help ease my aches or the bad dreams that shall soon assail me.'

Sabrina didn't know much about what happened when an alcoholic suddenly stopped drinking, but she imagined it wouldn't be pleasant. The alternative wasn't an option though. 'You're in the right place to be helped with those though, Fred. You'll see.'

'Ah, the optimism and faith that all will be well in the world belong only to the young, I'm afraid. Still, it is a wonderous thing to behold, but sadly it is not enough.'

Sabrina decided not to dilly dally. 'How did you wind up sleeping rough, Fred? Was it because of the drinking?'

'Ah, Sabrina, my girl. The drinking is merely the medicine that came after the cause.'

'What was your life like then, Fred, before you started drinking?'

Fred's sigh was weary, and he closed his eyes.

Sabrina glanced at Florence. Perhaps she'd best leave it for now. He'd been at death's door the day before. It was too soon. Just as she was about to voice this, however, Fred's eyes sprang open, and he fixed his attention, first on Sabrina, then Florence.

'There is no pain greater than that of a broken heart and no cure. At least not for me. The only thing that eased my suffering was that which is found in a bottle.'

'Tell us what happened, Fred?' Sabrina picked up his hand and cradled it.

'My angel and Florence Nightingale, I'm afraid I don't know where to start. Nor do I have the energy this evening.' His head seemed to sink into the pillows.

Sabrina bit her bottom lip. It wasn't fair to push him.

Florence mouthed at her, 'We should go.'

Still, Sabrina hesitated, but the voice that sounded at the end of the bed saw her get up from her pew.

'I think you've worn my favourite patient out. He needs his rest.' Nurse Daly might have been the same age as Sabrina and Florence, the owner of endearing dimples and a cheery Irish lilt, but her manner meant business.

'I'll come and see you after work tomorrow, Fred,' Sabrina said, patting his hand one last time.

'I shall look forward to it, Sabrina, my girl.'

Nurse Daly was scribbling something on the chart at the end of the bed. She glanced up as Sabrina and Florence made to leave.

'He's doing well. So don't be worrying now. I'll keep an eye on this old charmer for you.'

Sabrina flashed her a grateful smile. Maybe tomorrow Fred would be well enough to confide in her. Right now, though, her stomach was letting her know it was time to go and meet Adam.

Chapter Eighteen

'He was so close to telling me about his life, Adam.' Sabrina sighed with the frustration of having to get through the entire day at work tomorrow before she could head up to the Royal to see Fred once more. 'I hope he's up to talking tomorrow. I won't sleep tonight, you know, for wondering what happened to him when he was younger.'

'Maybe nothing happened, Sabrina.' Adam shrugged, dipping a chip into the sauce. 'Have you thought of that? Maybe he's an alcoholic, and that's all there is to it. He drank himself to where he wound up.'

'No, there's more to it than that.' She shook her head. 'He said it himself this evening that the drink was the medicine but what went before was the cause. Someone broke his heart.'

Adam shuffled the open parcel of fish 'n' chips towards her and their salty aroma wafted forth. 'C'mon, have some before they get cold. Nothing worse than soggy chips.'

He'd roared up outside the Royal on his gleaming Triumph after Sabrina had telephoned him to say she'd been to see Fred. Florence had made noises about Sir Galahad on his charger before grabbing Sabrina's arm. 'You won't say anything, will you? About what happened with Tim.'

Sabrina hadn't hesitated with her reply. 'Of course, I won't.' Privately though, she'd wondered if Tim might have already filled the lads in. He was a braggart when it came to his prowess with the ladies—with most things when it came down to it. She hoped for Tony's and Flo's sake he hadn't. But, either way, Adam wouldn't be hearing it from her.

Sabrina had donned the sunglasses she never left home without after the first time she clambered on the back of Adam's bike. She'd wound up being a dead ringer for a relation of Alice Cooper's by the time she'd waltzed into the fish and chippy on their first official date thanks to the wind making her eyes stream.

'Very cool. I'm going to get a pair off the market too.' Florence admired the knock-off Ray-Bans before waving Sabrina and Adam off in a cloud of exhaust fumes.

Adam had pulled up outside Clive's and run in to pick up their usual order while Sabrina stayed with the bike before coming here to what they thought of as their place, Everton Brow. It had been made official when Adam had carved their names, separated by a love heart with an arrow shot through it, into the bench where they were sitting now waiting for the sun to set.

Sabrina plucked a vinegar-soaked chip and bit into it, staring at the cityscape thoughtfully. The sun dipped a little lower, and a breeze blew up from nowhere, but it had no bite to it. A man walking a frisky dog or was it the other way around, cut across her line of sight, and she smiled, watching its lolloping gait. Laughter floated past from the direction of the car park.

'You'd have made a good bizzy, do you know that?' Adam wagged a chip at her.

'Do you think so?' Sabrina frowned, trying to imagine herself in a sensible WPC's uniform walking the beat but couldn't. 'Why?'

'You've gorra nose for getting to the bottom of things, that's why and you don't give up until you do. You would have climbed the ranks in no time.' He snaffled his chip and picked up his piece of battered cod.

'Are you saying I'm a nosy parker, Adam Taylor?' She squared her shoulders with mock indignance and he grinned.

'A proper curtain twitcher, Sabrina Flooks.'

She batted at him playfully.

'Oi, steady on, I nearly lost me fish then!'

'Serves you right.'

'I'm teasing, Nancy Drew. I luv your determination.'

She reached up and wiped the side of his mouth with a paper napkin. 'Sauce.'

Adam gave her a sheepish smile and carried on eating, done teasing her for the moment.

What he'd said was true, she thought, picking up the remaining piece of fish. She hadn't given up looking for answers when it came to her mother, and she wouldn't give up when it came to Fred either. Her mind flitted to Aunt Evie and Ray Taylor. That would have to wait for another day. One thing at a time.

'Are you going to eat that or just look at it?' Adam's eyes, more black than brown in the dusk light, danced.

She chomped into it, savouring the crisp batter and flaky fish.

'How did the rehearsal go? Did Linda show?'

Sabrina held her breath. Was this when he'd drop knowing about what had transpired between Flo and Tim on Friday night into the conversation? Or at least, Tim's version of what happened. She nodded, but he didn't say anything further, and so she told him about the kimono style dress Esmerelda had put her in and how she wasn't best pleased.

'I'm more interested in what she's got me bird wearing.' His grin was wolfish.

'You'll have to wait and see, won't you.' Sabrina laughed. She had him laughing a minute later when she got up and did an impersonation of Janice stalking down the runway in the heels she'd brought along for the rehearsal then sat back down to catch her breath.

'Adam, how would you feel if your dad married someone else?' Sabrina was as surprised by the question as he was. It was one out of the box.

'What brought that on?'

'I dunno.' It was true. However, Aunt Evie's face was still hovering on the periphery of her mind's eye for whatever reason. She didn't meet his gaze as she bit into the cod, savouring the crisp batter and flaky fish for a moment.

Adam's shrug was nonchalant. 'Well, as far as I'm concerned, what the arl fella does with his life is up to him. Same as what I do with mine is up to me. But if he were to get married again, it wouldn't bother me. Hopefully, he'd treat the lucky bride better than he did me mam.'

Sabrina nodded slowly. She didn't believe his easy-going response for a second. Still waters ran deep when it came to his dad, which was why he became so prickly when he talked about him. There was love there, though. She was sure of that. It had simply been buried under the heartbreak of losing his mam.

Adam scoffed another few chips before speaking. 'I don't think he will though.'

'Why not?'

'Because he's had someone on the side for years. Remember what I told you? How I overheard me mam telling Aunty Jean, she was sure he luved someone else?'

'Course I do.' Sabrina began to feel a little queasy at the turn the conversation had taken, but she took another bite of the fish anyway. 'I've been thinking about that though, Adam, and maybe there wasn't anyone else. Maybe your dad was too caught up with the business.' Sabrina had no idea what running a property business would entail. She imagined keeping an eye on tenants and ensuring rents were collected on time would keep you busy, though and back then, Ray Taylor was running a one-man band. 'You said he was always working when you were a lad. So maybe she felt neglected.'

'That's a lot of maybes, and no,' he shook his head vehemently, 'it wasn't that.' He pushed the chip paper away from him as though he'd lost interest in his dinner.

'But how do you know?' Sabrina persisted. 'You were only young.' She watched as his jaw muscles tightened, realising she was on shaky ground.

'Because I've seen the receipts, that's how. You're not the only one who could have been a bizzy, Sab. Me dad, tight arl bugger, never throws anything like that out. He keeps it for the tax man, and I went through them. All of them.'

Sabrina continued to chomp the fish despite her stomach churning. 'I don't understand. What were the receipts for?' She hoped she didn't regret having asked.

'For the flowers. Me dad buys whoever she is flowers, don't he? Same date every year. Never misses. He's done it for the past decade. Probably longer for all I know, but me mam was still alive ten years ago.' Adam fixed his stony gaze firmly ahead of him. 'It could be an anniversary, a birthday. I dunno, and I don't want to either.'

Sabrina did though, even if she was frightened of what she might learn.

'C'mon, don't waste that little bit,' Adam said gruffly, his eyes flicking to the remaining piece of cod she'd forgotten she had in her hand.

Sabrina didn't want it, but she stuffed it in her mouth anyway, barely tasting it before she swallowed. 'What date does he buy the flowers?'

'Why does it matter?'

'It doesn't.' Her voice was thick, and she felt like the cod was lodged in her throat. 'Just being a nosy parker, I guess.'

He managed a smile at that. 'The eighteenth of September.'

Sabrina began to cough, and Adam tore the tab off one of the cans of lager he'd brought with him, passing it to her. 'Ger this down you.' Concern flickered in his expression.

Sabrina grasped the can and, lifting it to her mouth, felt the fizz go up her nose before she took a sip. She swallowed, and after another small sip, the coughing subsided. She took a gulp, partly to be sure the food had gone down and partly to steady her nerves.

'Ahright now?'

Sabrina nodded. 'It went down the wrong way, is all.' She wiped her eyes and gave him a reassuring smile, surprised the heat that had suffused her body at hearing that date wasn't radiating off her. She'd lied. She wasn't okay—far from it because September eighteenth was Aunt Evie's birthday and Ray Taylor presented her with a bunch of her favourite hydrangeas every year. Given the time of year, where he managed to find them was always a mystery to Sabrina but then so much about Aunt Evie's and Ray's relationship was. She knew her aunt, though. There was no way she'd been Ray's fancy woman all these years.

She risked a glance at Adam. He was drinking his can watching as the sun began to put on its final show. There was a tenseness to him that hadn't been there before, and she regretted bringing the topic of his father up. She balled up the greasy paper and settled back in her seat, allowing the canopy of yellow and orange overhead to soothe her.

The silence stretched between them until Adam broke it. 'It's different every time.'

THE SUMMER POSY

He sounded more himself, Sabrina thought, relieved, as she stole a sidelong glance at him. He was staring at the outline of the buildings that made up their city. 'It's like a golden mirage,' she offered, proud of her poetic efforts.

Adam took her hand in his. 'This is it, Sabs. This is all I want. You and me. I luv you, girl.'

'I luv you too.'

Sabrina twisted to face him, uncertain of where he was headed.

Adam stood up, and then she watched bewildered as he got down on one knee, picking her hand up again.

'What are you doing?'

'Sabrina Flooks, will you marry me?'

For a moment, Sabrina was too stunned to speak. Adam's spur of the moment proposal wasn't what she'd daydreamed over, but he wasn't the sort for grand gestures. All she wanted was for them to be together, too. Surely that meant more than champagne and a diamond ring or a signwriter in the sky.

'Put me out of me misery, girl.' He gave her an uncertain smile.

'You mean it? You want us to get married?'

Adam nodded.

This was really happening, Sabrina thought, knowing what her answer would be. 'Yes. I would luv to marry you.'

They beamed at one another stupidly for a moment, and then Adam reached over to the bench and picked something up. 'I don't have a ring, but here, let's make it official.'

Sabrina held her hand out, and he slid the tab from the lager can on her finger. She laughed and wiggled her finger. 'That's it then. We're engaged.'

'We're engaged.' Adam laughed with her.

A cheer went up, followed by clapping from a couple out for an evening stroll who'd borne witness to the exchange as Sabrina leaned forward to kiss her fiancé.

Chapter Nineteen

Evelyn fed the swathe of green bridesmaids' fabric through the Singer and pondered, not for the first time since she'd opened Brides of Bold Street, there was no accounting for taste. She'd seen styles come and go. Short, long, full and fitted and now this.

The voluminous material she was currently working with was putting her in mind of her time at Littlewood's, sewing parachutes during the war. It might be all the rage, but she knew from experience that the shiny satin tended to look crushed by the time the wedding photographs were being snapped. Then there were the enormous puffball sleeves Sabrina was currently engaged in cutting out. They'd dwarf the poor bridesmaids. As for the bride, Chrissy Bolan, well, she was in danger of looking like Ida's crocheted blue toilet paper doll.

All that was missing for Chrissy to be a dead ringer was the white bonnet with blue trim.

Evelyn knew Chrissy's grandmother, Reeny, from bingo, and it had been her that had sent Chrissy along with her mother and sisters to Brides of Bold Street. They were like those Russian stacking dolls, Evelyn had thought upon meeting the younger Bolans. Instead of size, they went down in age, and they were equally as brassy with as much to say for themselves as Reeny.

The seam finished, she lifted the foot on the sewing machine and snipped the matching green thread free. It must be getting on towards cup of tea time, she thought, side-eyeing Sabrina, who'd moved on to the second sleeve. She'd attach the infernal things after a brew and not before, she decided. But then, she clocked the smile dancing at the corners of Sabrina's mouth. She had a dreamy expression too, which suggested she shouldn't be let loose on a bolt of fabric with a pair of scissors.

The humming sprang to mind. Sabrina had been making breakfast, and Evelyn had thought her humming was odd given she wasn't a hummer. A caterwauler when a song she liked came on the radio, yes, but not a hummer. It had slipped from her mind, though, as she got ready for the day ahead. Now her instincts were telling her something was afoot. Sabrina was far too cheerful given it was only ten o'clock and Monday to boot. She'd soon get to the bottom of it. 'Sabrina Flooks, what's got into you this morning?'

'What do you mean?' Sabrina stopped cutting, and when she looked over at her aunt, she was all wide-eyed and innocent, but Evelyn wasn't fooled. She knew that look of old.

'The humming earlier and look at you sitting there with a face on you like you've just been told you've won the pools. What's going on?'

'Am I not allowed to be in a good mood then?'

'A good mood, yes, but given that's a rare occurrence on a Monday morning, my money's on something having happened and you're, for whatever reason, not telling me.'

'You've gorra suspicious mind, Aunt Evie.' The pips on the radio sounded. 'Ten o'clock. Cup of tea time. I'll put the kettle on.'

Sabrina fled upstairs before Evelyn could drill her further.

Evelyn decided it had been an odd day, and she was feeling out of sorts as she pressed the last of Chrissy Bolan's bridesmaids' dresses. Swivelling the iron over the fabric she'd turned inside out, she knew she'd be glad to see the back of them.

For one thing, the day had been unusually hectic given it was the start of the week, and for another, Sabrina's Cheshire grin was beginning to get on her wick. She didn't like not being in the know, and there'd been no chance to press her further either because Sabrina had been busy out the front of the shop for the best part of the day.

The familiar sound of the till pinging open saw her glance at the clock on the wall. Closing time, she thought hearing the distinctive chinking as Sabrina began counting the coins. She'd mentioned plans to go up to the Royal to see Fred that evening, but she'd be wanting her tea first. A jacket potato would do them nicely, given there were potatoes that needed using. She moved the bottle green fabric across the board to begin the delicate manoeuvring required for pressing the sleeves and resolved to collar her as to what was going on before she left the flat.

Evelyn was folding the ironing board when she heard the door jangling, signalling someone had waltzed into the shop despite it being ten minutes past closing time. Adam or Florence, perhaps? It wasn't likely to be Esmerelda, not on a Monday. Wednesday was their night to put the world to rights.

As it turned out, it was Adam because as Evelyn returned from having put the ironing board back in the storage cupboard near the stairs, she was confronted by not one but two grinning Cheshire cats holding hands.

'Aunt Evie, we've got something to tell you.'

Evelyn took in their shining faces, but before she could gather her thoughts, Adam cleared his throat and spoke up. 'Erm, Miss Flooks, I want you to know I think the world of Sabrina.'

She saw Sabrina give his hand a squeeze encouraging him to carry on.

'And, erm, well, last night I asked her if she'd do me the honour of becoming me wife.'

So that was it, Evelyn thought, understanding why sheer delight was radiating off the pair of them.

'And I said yes!' Sabrina jumped up and down, clapping her hands. 'Isn't it wonderful? I've been dying to tell you all day, Aunt Evie, but Adam wanted to be here when I did. We haven't got the ring yet, but we thought we'd have a look around the jewellers on Saturday afternoon.' She was bubbling with the excitement of it all.

'I wasn't sure if I should have asked your permission first.' Adam's smile faltered as he tried to gauge the still silent Evelyn's reaction to their news. 'And I know it's arse-about-face, Miss Flooks.'

Sabrina coughed.

'Erm, what I meant was it's a back to front way of doing things, but it was spontaneous on my part, and I'd like your permission to marry Sabrina before we tell anyone else and make it official.'

'I told him he was being old-fashioned.' Sabrina was beginning to look antsy. Aunt Evie had warmed to Adam, but it was a slow burn, and this was a big move forward. 'I haven't even told Flo yet.' Sabrina added her tone, telling her aunt just how hard it had been to keep the news to herself all day.

'I promise I'll always look after her,' Adam added, hoping to soften her up.

His voice ebbed away, and Evelyn drew breath, her outward calm belying the simultaneous joy and fear their announcement had sent swirling through her. She'd known it was only a matter of a time until it came. She knew too that Sabrina and Adam fit together perfectly like pieces in a puzzle, but it had come sooner rather than later. 'Can I get a word in now?' She thrust her hands into the pockets of Monday's green shop coat.

They glanced at each other and nodded.

Adam was a good lad and he loved the bones off Sabrina. There was nothing for it. 'Adam, lad, I give you my permission and you both my blessing.' For a moment, the image of Sabrina, a little girl lost, floated before her. How was she old enough to get married? When had that happened?

Adam's shoulders slumped with relief, and he felt Sabrina squeeze his hand once more. He'd been worried that Evelyn, who could be prickly with him at times, wouldn't be as enthusiastic about their engagement as they were. He knew Sabrina well enough to know that what her aunt thought mattered deeply. He desperately wanted her approval.

Evelyn made a show of taking off her glasses and huffing on them before polishing the lenses against her chest. It was an opportunity to blink away the tears that had suddenly welled. Still, her eyes were overly bright behind her glasses once she'd pushed them back on. She looked from one to the other and cleared her throat. 'I'm very happy for the pair of you.' She meant it from the bottom of her heart despite her trepidation. 'This calls for a celebration, but there is one thing, Adam,'

'Yes?' he asked anxiously.

'I think you should stop calling me Miss Flooks now we're to be family. Aunt Evie will do nicely.'

Sabrina closed the distance between her and her aunt and hugged her tight. 'I luv you!'

Evelyn felt the tears threaten once more and patted her back before blustering that sherry was the order of the day. The trio trooped up the stairs.

The sherry tray was retrieved, and Evelyn pulled out the stopper, releasing the sweet, boozy scent. She poured generous tots into three cut crystal glasses before passing them to Adam first and then Sabrina before raising her own. 'To the pair of you.'

'Ta, Aunt Evie,' Sabrina said as they clinked their glasses.

Adam being a lager man through and through, managed not to grimace upon his first sip and decided it wasn't too bad after all by the third.

'Well, I didn't expect to be partaking in a sherry on a Monday night.' Evelyn's cheeks had pinkened. She'd have her ciggy after they'd had their tea, and Sabrina and Adam had got on their way. It would be then she'd be fully able to digest the news.

'Neither did I,' Sabrina added, affixing the silly look she'd worn all day on Adam, whose grin was equally foolish.

There was something Evelyn needed to do. She put her near-empty glass down on the silver tray. 'I'll be back in a jiffy.' She disappeared into her bedroom.

Sabrina shrugged at Adam. She hadn't a clue what her aunt was up to.

'It's not bad this,' Adam said as he drained the glass, and by the time he'd put it back on the tray, Evelyn was back in the room.

She was clutching a red velvet pouch in her hand. 'I'll understand if it's not what you had in mind, luv,' she directed at Sabrina, 'but it belonged to me mam, given to her by her mam. I'd like you to have it whether you choose to wear it as your engagement ring or not.' She held the pouch out to Sabrina.

Sabrina took it and undid the pink ribbon, keeping the contents secure. She tipped it up, and a ring fell into the palm of her hand. You could have heard a pin drop in the room as she stared at the yellow gold, diamond and sapphire ring. The diamonds formed the petals of a flower, the sapphire the centrepiece. Aunt Evie rarely spoke about her mam and Sabrina hadn't known she'd had anything of hers in her possession, let alone an heirloom like this.

Evelyn watched Sabrina's face closely. The ring was the only thing she had to remember her mam by. That and the legacy of Brides of Bold Street because it had been her mam whose knee she'd sat at learning to sew. It fitted that Sabrina have it now.

Sabrina gazed up at her aunt with eyes full of emotion and her voice was barely above a whisper as she breathed, 'I luv it, Aunt Evie. I'll treasure it. Adam?' She held the ring out to him, hoping she wouldn't have to spell out what she wanted him to do.

This time as Adam slid the ring on Sabrina's finger, Evelyn couldn't stop a tear from escaping.

Evelyn ground out her ciggy. Sabrina and Adam had left to tell Ray, Florence and the Teesdales, who were as good as family to her, their news. It was time to fetch the writing things she'd secreted away.

Once she had the pen and pad, she pulled a chair out from the table and sat down. The sherry was still warming her stomach despite the jacket potato they'd had to soak it up. Adam had insisted on seeing to the dinner things while she and Sabrina put their feet up in the living room. She'd listened with half an ear as Sabrina chattered on about whether they should have an engagement party, all the while angling her ring so as it sparkled under the light.

Now, Evelyn picked up the pen and tapped it thoughtfully against her chin. She was nearly finished jotting down her and Ray's shared story, and she'd made her mind up to tuck the letter away in the bag Sabrina would pack for the Isle of Man. It would be good for her to have space to soak in what she'd learnt. Evelyn only hoped it didn't sour things between her and Adam.

Oh, she'd had her misgivings when she'd first learned who Adam was alright. After all, Liverpool was a big city, and out of all the lads Sabrina could have chosen, she'd picked Ray Taylor's son. Perhaps it was fate. Adam was like his dad in many ways, fiercely loyal for one thing, but he lacked his self-assured brashness. Evelyn knew it was a trait that had been a necessary survival tool when they were both young.

Adam hadn't had it easy losing his mam, but he hadn't had to fight for everything he had either. Like his father, he had a kind heart. Only Adam wore his on his sleeve, and you had to dig deep to find Ray's, but it was there. She knew this for a fact.

Evelyn recalled her conversation with Ray over Adam and Sabrina stepping out together. They'd checked Sabrina was out of earshot before he'd told her her concerns were unwarranted. 'They're not us, Evie, me girl,' he'd said, and she'd wondered what he saw when he looked at her. The woman in her seventies or the girl she'd been when they first met.

Could the sins of the past be washed away with this new union? she wondered, beginning to write. She could only hope.

Chapter Twenty

Sabrina sat on the back of Adam's Triumph with her arms wrapped tightly around his middle as he darted between cars in the direction of the Royal. Winter was a distant memory now, and the nights were stretching out deliciously longer.

Ray Taylor had greeted the news of his son's and Sabrina's engagement with enthusiasm, slapping his son on the back as he told him he'd done well for himself. Sabrina had seen Adam's body stiffen at the gesture, but then she'd been propelled forward and kissed on both cheeks by her future father-in-law as he welcomed her to the family.

As the motorbike slowed and then idled at the lights, Sabrina marvelled over the strange way life sometimes worked because for as long as she could remember, Ray Taylor had been calling into Brides of Bold Street. Never in a million years would she have imagined herself one day being related to him by marriage. She grimaced, remembering the burn from Ray's finest malt he'd insisted on pouring to toast their engagement.

'Oi.' Adam turned his head slightly as Sabrina pinched him, shouting over the noise of the engine. 'What was that for?'

'I'm making sure this is all happening,' she informed him and grinned as he yelled back, 'You've not changed your mind, have you?'

'No chance!'

The lights changed, and she snuggled back in to mull over the excitement of sharing their news.

'That's a beauty,' Ray had said, admiring Sabrina's ring. She'd been surprised to see his eyes, so like his son's, grow suspiciously bright.

'It belonged to Aunt Evie's mam. She wanted me to have it.'

He nodded, and an odd expression had flitted across features that had lived a life, but she couldn't read it; she'd sensed Adam was keen to get on their way. But, on the other hand, there was no missing the hurt that flared briefly in Ray's eyes as they left, despite his eagerness to pour a second round. What would it take to help Adam make peace with his dad? Sabrina wondered, tightening her grip around his waist as he slowed suddenly for the car that had decided to turn without indicating. He'd be calling the driver something unrepeatable, no doubt, she thought. They were nearly at the hospital now. Florence was as desperate to know Fred's story as she was and she'd promised to telephone her if she managed to get it out of him.

The memory of the Teesdales' enthusiasm upon hearing of their engagement had her smiling. Once they'd all recovered from Florence's initial squeal of delight, Mr Teesdale had insisted on popping down to the corner shop to see what they had in the way of a bottle of celebratory bubbles. The plonk he carted back was cheap with an acrid aftertaste, but Sabrina didn't care in the least. The Teesdales were her second family, and she could see the pride in Mr Teesdale's face and the tears in Mrs Teesdale's eyes as they congratulated her and Adam. The twins, too, had wheedled a tiny mouthful each so they could join in the toast. They'd all laughed as they pulled faces at the taste.

'Can we be your flower girls, Sabrina?' Teresa had demanded more than asked, Shona backing her up.

Florence had jumped in before Sabrina could reply that it was a given to say, 'Oi, youse two, I'm head bridesmaid, which means it's up to me who gets to walk down the aisle with the bride. So you'd better think twice next time you're thinking of nicking me stuff, ahright?'

Their earnest expressions as they crossed their hearts and promised to die that they'd leave Florence's things alone had been comical.

By the time Adam stilled the Triumph's engine outside the hospital, the fresh blast of air from riding pillion had shaken off the fuzzy effects of the mixed bag of alcohol she'd consumed. She was glad she'd refused the last drop of fizz Mr Teesdale had offered around, downing it himself in the end.

'Shall I come up with you?' Adam's question was muffled behind his helmet.

'No,' Sabrina said, pulling hers off and shaking her hair out. She handed it to him and then patted the bag slung across her chest to reassure herself she'd not forgotten the chocolates she'd raced out to buy at lunchtime. It had been good to have an excuse to get away from Aunt Evie for a while. She'd been fit to burst with her news and wary of blurting it out. 'You'll only be fretting about leaving your bike parked around here the whole time. Besides, I think there's more chance of me getting Fred to talk to me if I'm on my own.' She glanced at her watch. She had an hour until visiting hours finished, and she was keen to get up there. 'Could yer pick me up in an hour?'

'Yeah. I'll head over to Tony's. Tim said he was calling around tonight because Tony's having problems with his regulator.'

A car tooted behind them and Sabrina put her hand on his before he could give the driver a rude finger sign. Adam winked at her under the visor and gunned the engine before roaring off in a cloud of exhaust fumes. She hurried inside the building, which never seemed to sleep with its fluorescent lights and busy waiting area. However, the lift was empty and exiting on Fred's floor, she spied his nurse and hurried towards her. 'How's Fred doing, Nurse Daly?'

The nurse smiled her greeting, the clipboard she was carrying hugged to her chest. 'He'll be pleased to see you. You'll be a welcome distraction because he's not so good tonight. His blood pressure's up, and he's had some nausea and vomiting. He had a bad night last night, too, with the nightmares. It's to be expected given his alcohol dependency.'

Sabrina thanked her, leaving her to carry on with her rounds as she entered the ward.

It was quieter than the previous afternoon when she'd called to see him with Florence in tow. A silver-haired woman was holding the hand of a gentleman who was wheezing painfully. Around another bed, a young family had gathered, and she smiled, witnessing one of the children steal a handful of the grapes their parents must have brought in.

'Hiya, Fred.' Sabrina sat down on the seat next to his bed noticing the beads of sweat decorating his forehead.

'Sabrina, my girl, you came back,' Fred declared with a tremor in his ordinarily booming voice.

'I said I would.' She grinned. 'Are they looking after you then? And more to the point are you behaving yourself?'

'I'm a model patient, but Nurse Daly, for all her jolly Irish brogue, has a heart of stone.'

'I take it she wouldn't sneak you in a bottle of whisky then?'

Fred looked sheepish and Sabrina remembered the chocolates. She dug them out of her bag, holding them out to him, 'Here you go, Thorntons' finest no less.'

Fred rallied a little, taking the box from her with a shaking hand. 'I don't suppose they're liqueurs?'

'Caramels.' Sabrina laughed. 'You're terrible, Fred.'

'Sabrina my angel, God loves a trier.'

She caught a glimpse of the Fred she knew and loved. 'I've brought you some good news.'

He visibly perked. 'Do tell.'

Sabrina couldn't stop the grin spreading across her face as she held out her left hand and wiggled her fingers.

'Your young man Aaron proposed, and you said yes. Angel girl, this is a joyous occasion. It calls for champagne!'

'Water will do, Fred, and it's Adam,' she said, eyeing the jug on the bedside cabinet. She told him about Adam's unexpected proposal on Everton Brow and Aunt Evie gifting her the ring that had belonged to her mother before reaching over and picking up his hand. 'Do you feel up to talking?' Her tone was hopeful.

'That's what we've been doing, my girl.'

'Not about me, about you. What happened, Fred? How did you wind up on the streets?'

'What's been and gone is best forgotten.'

'But I don't think it is forgotten, Fred. I think you carry it with you.'

Fred lay with his head resting on the pillows, and the silence stretched between them. Sabrina had decided that perhaps he was a closed book, and she should leave it alone if that was what he wanted when she saw his eyes glaze as though he were seeing something other than the ceiling above him.

'It was all such a long time ago, Sabrina.'

She kept a tight hold of his hand as he began to talk.

Chapter Twenty-one

'I don't remember when I knew I wasn't like the other boys.' Fred's voice was quiet, and Sabrina strained forward in her seat. She glared down at the family whose baby was starting to cry as they said their goodbyes to the patient they'd come to visit. She didn't want to miss a word of what Fred had to say, and she shifted her chair as close to his bed as she could without toppling onto him.

'I must have been quite young because I recall that while I wanted to daydream, the other boys at school liked to roughhouse one another. They teased me mercilessly for not joining in. In his short pants and cap, Frederick Markham was not a popular little boy, I'm afraid.'

Poor Fred, Sabrina thought, squeezing his hand gently as she tried and failed to imagine him as a child.

'I learned to disassociate myself, Sabrina, my girl. I rose above it.'

'Still, it must have been awful. Didn't you have anyone who stuck up for you?'

'Oh, my mother tried, but Father quashed her efforts. Lord Arthur Markham was a bully. He must have sensed I was different too, given his concerted efforts throughout my childhood to toughen me up because I did not fit the mould of who he thought his son should be.' There was bitterness in his voice as he drifted in his memories.

His father was a lord! Sabrina tried to process this unexpected information. It was a relief to see the family shuffling out of the ward, taking the grape thief and the little one whose face was screwed up and turning purple as the howls revved up.

'I was his only son, you see. I don't think he ever forgave me for being a disappointment to him. I tried for the longest while to win his approval, but I couldn't be someone I wasn't. So then, one day, I gave up.'

'Oh, Fred.'

'It wasn't all bad.'

Sabrina felt him press her hand back.

'I had three sisters, and I was happiest when I was in their company.' One side of his mouth twitched upward. 'Oh, but we had fun, my sisters and I. We loved playacting and dressing up.' His chest rattled as he took a deep breath, but a richer timbre sneaked through when he spoke. 'May I introduce Miss Bettina, Miss Juniper and Miss Alicia Markham.' It was uttered with the theatrical flourish Sabrina had grown used to, and it cheered her instantly. 'And, I, well, I wasn't merely Frederick. I became Master Frederico, maestro of the nursery. Betty, June, Alicia and I were transformed when we put on our shows.'

Sabrina smiled at Fred's imagery of the four Markham siblings performing together.

'We were fortunate enough to live in a rather grand house that had been in the family for generations, and we found an avid audience for our performances in Nanny Tuthill and the housemaid, Florrie. So the seeds for my future passion were, as they say, sewn. My father was in the House of Lords, and I was expected to follow in his footsteps, but I had caught the bug, and when I was supposed to be studying law at Oxford, I was immersing myself in amateur dramatics. My time there was an awakening. I'd found my people, and I felt at ease in my skin. I knew with absolute certainty what I wanted to do with my life. What I must do.' His voice rasped, and Sabrina, eager for him to continue, hastily poured him some water.

'Here we are, Fred, sip this.'

'Vodka or perhaps a gin? Although gin is apt to make me maudlin. My mother was a gin drinker, in a teacup, you understand, so nobody knew she was partaking of a tipple before midday. So there's a predisposition to liking a drop in my family.' He studied Sabrina's face for a moment taking in her steely resolve. 'Water it is then. Not quite the nectar of the Gods I was hoping for, but if you refuse me anything else, it will have to suffice.'

'Oh shurrup and drink it, Fred.' Sabrina smiled, holding it to his mouth because she didn't trust his shaking hands.

Once he'd had a few sips, Fred settled himself back into his story. 'I auditioned and won a place at the Royal Academy of Drama and Art, dropping out of Oxford without telling my family. When my father found out, I was given an ultimatum to stop my ridiculous pursuit and return to my studies or he'd cut me off. I threw caution to the wind and chose the latter. And voila! My new life began.'

'But how did you live? You know while you were at the Royal worever?'

'RADA, darling girl, RADA. I picked up whatever work I could find, lived on yesterday's bread and jam and slept on the floor of a fellow alumni's flat. And it was the most wonderful time of my life. I was amongst kindred spirits and free to be whoever I wanted.'

'What about your sisters though, you must have missed them?'

Sadness settled into the crevices of Fred's face. 'Father forbade them from coming to see me, but Betty was always the bravest of the three. She'd come to my shows irrespective of what he had to say about it.'

'So you performed in London then?'

'The Savoy, The Theatre Royal,' he bandied. 'Oh yes, Sabrina, the West End was my old stomping ground. I trod the boards with some of the greats of the day. Laurence Olivier, Michael Hordern and Peter Cushing before he abandoned us, lured by the bright lights of Hollywood. Of course, it all came to a grinding halt when we were sent off to war. Life was interrupted shall we say.'

Sabrina wondered how the genteel Fred she was meeting through the tale he was telling her had managed to survive the fighting.

'I was in the RAF. Pilot Officer Frederick Markham. He raised his hand in a salute. 'Don't look so surprised, Sabrina, my girl.'

She rearranged her features, not knowing why she should be surprised. She'd always known there was so much more to Fred than the homeless man she supplied with breakfast.

'I was there for the Battle of Britain.' He shuddered. 'The bastard Jerries shot me down, and I was honourably discharged from service, which is how I came to be in Liverpool. It never leaves you, you know, Sabrina. The horror. I forgot all about Mother, Betty, June and Alicia because I'm afraid I wasn't right upstairs for the longest while. However, there was a solace to be found for the malaise that wouldn't leave me. It came only from the contents of a bottle of whatever I could get my hands on or when I was back on the stage.'

'So that's how you came to be performing at the Shakespeare Theatre in nineteen forty-five.'

'Lady Here's A Laugh,' Fred stated, and Sabrina was rapt as he began to recite lines, presumably from the play, but as his monologue turned into a rattling cough, she poured him another water. This time it took more than a few sips to settle him and Nurse Daly appeared, seemingly from thin air, to check on him. Sabrina was frightened she'd be told she should let him rest but after fussing around checking his IV line, she left them to continue their conversation.

'How did you manage your performances if you were drinking though, Fred?' Sabrina asked once the nurse was out of earshot.

'I found a happy medium to juggle both, my dear. The drink wasn't all-consuming because I was happy when I was on stage. I was someone else once more, and I could forget the blasted war ever happened.' Fred's lids fluttered shut. 'Ah, the smells of that world, Sabrina. Such wonderful smells. Musky, velvet with a waxy, powder undertone. There's nothing quite like it.'

Sabrina pictured thick, red velvet drapes and actors running around with faces caked in stage makeup.

'And then I fell in love and the spectres that haunted me were chased away. But it was a secret love, a forbidden love.'

'Was she married?' Sabrina probed.

Fred looked at her sadly. 'Not she, my angel. Never she.'

The penny dropped, and Sabrina felt her face grow hot at her naivety.

'He was married, and when his wife found out about us, she threatened to go to the police if my love didn't agree to relocate and to cease all communication with me. When he took his own life, that, my dear, was the proverbial straw that broke the camel's back. We have come full circle.'

Sabrina, distressed, tried to find the right words but in the end, all she said was, 'Fred, I'm so sorry.'

She laid her head on his chest and stayed there for the longest time.

Chapter Twenty-two

Come Friday night, the backroom of Esmerelda's Emporium had been transformed into a dressing room, and the atmosphere was alive with excitement and nerves. Droplets of Silhouette hairspray and the Coty perfume Wild Musk Janice had doused herself and whoever else asked for a squirt floated on the air.

The clock ticking away on the wall said it was fifteen minutes until showtime, and Sabrina took a deep breath, or as deep as she could manage in her electric blue dress, to quiet the nerves that had suddenly assailed her. She could feel the weight of her eyelashes heavy with the lashings of mascara they were coated in.

The two glamour girls from George Henry Lee's cosmetic counters worked wonders on Carol and Gina. Meanwhile, the stylists from Sassy Scissors were backcombing and spraying Sharon and Joyce's hair.

As she waited her turn, decked out in what Florence had stated was a wee yellow kimono, Linda was puffing impatiently on a cigarette. She'd arrived late and was the last in the conveyer belt line set up for hair and makeup. Without her usual warpaint on, she looked pasty, Sabrina thought, idly turning her attention to Bossy Bev, who was holding a card out to her.

'These are the shades and products used on you today, Sabrina. I hope you don't plan on chewing sweets when it's your turn to walk the red carpet.'

Sabrina hastily chewed and swallowed her Opal Fruit.

'Eee, give us one of those, Bev luv, I've never looked so glam in me life.' Janice, resplendent in a billowing, purple caftan, struck a pose teetering in her heels. 'I can see the headline now, from Bootle Meter Maid to Liverpool Femme Fatale.'

'You could hide a fella up that outfit, and no one would ever know,' Florence remarked, causing a ripple of laughter from her fellow Tootlers.

Sabrina giggled as Bev shook her head and dug out the applicable beauty card. She'd taken it upon herself to distribute them on behalf of their cosmetic hair team. At least it had put a stop to her swanning about, randomly grabbing them by the shoulders to trill, Shoulders back, tummy's in, girls, Sabrina thought, taking the card.

Gina, who'd remembered her camera, had been put in charge of snapping them for posterity as they got off the hair and makeup chairs. Sabrina had made sure her ring was clearly on show when her turn came and had spent the next ten minutes having it admired and lapping up the congratulations.

Bev was adamant she would have a wall of fame for the Tootlers in the community centre where the weekly Weight Watchers meetings were held.

Sabrina had barely recognised herself in the mirror when she'd sat down to have her hair teased into an elaborate updo by Penny from Sassy Scissors. Florence, sitting next to her, having her short blonde hair primped by John-Paul at the time, met her eyes in the free-standing mirror they were plopped in front of and grinned. She too was transformed with bold slashes of magenta blush, matching lips and lethal hair.

'That's not a dress. It's a flamin' leather sausage casing Esmerelda's got you squeezed into,' Aunt Evie mumbled, on account of the pins she was holding in her mouth, as she looked up from the task of re-pinning the hem of Patty's dress.

Patty had somehow managed to dislodge Sabrina's effort at the dress rehearsal the previous Sunday to ensure she didn't go head over heels when the time came for her to glide down the strip of carpet. Esmerelda had laid the red runner down to indicate where they were to walk in the centre of the shop floor. Their Axminster runway, one of the Tootlers had stated.

Sabrina was too worried about how she would walk, let alone stride down the runway in her dress to pay her aunt any heed. The blue leather was a dress for mincing along in. She was only surprised Aunt Evie was passing remark this late in the day, but then she'd been busy since she'd arrived, with an emergency repair having to be done on Peggy's jumpsuit when she tore the seam under the arm. The suit was a tight call, but she'd been insistent on wearing it.

As for Esmerelda, she was nowhere to be seen, so Sabrina pushed her way through the cramped quarters to the door separating them from the shop floor. A peek through the crack revealed the emporium had filled up since the last time she'd looked. The area, usually a chaotic, exotic jumble, had been transformed, with the shelves pushed towards the walls. Who knew they were on wheels? An open space was left in the middle of the shop floor and a row of chairs two deep lined both sides of the strip of carpet. Every seat was filled by a woman chatting and holding a bubble filled flute.

Esmerelda was working the room in a turquoise blue ensemble that reminded Sabrina of the glossy pictures of seaside resorts in the travel agent's window. Cigarette smoke circled over the gathered group, and near the entrance, a darting movement caught her eye. Tim, Tony and Adam were ribbing one another and she tried to catch Adam's eye, but he was too busy fending off a mock punch from Tim.

'Give us a look.' Florence's voice made her jump and Sabrina moved aside to let her press her eye to the crack. 'I'm even more nervous now. Tim's out there,' she hissed, stepping back.

Florence had avoided The Swan like the plague since the previous Friday.

'Of course, he is. Linda's here, isn't she? Don't worry. He'll have forgotten all about it.'

'I wish I could forget about it. Any more thoughts on how we're going to set about finding Fred's sisters?' Florence asked, abruptly changing the subject.

The sole topics of the two friends conversation all week had been about Fred, and Sabrina and Adam's engagement. Between them, they'd decided there was nothing else for it but to try and locate Fred's sisters. It was the best hope for his future because surely if they knew where he was, they'd look after him, they'd decided. He'd been close to them when he was young after all, and his father would be dead now, so there'd be nothing standing in the way of a reunion. The only problem was searching for them especially given the likelihood of them having married and no longer being Markhams.

Sabrina nipped at her bottom lip as she mulled this over. She'd been to see Fred every evening, hoping to glean more clues as to how she might trace his family, but he'd turned the topic to her and her engagement each time she'd steered him towards the subject. Some things were too painful to keep touching, she supposed.

'Don't do that. You'll ruin your lipstick,' Florence reprimanded.

She was right, Sabrina thought, duly releasing her lip and giving a slight shrug. 'Aunt Evie says all the births, deaths and marriage records are held in London. Fred said he was from a village close to London too, which means the parish register is out.'

'Well, I spoke to Mam about it, and she suggested we start with the library. You know, me aunty Mavis?'

'Who always smells of lilac?'

'That's her. She was on about doing the family tree but only because she'd gor it into her head that Great Nana Elsie had a fling with some toff, and she wondered if there was a secret inheritance lying about somewhere. We all reckon it was far more likely Great Nana Elsie had a fling with the butler, not the lord of the manor, especially since we've not heard a peep more from her about it. Anyway, Mam said she began her search at the library, checking census records on the microfiche thing-a-me.'

Sabrina brightened. 'That sounds like a good place to start. The sooner the better because Fred can't go back on the streets again once he's discharged.' So they decided to pay a visit to the library the following afternoon.

'What about Fred? Will you tell him what we're up to?' Florence asked.

'No, but only because he'd tell me too much water's gone under the bridge and to leave things be.'

Esmerelda swept into the small space, silencing them, and all eyes swivelled towards her.

'Five minutes, ladies!' she announced, a majestic teal dragon exhaling a cloud of smoke.

Chapter Twenty-Three

The eclectic rhythm of conga drums sounded. It was Florence's cue to take to the runway. She was the first to take a turn, and was trying to visualise herself sailing down the runner with her head held high, her feet confidently placing themselves one in front of the other, but Bossy Bev was sabotaging her thoughts.

'Remember, Florence, shoulders back, tummy in.

Sabrina thought it was like watching Rocky's coach try to coax him back into the boxing ring as Bev massaged Flo's shoulders.

'You've got this, Flo,' she said as Bossy Bev upped the shoulder work. 'You're a leopard stalking your prey, girl. Count of three. One, two, three.' Sabrina gave her a gentle push towards the door before stepping back into line, leaving Bev to start on poor Janice. The rest of the Tootlers jostled one another, trying to catch a glimpse of Florence's modelling debut from the partially open door, but it was impossible.

'If you lot aren't careful, you'll spill out into the shop. You'd have been hopeless queuing in the war when we had to form an orderly line,' Evelyn tutted.

Sabrina didn't care, being too nervous on Flo's behalf to watch anyway. She wished she had her Opal Fruits to hand, but they were in the pocket of her jeans, and she didn't dare step out of line. She could hear Tony though, cheering Flo on, and the look on her face when she sailed back into the room glowing told her she'd pulled it off.

'It was amazin'. I felt like Jerry Hall,' Florence gushed before flopping down in a chair designated for makeup. 'Do what Esmerelda said and concentrate on something straight ahead of you.' Her shoulders slumped forwards as the adrenaline began to seep from her body.

Janice was next, and Sabrina couldn't resist peeking to see how she managed her heels. While she wasn't gliding exactly, there was a vast improvement to the drunk stork of the dress rehearsal reminding Sabrina instead of Mick Jagger strutting on stage. As Janice turned and began her return trip, her heart began to bang against her chest, and she felt simultaneously hot and cold as she tried to concentrate on her breathing.

'You're not giving birth, girl.' Gina nudged her from behind, causing the others to giggle nervously.

Sabrina killed the huffing tiny breaths, shook Bev off, and then she was on!

One foot in front of the other, eyes fixed straight ahead, mincing forth to the beat of the drums. All eyes were on her, and upon reaching the end of the carpet, she couldn't help but glance towards Adam, who mouthed 'WOW' as she spun about and, with an extra wiggle in her hips, headed back to where she'd come from.

'I couldn't watch you,' Florence said, adding, 'I was too nervous.'

Sabrina sank into the seat next to her. 'Me too, with you. It was flippin' amazin', though!'

'I know.'

They grinned at each other.

'I feel as though I could climb Mount Everest right now,' Sabrina piped up.

'Me too,' Florence echoed

'Not in those dresses you couldn't,' Evelyn muttered.

The nervous energy of earlier had been replaced by elation as the Tootlers, on a natural high, piled back into the small space at the rear of Esmerelda's Emporium to change back into their civvies. They'd struck one last pose along with their hair and make-up team for a photograph snapped by the reporter who'd shown up from *The Echo*, leaving Esmerelda and Bossy Bev to compete for his attention. His head was swivelling from one woman to the other as he scribbled shorthand notes for his story.

Esmerelda's customers were either polishing off their bubbles or beginning to browse the racks of vibrant coloured clobber she'd pulled out from against the wall as the drumbeats faded and the last of the Tootlers vanished back into the storeroom.

The lads had already left, having arranged to meet the girls down at The Swan in a little while.

'Don't forget to mention Sassy Scissors and the Max Factor girls from George Henry Lewis's in your story,' Florence called over to the reporter before closing the door behind them to where Evelyn was already buzzing about unpegging, unpinning and unzipping.

Sabrina was wondering if she'd have to be cut out of her dress when Florence announced overtop of the babble that a celebratory drink was in order and, given The Swan's proximity, that's where they should head. A cheer went up because no one wanted to waste their glam looks by heading straight home.

'I'm going to sleep with my face on,' Janice announced, slipping her sensible shoes back on.

'It might see some action in your camp, Jan, girl.' Peggy winked.

'Not if I put a headscarf on to stop my hair getting ruined,' she retorted.

Ribald cackling sounded in the small space and Sabrina grinned, seeing Aunt Evie suppress a smile.

Linda scarpered as soon as she'd zipped her jeans up, eager to get to the pub and the rest of the Tootlers weren't far behind. They followed her lead out of the back door to Wood Street. Sabrina and Florence volunteered to stay behind to help Evelyn hang the last of the discarded fashion show items back onto the rack.

'I wonder what will happen with this lot now?' Sabrina said, sliding Linda's kimono, which she'd left in a heap on the floor, along with the jacket onto a hanger. 'Esmerelda can hardly sell them now they've been worn. And,' she sniffed, 'they all reek of Janice's Coty.'

'They were samples,' Evelyn informed her and Florence. 'They'll go back to her suppliers.'

Florence peered into the Emporium, abandoning the floating emerald garment she'd been about to hang up. 'Esmerelda's bagging up gear left, right and centre out there. I think she'll be dead chuffed how it's all gone tonight. She must have made a tidy profit.' She resumed her task. 'I told her we'd be heading down The Swan, and she said she'll duck in with the silk scarves for us as promised. Hopefully, she'll stand us all a round too.'

'Aunt Evie, will you come?' It was a question Sabrina fully expected to be met with a resounding no even as she added the sweetener. 'I'll buy you a bottle of Babycham.'

'Babycham, you say?' Evelyn replied. 'Well then, I might be persuaded. Besides, Ida's invited her neighbour to the bingo tonight, and the last time she came, she took home the rolled beef roast.' Her clipped manner suggested she was still annoyed with her old friend for allowing her neighbour to tag along in the first place.

'Surprise!'

Sabrina blinked as she stood in the doorway of The Swan. A banner was strewn across the bar with 'Congratulations on your Engagement' emblazoned on it. Colourful clusters of dangling balloons bobbed about and, once she'd got over her initial shock, she registered the sea of faces, all grinning from ear to ear at the stunned expression on her face.

Adam peeled away from the group of lads by the bar and moved towards her.

'Whose idea—' she was silenced by a kiss which saw a cheer go up.

'Mine,' Adam said when he'd finished planting one on her. 'But I couldn't have pulled it off without those two.' He gestured to Florence and Aunt Evie; they were standing nearby with their arms linked, both looking thoroughly pleased with themselves.

The shock was subsiding as warmth flooded her that he'd gone to the effort of arranging a surprise party to celebrate their engagement. 'Thank you,' she managed to choke as unexpected tears sprang forth.

'All the Tootlers were in on it too,' Florence announced proudly, edging in on the conversation.

'I should have known something was up when you agreed to come with us,' Sabrina said to her aunt, fluttering her lashes in an attempt to bat the tears away.

'Ida's already here,' Evelyn stated slyly, 'As if we'd forfeit your do for the bingo. And as I recall, there was a Babycham in it for me.' She inclined her head towards the bar.

'We have a free bar until nine,' Adam said, pulling Sabrina over to where Mickey was already pulling her a pint of her usual. 'And there are a few guests here desperate to say hello.'

Sabrina took a moment to scan the familiar faces and saw the Teesdales all waving madly at her from the table they'd commandeered. The twins had a bag of crisps each and a glass of pop in front of them. She waved back and looked past them to a face she'd not seen for a while and delight suffused her. It was Jane who she'd met on her first foray back in time when she'd stepped into the nineteen twenties. Oh, and there was Bernie too from the nineteen sixties!

'This is amazin',' Sabrina breathed.

'You're amazin', Adam replied. 'I know my proposal wasn't the most romantic, and I wanted to do something special for you.'

'Well, you have.' Sabrina kissed him. Then taking the glass of fizz Mickey held out to her, she moved into the fold to greet her guests.

Chapter Twenty-four

Sabrina was on tenterhooks as she paced up and down the platform at Lime Street station. It was strange being away from the shop on a weekday afternoon, and she hoped Aunt Evie wasn't run off her feet in her absence. But given the nature of her mission, she'd been shooed on her way. Aunt Evie was adamant she'd manage perfectly well on her own.

Sabrina's stomach rumbled, and she eyed the newsagent's toying with the idea of a sandwich but then decided it would be a waste of money. She wouldn't be able to eat it, not in her current agitated state. So an Opal Fruit would have to do instead.

Overhead the intricate arch of meshed steel and glass was letting the early afternoon sun filter through and the screech of brakes, mingling aromas of ciggies, coffee, newspapers and fuel all seemed amplified as though in a dome.

She checked the station clock with its Roman numerals for the umpteenth time and then wandered through the tidal flow of people ebbing in and out of the station to gaze up at the Arrivals board. The train from Euston, London, was due in five minutes. It had been eight minutes last time she checked, but the three minutes that had ticked by in between felt like an age. Time had slowed, the way it always did when you were waiting for something or, in this case, someone.

Sabrina had come to collect Mrs Betty Markham-Swift, who would be looking for a girl with a teal silk scarf knotted about her hair. Esmerelda had chosen her colours well.

Where she'd been so confident she and Flo were doing the right thing in reaching out to Fred's family, now she was second-guessing their actions. Had they been playing God? Fred had made it clear he wanted everything he'd confided in her to stay in the past. She shook the worrying thoughts away, recalling how in the end, it had been surprisingly easy to find Fred's youngest sister.

She and Flo couldn't take the credit for doing so though. That was down to Sue, the Miss Marple librarian they'd lucked upon when they'd visited the Central Library on the Saturday afternoon after her surprise party, despite their slightly greenish tinge thanks to the celebrations the night before.

Sabrina had clinked more glasses than she could remember and had declared the engagement party the best night of her life to Adam, stumbling from the pub shortly after eleven.

As they'd arranged, Flo arrived at the shop dead on their Saturday closing time of one o'clock, waving to Aunt Evie as she tootled off in her red, yellow and white Liverpool supporter colours to catch the No. 17 to Anfield Stadium. She'd been armed with a big bottle of Lucozade which they'd guzzled greedily, hoping for a second wind but all it did was give them wind.

They'd forgotten all about feeling under the weather as, with growing excitement, they watched over Sue, the librarian's shoulder.

The older woman was whizzing through the census records on the microfiche at a dizzying speed, relishing playing detective. Then, at last, her hand froze, and she peered closer at the screen scanning the information before announcing she'd located a Lord Frederick Markham of Headley Hall. She went on to say that the hall was located near the village of Shere in Surrey. 'Does that help, girls?'

Sabrina and Florence had nodded excitedly as they thought, jackpot! All that was left for them to do was telephone BT directory enquiries for the phone number for Headley Hall. Even if the family was no longer in residence, someone was bound to know how to contact them.

A woman hurrying down the platform, dragging two children along with her, shoved past Sabrina, nearly knocking her bag from her shoulder. She muttered a sorry as she half ran, half walked with her children's plump little legs spinning around in overdrive. Sabrina righted the bag strap and replayed the unusual conversation she'd had earlier in the week, which had now brought her to Lime Street station.

It was with nerves twanging like a harp being plucked that she'd dialled the number to Headley Hall, the phone jammed against her ear. Florence sat in Aunt Evie's chair, leaning forward to listen in, chewing on her thumbnail.

'It's ringing,' Sabrina informed her friend. She was about to hang up on the eighth ring when a plummy voice answered.

Sabrina didn't know what she'd expected, and perhaps she'd watched too many episodes of *Upstairs Downstairs* with Aunt Evie when she was younger because it wasn't a housekeeper who answered at all. To her shock, the posh voice down the line belonged to one Mrs Betty Markham-Swift herself. Sabrina clapped her hand over the receiver and mouthed at Florence, 'It's her! It's Fred's sister.'

Florence's eyes were already resembling Bambi's, albeit bloodshot, but hearing this, they popped.

'Hello, are you there?' Betty Markham-Swift repeated, sounding perturbed by the silence.

'Oh yes, erm, hello.' Sabrina sat up straight in her chair and, enunciating her vowels like Aunt Evie said, 'My name's Sabrina Flooks and I'm contacting you regarding your brother Fred Markham.'

'Freddy?'

'Yeah, erm, yes. Freddy.'

'Have you found him?' The voice was breathless.

'Yes, that is I know where he is.'

'Oh, dear girl, I've waited such a long time for this. Please, give me a moment. I need to sit down.'

'Yes, of course.' Sabrina cupped her hand over the receiver once more. 'She's sitting down,' she whispered to Florence, who nodded sagely and replied, 'It must be a shock after all this time.'

'Are you there, dear?'

'Yes, I'm still here.'

'Please, tell me.'

Sabrina, who was picturing the queen on the other end of the line for some reason, imagined Betty Markham-Swift twisting the curly phone wire in her hand with a stoic yet hopeful expression, a corgi curled up at her feet, a fire flickering in the grate. 'He's here. In Liverpool, I mean. At the ozzy, erm, hospital. The Royal Liverpool Hospital.'

There was a clearing of the throat. 'Are you from the War Graves Commission, young lady?'

Taken aback by the question, Sabrina replied, 'No, I'm from Brides of Bold Street.'

'I beg your pardon?'

'I'm from Brides of Bold Street, here in Liverpool,' Sabrina repeated.

'If this a joke, it's in very poor taste.' The tone was sharp now.

'I'm not joking, Mrs Markham-Swift. Fred's in hospital. He had a heart attack.'

'We've no money, you know, if that's what you're after.' Her voice had grown shrill. 'I've read about your sort. Well, you're barking up the wrong tree. Headley Hall is a money pit with its leaking roof and rising damp.'

Sabrina gripped the phone even tighter. This was not going how she'd planned, and Florence was looking alarmed as she tried to get the gist of a one-sided conversation. 'I promise you, Mrs Markham-Swift, I'm telling you the truth. I thought you should know where Fred was, that's all.'

'Who exactly are you?'

'I'm Sabrina Flooks.'

'Yes, yes to Fred, I mean.'

'I'm a friend.' How much should she tell this woman about the life her brother had been leading? Sabrina decided there was no point sugar-coating the truth. 'Listen, Fred's had a sad time of it, and I don't think it's my place to get into all of that. But the thing is, Mrs Markham-Swift, he likes a drink, and he sleeps rough. Sometimes he sleeps a few doors down from where I live and so, I bring him his breakfast, and we chat. It was a week ago now I found him unconscious, and he's been in the ozzy ever since.'

'I, I don't understand.'

'He's in the hospital, Mrs Markham-Swift, and he's doing as well as can be expected, all things considered.' Sabrina tried to slow her speech but found herself rushing on, nonetheless. 'The thing is, he opened up about his past and told me about his childhood. How you all put on shows in the nursery for your nanny and the housemaid. You were Miss Bettina. I—' Sabrina was burbling. She glanced over at Florence, who nodded encouragingly. 'I mean, we that's me bezzie mate, Flo and I, decided we owed it to Fred to try and find his family. We don't want him winding up back on the streets, and he has nowhere else to go.'

'Fred's alive?'

It wasn't a question, so Sabrina stayed quiet.

'Father told us he was dead, you know. Killed on foreign soil during the war. Shot down over France, he said. I thought you were from the War Graves Commission telephoning to tell me you'd located where he was buried.'

Sabrina was glad she was sitting down too. What sort of a father would pretend his son was dead? And lie to his whole family. 'I'm sorry, Mrs Markham-Swift.'

'Betty, call me Betty, dear.' The frostiness was melting.

Once she'd convinced Betty that the brother she'd not seen in forty years was lying in a hospital bed in Liverpool, she hadn't hesitated in making arrangements to come to him.

Now an ear-piercing screech and whoosh of air saw Sabrina stand to attention. It was the London train pulling into the station. She began to scan the faces of the passengers being disgorged onto the platform. Betty had informed her she would be wearing a tweed blazer and skirt, which had fitted the queenly image Sabrina already had in place.

And there she was! A woman of middling height with a sensible chin-length metallic bob dressed like a Burberry advert as she stepped down from the train. Sabrina thought she must be baking in the heavy tweed two-piece as she moved towards her. 'Betty?' she asked hesitantly, knowing she couldn't be anyone else.

'Sabrina, dear girl, so kind of you to meet me. And what a becoming scarf.' The voice, while aristocratic, was also warm, and on closer inspection, Sabrina could see the family resemblance between brother and sister. It was there in the regal nose and sparkling eyes which rubbed away her sharp edges. She held her hand out, and Sabrina took it, receiving a firm, no-nonsense handshake.

'Erm, welcome to Liverpool.'

Betty cast a wary glance around her as if by landing in the north, she'd entered the wild west.

They walked outside to the taxi rank with Sabrina enquiring politely about how Betty's journey had been. However, once they were ensconced in the backseat of a taxi, Betty cut to the chase.

'I still can't believe Freddy's alive. I don't suppose I will until I see him for myself. I thought I was the only one left. Mother and Father have been gone for years now. I think it was losing Freddy that pushed Mother over the edge. She passed not long after the war. He was always her favourite. Such a cruel thing.' She shook her head, and the points of her bobbed hair swung back and forth. 'Inhuman is what I'd call it. I mean to tell a mother her son is dead. It broke her heart. Broke of all our hearts for that matter.'

Sabrina didn't know what to say, so she reached over and placed her hand on Betty's. The older woman appeared to be taken aback as she stared down at her hand. She wasn't the touchy-feely type, Sabrina surmised, noting she looked pleased by the gesture, nonetheless.

'I think you must be a very kind young lady to care as you do. You sew what you reap in this life though, Sabrina because our father died on the throne with his trousers around his ankles. The housemaid found him. He'd have hated such an undignified ending.' Satisfaction rang out clearly.

It might have been a just ending, but Sabrina couldn't bring herself to smile. She didn't know about being kind either. Although Adam had said the same thing to her. She'd have said she was being human, unlike the late Lord Markham.

Betty continued to talk. 'Alicia died last year. It was her heart. And June, well, that was terrible. A car accident while holidaying abroad ten years or so back.'

'Oh, I'm sorry to hear that.' It seemed unfair one family should suffer so much sadness.

A wistfulness passed over Betty's face for bygone days. 'Alicia and June never wanted anything to do with Headley Hall. Mother's demise wasn't graceful. Her drinking, you understand. There were too many sad memories for them. So, I took the old place on with my Theo and made happy ones.'

This time Sabrina smiled.

'I never intended to grow old at Headley. I thought I'd move far, far away and lead an exotic life in Marrakesh or the like, but then I met my Theo. He had no desire to live in a riad, and I found I was pleased to stay put in Surrey. We open the house to the public these days, and its' been used as a set for television programmes. The old ghosts have been banished.' She fixed a bright smile on Sabrina, and Sabrina noticed the peach lipstick on her teeth. 'I shall convince Freddy to come and live with us. Headley Hall is his home. He belongs there with Theo and me.'

'Erm, there's something I should tell you,' Sabrina said as the taxi pulled up outside the hospital entrance.

Betty, whose hand had been reaching inside her handbag, froze, her gaze swinging sharply to Sabrina.

'Fred doesn't know you're coming, Betty. It's going to come as a shock to him, I'm afraid. He told me to leave things alone.' She hoped he'd forgive her.

'Oh, don't worry about Freddy. You leave him to me, dear.' Betty said. 'And put your purse away. I've got this.'

'Shall I go in first and let him know you're here?' Sabrina asked as they reached the ward. She could break it to him gently, she thought, unsure how exactly she'd do that.

Betty made a noise that was a cross between pooh and pah. 'I've waited forty years for news of Freddy dear. I shan't wait a moment longer.' With that, she sailed into the ward, pausing only to swivel her head left and right as she searched for her brother. 'I say, Freddy, you're looking peaky,' she announced, striding over as though she'd seen him only the day before.

Fred, frail and sweating profusely, stared at the tweed apparition in front of him. He probably thought he was hallucinating, Sabrina realised. Nurse Daly had said the alcohol leaving his system could cause them.

'You're not seeing things, old boy. It's me.' Betty pulled out the chair and sat down. 'Oh, but we've got a lot of catching up to do.'

'Betty?' Fred rasped, not seeing Sabrina still in the doorway of the ward.

'Yes, I'm here now, Freddy. I've come to take you in hand.'

Sabrina watched the exchange through watery eyes. Fred kept repeating Betty's name. She waited, seeing the realisation he wasn't seeing things dawn on him in the way he reached for her. As they embraced, happy endorphins flooded her system.

Fred would be alright from here on in.

Part Three

Chapter Twenty-five

'Aunt Evie, how will you manage when Adam and I are married?' Sabrina, who was drying the dishes, turned to look at her aunt. She appeared lost in thought as she sat in her customary spot by the open window enjoying her ciggy.

Evelyn was thinking about two things. The first was that she'd enjoyed the pork chops they'd had for their dinner, although they'd been a tad on the chewy side for her dentures. The second was the letter and, realising she'd been spoken to, Evelyn ground out the cigarette.

The past was tugging her back more and more of late. The need to finish putting her story on paper was urgent, and she wished Sabrina would hurry up with the dishes and get herself down to the pub where she was due to meet her friends to discuss who was taking what to the Isle of Man.

If Evelyn was going to tuck the letter in the bag Sabrina packed to take to the island as she'd planned, then she needed to crack on with it. Now, here she was wittering on about how she'd manage when she moved out. Well, she'd nip her worries in the bud. 'Perfectly well, I should imagine, luv.'

'I meant when we move into a place of our own. I don't like to think of you on your own here.' The idea of Aunt Evelyn being here in their flat without her made Sabrina feel peculiar, and ever since Adam had brought up the subject of where they would live once they were wed, the question as to what would happen to Aunt Evie had been niggling at her. Who would make her porridge for instance? She knew precisely how her aunt liked it. And who'd take the washing to the laundromat? Or get down on their knees to give the lino a going over. Aunt Evie's knees weren't up to the task these days. She drew a breath feeling quite panicky.

'Sabrina Flooks,' Evelyn intervened, seeing Sabrina growing pink in the cheeks. 'I lived here on my own for thirty-odd years before you happened along.' Her accent slipped in her insistence. 'I gor up of a morning and made me own breakfast, and you could have eaten your dinner off me floors. All that while running a business singlehandedly. A business I saw through the depression and the war years, ta very much.'

Sabrina knew Aunt Evie had been and still was a force to be reckoned with. A woman before her time who'd never relied on a man. If she'd been born in a different century, she'd have been there at the forefront of the suffragette movement they'd learned about in history at school. And she hadn't finished making her point yet either, Sabrina realised.

'I'm quite capable of managing here on my own, ta very much. Besides, you're not emigrating, only getting somewhere of your own to live. So I'll still be seeing you every day downstairs in the shop.' Her lips pursed. 'Unless there's something you're not telling me?'

Sabrina shook her head. 'Of course not.'

'Right then.'

Sabrina turned back to the dishes in the drying rack, somewhat regretting having said anything.

'And, for your information, I'm looking forward to not being subjected to that *Top of the Pops* rubbish every Thursday evening,' Aunt Evie added for good measure, always eager for the last word.

'Well, you won't have to watch it tonight, will you?' Sabrina flung back as she rubbed at the dinner plate with the tea towel. Aunt Evie would miss her. She knew she would, despite her blustering. They had their routines, and they rubbed along nicely together. But what she said was true. She had managed before Sabrina had come into her life, and they would still see each other every day except Sundays. But still, she felt antsy, so what else was bothering her?

Evelyn's tone softened as she said, 'Change can be a good thing, you know. You'd do well to remember that.'

Aunt Evie had hit the nail on the head, Sabrina realised. She could read her like a book. Any change unsettled her and, given the traumatic events of her childhood, was it any wonder? It didn't matter that she was looking forward to her and Adam starting their married life in their own home. The thought of waking up next to him every morning gave her a delicious thrill, and she revelled in imagining them as an old married couple curled up on the sofa watching the tele together of an evening.

She didn't have big dreams, counting herself lucky to have found her passion in life from a young age and to be doing what she loved—creating beautiful wedding dresses. She made other women's dreams come true, and there was nothing else in the world she'd rather do. As for travel and broadening her horizons, in the last few years, she'd had enough adventures traversing time to last her a lifetime. All she wanted from now on was a simple life spent with the man she loved. Children would be lovely one day too. Despite this, she knew when the time came to move out of the little flat she'd called home for as long as she could remember, it would be as much a wrench for her as it would Aunt Evie.

Adam, who had first-hand access to property information, given the nature of his family business, was determined they'd scrape together a deposit for their own home. He'd said they'd not start their married life renting and was already talking about opening a joint bank account for their savings. Sabrina hoped he wasn't too hard a taskmaster on the saving front. It had never been her strong suit. All his talk of deposits and mortgages had made her feel properly grown-up. But, while his head was full of practical things like finances, hers was full of the wedding. Her dress, to be more precise.

Over the years, she'd designed her dream wedding dress time and time again, tweaking it as fashions and her tastes changed. In the quieter moments downstairs during the working day and when Aunt Evie's beady eyes weren't on her, she'd been sketching and re-sketching ideas. The perfect gown alluded her as yet though. As for Flo and the twins, she'd not even begun to think about what they'd wear. She'd sit down and pow-wow some ideas with Flo when they returned from the Isle of Man. According to Florence, the twins were already cutting out pictures of dresses they liked from their mam's Woman's Weekly. Mrs Teesdale had gone mad the other day when she'd put her feet up with a cuppa all set to enjoy her new magazine only to find the twins had been snipping at it!

Then there was the wedding itself to think about. Adam had made noises about a registry office service, while Aunt Evie thought it was a given they'd be wed at St James, the church she'd attended since forever.

If that were to happen, she and Adam would need to participate in weekly services at the church leading up to the wedding. Given Sabrina had trooped along with Aunt Evie until she'd been of an age to make her mind up as to whether she went or not, she didn't relish this idea. As for Adam, he wouldn't be ecstatic about marching along to church on a Sunday morning either. It was a dilemma because she didn't want to upset Aunt Evie. Accordingly, it was in the too-hard basket, and she'd resolved not to think about it again until they set an actual date.

That was another thing—the date. Sabrina wanted to be a summer bride, but that would mean waiting an entire year as there was no way the do she had in mind could be organised in the next few months. Did she want to wait that long? Her head began to spin at the thought of the honeymoon. She'd never been anywhere, and when a magnetic-like pull had seen her flicking through brochures in Thomas Cook, the agent had said Spain was a popular choice for honeymooners.

Sabrina Taylor née Flooks in Spain! She'd left with a brochure depicting a brilliant blue sea with whitewashed buildings tumbling down a hillside, their ochre tile roofs a splash of colour. It was secreted away in her bag to show Adam. She'd wait until the right moment though because she suspected he'd prioritise a house over a glamorous holiday.

As her thoughts threatened to spiral until she'd bitten off all her carefully shaped fingernails, not too long, not too short, she closed the cutlery drawer with a flick of her hip. 'There, that's me done. I'll go and smarten myself up.' Once she'd hung the tea towel to dry over the cooker handle, she disappeared off to her bedroom to fluff around with her hair and makeup.

Evelyn itched to retrieve the writing things she'd tucked away but instead made herself a cup of tea. By the time she'd settled herself down to drink it, Sabrina had reappeared looking glossy and primped. 'I'll be off then, Aunt Evie.' She leaned in and kissed her aunt's soft, powdered cheek feeling a swell of love as she did so.

'Enjoy yourself.'

Sabrina was halfway out of the door when Evelyn called after her. She spun around to hear what she wanted to say.

'Don't be worrying about me, luv. You've your own life to lead. It's the natural order of things.'

Sabrina gave a slight nod. She couldn't promise anything, and thundering down the stairs, she shouted back up them. 'Don't forget *Top of the Pops* is on at seven thirty!'

'Cheeky madam,' Evelyn called back, waiting until she heard the back door bang shut before unearthing her writing pad. She scanned over the last page she'd written, feeling herself being swept into the past.

Chapter Twenty-six

Evelyn, Liverpool, 1927

Evelyn let herself back into the house, pressing the door shut firmly behind her as she tried to catch her breath before she faced her mam and sisters. Her face was hot, and despite the chill outside, she was clammy. Her hands were trembling too, and holding them out for inspection, she wondered if the lad—what was his name? Roy? No, Ray. Ray Taylor, that was it, was heading back to join in with the trouble that had been unfolding. She hoped he'd be wise enough to steer clear of The Ship's Head and go home, wherever that may be but somehow doubted that would be the case. He was with the Lime Street Boys, after all. Everybody knew they were trouble.

They'd been halfway down Potter Street by the time he'd decided they could slow their run to a clipped walk, being a safe distance away now from the angry mob. He'd loosened the firm grasp he had of her arm. She could still feel the imprint of his fingers, and she rubbed at it knowing there'd be a bruise there in the morning. Still, it was a small price to pay for getting home in one piece. He'd ignored her protests that she would be fine to see herself to her door, and despite her agitation, she'd noticed he didn't walk so much as swagger. Either way, she'd been secretly glad of his insistence on escorting her because she was far from fine, and his cocky self-assurance was a comfort. Not that she'd have let on to him.

Breathing through her nose and exhaling through her mouth slowly, her racing pulse began to settle back into a more natural rhythm. How would she shake the wildness of those men who'd swarmed from the courts from her memory? They were like the rabid dog she'd once seen with spittle at the corners of its mouth. There'd been no reasoning with the animal and nothing for it but to send for the police. She'd not stayed around to see the poor dog shot. She'd not waited around when she and Ray had reached her house tonight either, mumbling a goodnight but forgetting her manners in her haste to get inside and shut the door on the last half hour. Oh well, she thought, there was no point berating herself. It was unlikely she'd ever see the lad again.

'Is that you, Evie?' Lizzie called out from the parlour.

'It is, Mam. I'm hanging me hat and coat up.' She did just that, taking one last calming breath before facing the music.

Her sisters were still sitting where she'd last seen them, on the sofa. Only Nellie had moved on to stitching a nightgown and Bea a shirt. Nellie's eyes were wide as she waited to hear what Mam would have to say about the way Evie had hared out of the door without so much as a by your leave. Bea, meanwhile, looked smug.

Evie scowled in her direction before the lie she'd prepared earlier tripped off her tongue, 'Sorry for rushing off as I did, Mam. I'd forgotten, you see. I promised Ida I'd call around after tea. She gorra a terrible tongue lashing from Mrs Wilson for being two minutes late this morning, and she was awfully upset all day.'

Lizzie eyed her daughter from the chair she'd twisted around in. Tendrils of hair had escaped the low roll she pinned her hair into each morning, and she tucked them impatiently behind her ears. Mrs Wilson was well known for having a vicious bite. If it had been Violet standing there telling her the same story, she'd not have believed a word of it but, Evie, well, Evie was as honest as the day was long. 'Be that as it may, you had me and your sisters worried, dashing out like so,' she chastised gently.

'Sorry, Mam. I'll think on next time,' Evelyn replied and, catching sight of Beatrice's disappointed face that her sister wasn't going to be on the receiving end of a tongue lashing, after all, pulled a face at her.

'Right, well don't just stand there, Evie,' Lizzie clucked. 'There's the beading work on Mrs Griffith's dress for you to be getting on with.'

Evelyn made her mind up as she retrieved her sewing things and the tin containing the hundreds of shiny beads to put the events of the evening behind her. She was home safe, and that was what mattered. If her dad was caught up in the fighting at The Ship's Head, then serve him right. He'd only be receiving a taste of his own medicine. She'd not be wasting her energy worrying about him. As for Violet, Evelyn knew her sister well enough to know she wouldn't be home until late. She'd tackle her then. Soon, what her sister got up to when she moved to the Birches wouldn't be her problem.

Despite her best efforts to stay awake, Evelyn was floating in that neverland of half-awake, half-asleep when she heard her mam's voice downstairs. She was doing her best to whisper but snatched phrases like 'who do you think you are, lady?' and 'what will people think?' floated up through the floorboards as she failed to keep her voice down. Bea next to her didn't stir, nor did Nellie, whose warm little toes were resting against the back of Evelyn's thighs.

Violet was home then, Evelyn deduced, and Mam would be wanting to know how she'd managed to afford her dress, let alone stockings and new shoes, not to mention where she'd been all dressed up like so. She'd not be happy about Vi galivanting out of the door in her coat either.

She heard a muffled response and hoped Vi wasn't giving her a mouthful back. Violet was the only one who'd dare to answer Mam back, which in Evelyn's opinion, wasn't fair given how hard she worked to put food on the table for them. Annoyance at her sister's selfishness flared.

Evelyn strained to hear the rest of what was being said but couldn't make it out, and so she lay in the semi-darkness of their bedroom waiting for her sister to appear.

It wasn't long before she heard creaking on the stairs. Their door squeaked open, and Violet tiptoed into their room like a thief creeping across a rooftop. Evelyn pushed herself up onto her elbows and glared at the shadow of her elder sister. Even from here, she could smell a heady perfume; it was competing with the stale smokiness of cigarettes, and, her nose twitched, alcohol. Violet had been drinking! It made her blood boil, given Vi had seen what the drink did to their dad night after night. No wonder Mam had been giving her what for.

'Where've you been?' she hissed.

Violet, who'd been in the process of unzipping her dress, jumped and stumbled back into the wall.

There was a sound like 'oof', and then she rubbed her elbow. 'Christ, Evie, don't do that! You didn't half frighten me. Why are you awake?'

'Waiting for you. Where've you been?'

'Mind your own business and go back to sleep.'

Next to Evelyn, Bea rolled over but didn't wake, and Nellie down the bottom of the bed smacked her lips together. Those two could sleep through anything, Evelyn thought, her cheeks heating up in annoyance. 'I followed you. So don't bother lying and saying you were at Lois's or Maggie's or whoever's. I know you weren't.'

The dress fell in a puddle on the floor, and Evelyn fought the urge to clamber over the top of Bea and rescue it.

'What do you mean you followed me?' Violet swayed for a moment before bending to retrieve it. She draped it over the end of the bed, then, sliding under the blankets, muttered how it was like ice.

'Just that. I wanted to see where you were going, and I saw you get in that man's motor car on the Vauxhall Road.' She decided not to mention what else had transpired because Violet would only tell her it served her right for spying on her.

Her sister propped herself up on one elbow, and even though she couldn't see Violet's eyes clearly, Evelyn knew she was glaring at her. She could feel them boring holes into her as she spat, 'You had no right to do that, Evelyn, you little sneak. Don't you dare breathe a word to Mam. He's a friend of mine, is all.'

Evelyn wasn't going to back down. 'Why isn't he picking you up here then if it's all so above-board? How come you haven't introduced him to Mam?'

'There are things you wouldn't understand.' Violet sniffed haughtily.

'I'm not a child, Violet, and I know if you have to skulk about, then he can't have your best interests at heart. Is he married? Is that why you're wearing silk dresses and stockings and stinking of expensive perfume?' Evelyn didn't know what she'd do if Violet said yes.

'He's not married. It's complicated, that's all.' Violet sighed, and the condescending sound riled Evelyn further.

'He was too old for you. I could see that much.' Evelyn was about to give up. There was always tomorrow to try and talk some sense into her. Besides, she could tell from Vi's self-righteous indignation that she wasn't going to get anywhere tonight, and she was tired. Morning would be here before she knew it.

Violet wasn't ready to give in yet though. 'Oh, and what would you know? You've no life of your own stuck here in this hovel we call home sewing all the hours God sends or down at that factory—dreaming you and Mam are going to turn things around. I don't want to waste my life on dreams. I want better for meself than this, and there's no crime in that.' She flopped back down on her pillow, huffing, 'You're like an old photograph, Evelyn. Faded and dull.'

Violet's words stung, and Evelyn forgot about her resolve to leave things be in favour of sleep as she shot back over the top of Bea. 'I won't be reliant on a man for my happiness, Vi. Not ever and you, well you'll come a cropper carrying on like a tart. It will be you who loses in the end because that flash Harry of yours will come out smelling like roses. His sort always does.'

Quick as a flash, Violet was up and reaching over, slapped her sister hard. 'I'm not a tart!'

Evelyn blinked in shock at the stinging blow, then she reared up and walloped her sister back. She yelped as Violet snatched hold of her hair, yanking it hard and, with her head bent, pulled herself onto her hands and knees, clambering over Beatrice, who'd finally stirred.

'Ger off me,' Beatrice grunted, and as the two sisters continued to wrestle, she managed to pull them apart.

'I don't know what's gor into the pair of you, but you'd better shurrup. Dad's home.'

The fight went out of the sisters, and they lay back down, panting. Beatrice was furious at being woken by such a kerfuffle and Nellie was crying softly.

'Shush, Nellie poppet, it's ahright. Go back to sleep.' Evie tried to comfort her sister as she wondered whether it had been a whistling night or a singing night.

Chapter Twenty-seven

Evelyn had her arm laced through Ida's. She had a spring in her step as they passed through the gates of the button factory despite the heavy clouds that greeted them. It was bone cold, and the chill whispered of snow. The coal fires burning across the city, doing their best to ward winter off, made the air thick and sooty. The smell settled over you like a cloak. It got into your pores, and for those not blessed with a strong constitution, the lungs too.

A week had passed since the incident with Violet and the two sisters still weren't speaking to one another, much to their mam's dismay, who'd hoped they'd patch it up before Violet left to live in at the Birches. She'd tried to worm out of them the reason why her two oldest daughters were at loggerheads, but both Evelyn's and Violet's lips were sealed. So, on that at least, they were united.

It wasn't out of sisterly loyalty on Evelyn's part, however. It was because she couldn't see what would be gained in telling their mam about Vi's fancy man. All it would do was cause her more worry, and she had enough on her plate. Evelyn knew Violet well enough to know it wouldn't matter what Mam said to her anyway. She wouldn't stop carrying on with whoever he was, not until she was good and ready.

Beatrice, of course, had relished telling their mam an exaggerated version of events that had kicked off the feud where words like bloodbath and madwomen were bandied about. Mam thankfully knew Beatrice well enough to take this with a pinch of salt. However, Evelyn's scalp was still tender where Violet had yanked her hair, the scratch mark down Violet's cheek only beginning to fade now.

Perhaps it was the soreness of her scalp acting as a reminder of the events before the fight because her thoughts had swung pendulum-like to Ray Taylor all week. She tried to stop them sneaking up on her but had no control over when and where they'd pop into her head. She wasn't sure why she couldn't banish him from her mind, but for whatever reason, she could still feel the pressure of his fingers on her arm. Nor could she shake the smell of the oil he'd slicked through his hair from her nostrils.

Evelyn and Ida were swept along with the sea of factory girls as she recalled the scene first thing that morning.

Violet, bundled into her coat, had set her case down in the passage and stepped through to the parlour to give their mam a fierce hug goodbye. She'd promised to come home every Sunday afternoon to see them all, but Evelyn doubted she would. Her sister thought she was set to close the chapter on her life in Potter Street, but she'd be back with her tail between her legs.

Vi had moved on to Bea, who'd been embraced briefly before sweeping little Nellie up. Their littlest sister's bottom lip had been wobbling, threatening to derail her determination to be brave. However, when it came to Evelyn, her nose had been firmly in the air. She'd pushed past her to retrieve her case, causing a tut of dismay from their mam.

She didn't care anyway, Evelyn told herself. Violet would do what she would do.

Whatever happened to her sister from here on in, at least her conscience would be clear because she'd tried to talk sense into her. Evelyn ignored the whispering voice that said she should have tried harder. Violet may have been blessed with beauty, but she'd been bypassed when it came to common sense.

The dark thoughts matched the sky, but the lightness in her step didn't falter because Violet had made her bed, at least for the time being, and she couldn't change that, but on the home front, things were at last set to change.

'What's got you skipping along?' Ida asked, eyeing her friend with curiosity stamped on her face. 'It's not the weather, that's for sure because it's freezin'. I reckon we're in for snow.'

Evelyn shivered and hoped there was enough coal to feed the fire.

'C'mon,' Ida urged. 'What's going on?'

'Mam gor two orders yesterday for evening dresses from friends of Mrs Griffiths.' Evelyn gushed, banishing all her worries. Mam had greeted her with the news that not one but two ladies' maids had tapped on their door while Evelyn had been at the factory. It was this she needed to pour her energies into. Turning their dreams of opening a dressmakers into a reality.

'That's grand, Evie.' Ida beamed.

Evelyn squeezed her friend's arm. 'It won't be long, Ida. You'll see. It's only the beginning. Me and Mam, we'll be opening our shop in no time.' Her eyes sparkled at the thought of it as she pictured the sign with gold lettering above a smart blue door, 'Flooks Dressmakers', Although the name was still very much open to debate.

They'd Mrs Griffiths to thank for things beginning to look up. According to Dot Clancy, the whimsical apricot chiffon dress had been a roaring success at the Grafton Ballroom's anniversary tea dance.

The lady's maid had called on Sunday afternoon. Evelyn hadn't recognised her when she first opened the door without her mob cap and uniform. It was her afternoon off, and she'd been kind enough to swing by to tell them how thrilled Mrs Griffiths had been with her gown.

'She's sure to tell all and sundry about Lizzie Flooks' exceptional dressmaking skills,' she'd said.

Evelyn had wanted to call her mam to come to the door and listen so she could hear first-hand what Dot was saying but knew she wouldn't have come if she had. The reason for this was because she was tucked away in the parlour nursing a fat lip. It had been a singing night the night before.

Evelyn relayed the good news once Dot had gone on her way and Lizzie had dropped the wet rag she'd been holding to her mouth to clap her hands delightedly. 'This is it, Evie! I know how women like Mrs Griffiths work. Word will spread, and the orders will roll in, and you'll be packing in that job of yours in no time.'

Evelyn wondered now why she hadn't thought to ask how Mam knew how women like Mrs Griffiths operated.

Ida nudged her. 'I wonder who that fella up ahead there's waiting for.'

Evelyn looked to where a lad was scuffing at the ground with the toe of his boots. There was something familiar about his assured stance as he stood with one hand thrust in the pocket of his coat, the other holding a smouldering cigarette in danger of burning his fingers. The penny dropped, as did her mouth. 'I think that's him,' she managed to splutter once she'd recovered from her initial shock.

'Who?'

'The lad I told you about.'

This time it was Ida whose eyes widened in shock. 'The Lime Street Boy. Are you sure?'

Evelyn risked a second glance, and this time she was sure. She nodded.

'What does he want with you?'

'I dunno, do I?' She was as bewildered as Ida and hadn't a clue how he'd known where she worked. She flashed back over their brief exchange but couldn't recall telling him anything about herself other than her name and that her dad was a bizzy.

'Your mam will go spare if she finds out you've been hanging about with the likes of him.'

'Ida, you sound like Bea, and I've hardly been hanging about with him. Besides, I didn't ask him to meet me. I haven't the foggiest how he even knows where I work.'

'Maybe he's waiting for someone else then,' Ida added hopefully.

At that moment, he spied the two girls, and his eyes narrowed as he gave Evelyn the once-over as if checking she was the same girl he'd seen home the other night.

Evelyn and Ida slowed their pace, watching as he flicked the cigarette onto the cobbles and ground it out with the heel of his boot. Then he held his hand up in a greeting. So much for waiting for someone else then, Evelyn thought.

He was dressed much the same as he'd been the night it had all been about to kick off at The Ship's Head she noted as they drew closer.

'You didn't say he was so handsome?' Ida breathed.

Evelyn elbowed her hard. 'That's because I was too bleedin' petrified as to what he wanted with me to notice. And don't you go getting any ideas either, I'm not the only one with a Mam who'd go spare if she thought I was hanging about with a lad from the Lime Street Boys.'

Was he good looking? Evelyn couldn't help but wonder, sizing him up from under her lashes as they drew nearer. Well, even if he did have a certain something about him, she wouldn't be swayed by a handsome face because no man would get in the way of her plans. With this in mind, she untangled herself from Ida and took a deep breath as he greeted her.

'Well, well, well, if it isn't Evelyn Flooks whose dad's a bizzy.' He doffed his bucko cap.

Ida shot her a quizzical glance which Evelyn ignored as she squared up to him, her chin jutting out as she demanded, 'How did you know where I work?' Her hands settled on her hips. 'And why are you here?'

'How do you know it's you I'm waiting for?' Ray replied with a grin that set off a hint of a dimple on his cheek.

Evelyn's face flamed. Had she got it wrong? Was it another girl from the factory he'd come to see? Something like disappointment flickered as she fumbled for a reply.

'I'm teasing. I wanted to see if you were ahright, like.'

'Well, now you've seen I am.'

'And I wanted to show you something.' Her brusqueness didn't in the least bit faze him.

'What?'

'It's a surprise.'

Evelyn didn't need to glance over at Ida to know her gaze would be swinging back and forth between them like a tennis ball being lobbed over the net, her mouth hanging open.

Ida wasn't the only one intrigued by quiet, mousy Evelyn Flook's conversation with a wide boy. The other girls she worked with stared as they filed past. No prizes for guessing who'd be the talk of the factory, Evelyn thought. But, to her surprise, she found she quite liked the idea and decided she'd act all mysterious when they quizzed her about him as they were sure to do.

'C'mon, Evie. We'd best be going,' Ida urged. She'd had enough of the show, and it was too cold to stand about bantering.

Violet's words echoed in Evelyn's ears. 'You've no life. You're faded and dull.' And she was as surprised as Ida when instead of walking off with her friend she said, 'You go on, Ida. I'll see you tomorrow.'

'Evie.' Ida held back uncertainly.

'I promise to look after Evelyn, Ida, is it?'

Ida mumbled a shy yes.

'Ray Taylor. Pleased to make your acquaintance.' He doffed his cap once more. 'And, Ida, Evelyn here can vouch that I'm a gentleman, can't you, Evelyn?'

Evelyn liked the way he said her name. It sounded different, somehow.

Ida turned worried eyes on her and she smiled at her friend reassuringly. Even if he did go around in a gang, he was a gentleman. He hadn't shown a hint of impropriety the other night apart from when he'd grabbed her arm, and he'd only done so to get her moving away from The Ship's Head. 'I'll be fine, Ida, you g'won.'

Chapter Twenty-eight

Ray held out his arm and Evelyn hesitated for a moment before taking it. She felt like somebody else because Evelyn Flooks would not go off with a lad she barely knew, let alone a lad like Ray for whom the scent of trouble hovered over his head like a halo. But, in for a penny in for a pound, she decided, holding her head high. If she was going to give the other girls something to talk about, she might as well make it something worth their while.

They set off at a quick pace because it was too cold for strolling.

Ray steered her to the left when they reached the end of the lane, where she would usually turn right to catch the tram.

Evelyn twisted her head to look back over her shoulder and spied Ida, who'd tagged on with Nessa and Millie, a little way down the road. For a moment, she toyed with telling Ray she'd forgotten her promise to go straight home after work, because it wasn't too late.

The moment passed though and turning back, she kept in step with Ray as he strode along, keen to get to wherever it was they were going.

'Where is it we're off to?' she asked, trying her luck a second time.

'I told you it's a surprise, and if I tell you then it won't be one anymore,' Ray replied amicably.

Evelyn changed tack. 'How did you know where I work?'

He tapped the side of his nose. 'Us Lime Street Boys have our ways.'

She frowned. Ray made it sound as if he'd twisted someone's arm to get them to say where she could be found.

He laughed at her expression. 'Don't worry. I didn't rough anyone up. I knew where you lived, so I went to Potter Street this afternoon, and the woman next to yours told me I'd find you down at the button factory.'

Mrs Murphy next door would have a field day with this, Evelyn thought glumly. The news that one of the Flooks girls had a Lime Street Boy looking for her would spread like wildfire up and down Potter Street. It was bound to get back to Mam too. Evelyn knew only too well there was more than one woman in their street who'd be glad to bring Lizzie Flooks down a peg or two by informing her who her daughter was getting about with.

Ray was asking her what she did at the factory, she realised, deciding it was too late to be worrying about what Mam would say now. 'I work on the power press,' she told him, relaying the gruesome stories she'd been told of girls who'd gone before her having lost fingers on the job. 'It's only temporary though because me mam and I are going into business soon.'

Ray raised an eyebrow out that. 'What sort of business?'

'Dressmaking. We're going to open a shop.' First, Evelyn told him about her mam's prowess on the sewing machine and how she'd learned at her knee and loved it. Then, opening up, she told him about their luck with Mrs Griffiths and how her word of mouth as to the mother and daughter dressmaking duo would pave the way for them to afford to rent premises. Her eyes shone as she said, 'We won't have to work out of the parlour anymore, and when we've our shop, we'll be able to compete with the likes of Cripps and the department stores.'

The more she talked, the more real the prospect became, and she refused to entertain thoughts about how her dad would take to her mam going into business. It was something she and Mam never discussed. They both knew he'd take umbrage, seeing it as a slight on his ability to provide for his family even though he hadn't contributed in any meaningful way in a long time. The plan was for Mam to tuck the extra money away from the dresses she was sewing. It would go towards the deposit they'd need to make their dream a reality.

'I know about business,' Ray said airily. 'And, that's stiff competition you're talking about going up against.'

Evelyn bristled. She didn't appreciate him raining on her parade.

Feeling her tense beside him, Ray said, 'Don't get mardy. I'm not saying it ain't a good idea, but I am saying if you're going to do it, then you'll need to find a point of difference. Summat to set you apart from your competitors.'

It made sense, Evelyn thought, rolling his words around in her head and then coming up with an idea. 'Maybe we could specialise in evening gowns. That's what's got the ball rolling for us.'

'I'd have thought Blacklers, Lewis's and the like would have a monopoly on those.'

'They do, but Mam's got more talent in her little finger on that old Singer of hers than all their machinists put together.' It was true, Evelyn thought. She didn't even need a pattern and held ideas in her head to rival any of the London or Paris fashion houses.

'It's still competition, though, innit? So why make things tougher than they need be? No,' he shook his head, 'You need an opening of your own. A corner of the market that's not been tapped into as much.'

Evelyn thought hard, and then it came to her. 'A bridal shop!' she exclaimed excitedly.

'Bingo.' Ray winked at her.

Evelyn grinned at him. It was perfect. They could make a name for themselves by creating the most beautiful wedding gowns the city had ever seen. She was tingling with excitement and couldn't wait to share the idea with Mam when she got home.

Poor Violet, she thought idly. She might think the answer to a better lot in life lay in finding a man to latch on to, but Evelyn believed in hard graft. This would change things for them.

'And how come you know so much about business then? Evelyn asked. 'And don't tap the side of your nose again!' she said, jumping in before he could do just that.

Ray laughed. She liked his laugh. It was a slow rumbling that came from deep within him.

'It's common sense innit, and I've plenty of that. You've gorra look at the different angles.'

Was he suggesting she was silly then? Again she bristled. 'Well, if you've got so much common sense, why do you run with a gang? That doesn't seem very sensible to me.'

Ray looked at her as though the answer was obvious. 'You're a touchy Judy int ya. Cos it's a way of getting out.'

'What do you mean?'

He shrugged. 'You're born into what you're born into, and I wasn't born into a lot. I'm one of four, all girls 'cept for me. I was ten years old, too young to work and too old for learnin' when me dad died.

Mam struggled after that. She did her best to keep us together, worked herself to the bone and died trying. So me sisters and I were farmed out, and I dunno where they wound up, but I didn't much like where I went. The Lime Street Boys are me family now. And I've got it figured out. You need money to better yourself. The sort of money I could never make working in a factory or the like. Us lads, we're like Robin Hoods. We rob from the rich and give to the poor.' He gave her a cheeky wink.

Sabrina raised an eyebrow. She'd not heard that before, and the papers never had anything good to say about any of the gangs.

Ray gave that low rumbling laugh again. 'Ahright, we ain't that saintly, but we do look after our own. I've got a tidy sum stashed now, and it's mounting up all the time. So I'm going to put it into property. That's where the real money's at. And then when I've got enough of it behind me, I'll go respectable like.'

Evelyn believed him. Ray struck her as someone who'd been knocked down and wouldn't let it happen again. He was on the right side of stubborn to make his dreams happen. It was something they had in common.

Darkness proper would be upon them soon, and the rabbit warren of streets Ray had been leading her up and down, had given way to a leafy square, beyond which stretched a wide, tree-lined avenue. Poverty rubbed shoulders with squalor here in the city they called home. One was only a breath away from the other, Evelyn mused as they passed through the square to meander past the grand Georgian houses with proud Corinthian columns standing sentry at their entrances. Gardens and driveways were encased within lacy wrought iron. It was worlds away from the one she inhabited down Potter Street and was the world Vi hankered after.

Had Ray brought her to come and ogle the wealthy homes of the city's bankers and merchants? Was that was this was all about. Or perhaps he would show her which house he had designs on because his ideas were lofty enough.

Before she could ask him, though, he'd swung his gaze left and right before pulling her into a narrow lane running between two particularly imposing houses. It was dark down here without the glow of the gas lamps that had been flickering on. She could barely see the sky above her head as the walls of the buildings on either side of them threatened to close in on her. Evelyn was beginning to think she'd no common sense after all. If she'd had an ounce of it, she wouldn't have agreed to accompany Ray this evening.

It was too narrow to walk side by side, and Ray led the way. Enough was enough, Evelyn decided, tugging on his arm. He looked back over his shoulder, and she could see the whites of his eyes and teeth as he grinned at her in the faltering light. It gave him a wolfish look which did nothing to reassure her.

'We're nearly there.'

She strained to see past his burly frame, but there was nothing there but a brick wall. The lane was a dead end.

'What sorta game are you playing, Ray Taylor, because if—'

Ray interrupted her, 'I'm not playing games. That's where we're going. Over the top of that wall.'

'Over my dead body!' Evelyn spluttered.

Evelyn couldn't believe she was doing this. She had one foot in Ray's cupped hands while her hands were clutching the bricks at the top of the wall.

The last time she'd been in this position, it had been Vi crouched down in the jiggers to hoist Evelyn up to peek over the sagging wall into Ma Kenny's tumbledown yard. They'd managed to convince themselves she was a witch, and if she'd a black cat skulking about in her yard, then that would be all the proof needed.

'One, two, three.' Ray hefted her up, and she swung her other leg over the wall, so she was sitting astride it in a most unladylike manner. He shimmied up alongside her, and Evelyn gazed down at what he'd brought her to see.

'Magic, innit?'

Evelyn nodded slowly. The light was different. The sky had taken on an almost pinkish hue, and she felt something icy land on her face.

'Snow,' Ray stated, reaching forward and wiping it off her cheek. Evelyn was too intent on the walled garden and a greenhouse like a smaller version of the ones in Calderstones Park below her to pay it much heed. It looked like a glass palace set in its grounds.

'C'mon.' Ray jumped down, landing on the damp, clipped grass with a soft thud. He held his arm out, and Evelyn launched forward. Once her feet were on the ground, she let him take her hand, already knowing what he was going to do.

The door to the greenhouse was unlocked, something Ray didn't seem surprised by as he held it open for her. She glanced over her shoulder to the arch in the wall. It must lead to another of the big homes like the ones dotting the street they'd turned off. However, there was no sign of life and, keen to see what was housed inside the greenhouse, she stepped inside. Ray pulled the door behind them closed quickly, not wanting to let the frigid air in.

It was as though she'd stepped into another country, Evelyn thought as the close, warm air enveloped her. Her senses were struggling to comprehend the intoxicating fragrance filling her nostrils that were simultaneously spicy, sweet and exotic. Tinkling water was the only noise breaking the overwhelming hush aside from her and Ray's breathing. She could see shadowy alien shapes on either side of her and a marble statue of a nymph glowing eerily amidst them. The rasp of a flint broke the silence, and as Ray held his lighter aloft, she gasped. They were surrounded by the most glorious array of flowers she'd ever seen. There were vibrant shades of yellow, pink, red and purple and softer peaches, lemon, and white.

'It's an orchid house,' Ray explained, enjoying the wonder dancing in her eyes.

Evelyn tried to soak it all in. She wanted to imprint it to her memory to bring out when the world seemed dull and grey before the lighter grew too hot, and Ray had to extinguish the flame. At the end of the path they were on was a stone bench seat, and in the foliage behind it was the small fountain responsible for the tinkling sound. As the light ebbed and died, she followed him down to the seat feeling its cold surface solid beneath her despite her coat. She allowed a sliver of reality in. 'What will we do if someone comes and finds us here?'

'They won't,' Ray said with the self-assurance that gave her confidence.

'You seem awfully certain.'

'I am. The family's in America, and the house is all shut up. The only person who comes in here is the gardener, and he's hardly likely to call in this time of the night. It's a shame to waste all this beauty, don't you reckon?'

Evelyn nodded. It was. Then something else occurred to her. 'How do you know all that?'

Ray tapped the side of his nose and she thought of the stories Vi had brought home about the burgling spree plaguing the upper classes. This time she decided not to ask him to elaborate further. She didn't want anything to spoil this moment or this place.

'I told you about me mam and what happened. What's your story, Evelyn Flooks? Because I ain't convinced your dad's a bizzy.'

Evelyn thought about her dad, and her stomach twisted. 'Me dad's a mean drunk who hits me, mam and any of us if we're stupid enough to get in his way.' Then she began opening up like the flowers she could still see reflected on the insides of her eyelids.

Evelyn had never spoken frankly about how bad it was with anyone. Mam had forbidden them all to talk about what a brute Jack Flooks was outside their home. As though not mentioning it would make the bruises fade quicker.

She'd given Ida snapshots of what life was like for them behind the closed door of their Potter Street house. But she'd never confided how they all walked on eggshells when her father banged through the door, how she lay awake night after night waiting to hear if it was a whistling night or a singing night. What it felt like to listen to him doling it out to their mam and not being able to do a thing about it.

She talked and talked, and only when she'd finished talking, exhausted and spent by her confession, did she become aware of Ray holding her hand.

Chapter Twenty-nine

ONE YEAR LATER

The wind was whipping itself into a frenzy, and brittle brown leaves scudded along the pavement past Evelyn as she pulled her coat tighter around her. She'd stitched patches onto the elbows of her old navy coat so it would see her through another season, and Ray, noticing how worn it was, had wanted to buy her a new one. He wanted to buy her lots of things, and she'd told him he was like a magpie attracted to shiny things. But, she'd also told him to save his money because she couldn't be bought. She wasn't Violet.

Their time would come when she'd dress in the latest fashions, and he'd squire her to dances where they could kick their heels up without a care in the world. They had to be patient, that was all.

Evelyn also knew the money Ray was so keen to splash about didn't come from hard graft down at the docks, or anywhere else for that matter. She didn't like to think about how he came by it and was determined to make her own money.

The seasons had turned full circle since they'd first met. The orchids in their special place, the greenhouse, had withered, fallen, lain dormant and flowered once more. Now, winter was here again and Ray was still her secret. But, despite his protests about the clandestine nature of their courtship, Evelyn was adamant she'd not give her mam any cause for worrying about her. She worried enough about Violet and the scarcity of her visits home since she'd left to live in at the Birches.

Evelyn knew how much it hurt Lizzie that her eldest child thought her family beneath her these days, although, to the best of Evelyn's knowledge, Violet was still a lady's maid to Rose Birch. Where Vi got her delusions of grandeur from, she didn't know, and whoever the man she'd seen her sister with was, he'd not whisked her down the aisle and off to a glamorous new life.

Violet hadn't softened where Evelyn was concerned either. She barely tossed a word in her direction on her rare visits home, upsetting their mother, and as dearly as Evelyn would have liked to explain to her what had happened to cause their rift, she knew she couldn't. Mam would only worry more about Vi getting into trouble and losing her job, or worse, her good name. So, if she were to find out Evelyn was smitten with a Lime Street Boy, it would serve to give her a headache she didn't need.

Lizzie Flooks was nobody's fool though, and Evelyn knew she suspected she was courting.

It hadn't been easy fending off her questions as to who the swaggering lad was looking for her the evening Ray had first brought her to the orchid house, and she hadn't liked fibbing. Needs must, though, and she'd managed to convince her mam it was Ida he was sweet on. He'd wanted to ask her what she thought his chances were with her friend, Evelyn had explained.

'I hope you told him not to waste his time,' Lizzie Flooks had sniffed. 'His sort's trouble. Hooligans, the lot of them. She'd do well to steer clear.'

Ida was the only person who knew about them, and she kept it to herself. Despite her misgivings, she'd agreed to go along with Evie's fibs, and as such, Lizzie thought it was Ida, her daughter was meeting when she didn't come straight home from work.

This deception of theirs was another reason she didn't want Ray splashing his money about because their relationship would stay a secret until he severed ties with the gang and went respectable. When that happened, she'd happily shout about being Ray Taylor's girl. But, until then, a secret they'd stay.

The gas lights took the edge off the encroaching darkness, and Evelyn touched a finger to her lips as she hurried on towards home. They still tingled with the goodnight kiss they'd shared on the corner of Kiln and Moor Streets. It was their custom to part ways there, close enough to Potter Street for Ray to feel happy, leaving her to walk the short distance home and far enough away not to get the women in her neighbourhood's tongues wagging.

Evelyn clutched hold of her hat, feeling it lift off her head despite the pins used to secure it. Her eyes felt gritty from the wind, and she squinted into it. Noises always seemed more pronounced at night, and she jumped at the sudden parp of a horn.

In the distance, she could hear the bells and rumble of a tram. A dog barked and she caught snatches of voices chattering over the whistling of the wind. Even the smells were more pungent, she thought, spying a suspicious dark mound near the gutter. Horse poo. Her nose curled as a whiff assailed her. As for the coal fire smoke, it was a permanent black cloak this time of year.

Her thoughts returned to Ray. It wasn't just the sneaky nature of their time together that irked him; it was the fleetingness of it because Evelyn worked all the hours under the sun. Between the factory and her evenings spent helping her mam, she barely had a moment to catch her breath, let alone conduct a courtship. Her mam's prediction that they'd have more work coming in than they could manage after the success of Mrs Griffiths' dress had been prophetic. There'd been a steady stream of ladies' maids making their way to Potter Street armed with patterns and fabric and, more importantly, money ever since.

Evelyn fancied the good Lord was on their side because it was a miracle they'd managed to keep their burgeoning cottage industry from her dad. If he'd had an inkling about the notes stuffed in the tin Mam kept hidden under a loose floorboard, he would have long since squandered them at an alehouse. She kept her mother's engagement ring tucked away there too, inside its red velvet pouch, knowing he'd pawn it if he were to lay eyes on it.

Evelyn and her sisters had not had the opportunity to meet their nan. Or any of their mam's family, for that matter. All they knew was she had passed away when Mam was young, and her ring had been bequeathed to their mam as the only daughter. She'd let them all try it on once. Oh, how they'd admired the sparkling jewel! Lizzie Flooks would not be drawn further on the subject of her estranged family despite her girls' best efforts, and as for their father's side of the family, they were all in Ireland.

Evelyn held onto the belief that things would change once she and her mam opened their shop. They wouldn't have to work such long hours because she wouldn't have to trudge off to the button factory anymore, and Mam could stop supplementing the dressmaking by taking in mending. Then, that very morning, Mam had whispered to her they'd have enough put by before the winter was out for a deposit on modest premises.

She'd relayed this to Ray as they'd snuggled together on the stone bench in the orchid house. Her head had been resting on his chest, the trickling water from the fountain behind them a hypnotic constant.

His question had reverberated through the fabric of his button jacket. 'Do you promise, Evie?'

She'd promised.

At first, her mam had been uncertain when Evelyn, seemingly out of the blue, had suggested they needed to find a niche in the world of dressmaking for their business. They could do this by creating made to measure bridal gowns for the ladies of Liverpool, she'd declared.

Lizzie had listened to Evelyn's reasoning though, and after pondering over it, had seen sense in what she was saying. If she'd wondered how Evelyn had come up with such a notion, she'd not asked, merely saying, 'Well, I don't see why if we can sew an evening gown, we can't sew a wedding dress.'

A battered old ginger tom watched Evelyn's progress down Potter Street from a front door stoop, but she barely noticed him. filled as she was with jubilation at the thought of their dressmakers.

She'd see more of Ray, and she'd never have to listen to the clanking and clanging that rang in her ears long after the bell that signalled her working day at the factory was done again.

At last, Mam would lose the dark circles under her eyes and the wariness that lurked within them as she waited for Dad to burst in through the door.

His drinking was worse than ever, but he'd kept his fists to himself since he'd been set on by a group of lads outside the pub who'd warned him off hitting his wife and daughters.

Ray had never said it was him and his gang behind it, but Evelyn had known. There might have been a reprieve from his violence, but with no outlet for his rage, it bubbled beneath the surface and there was the fear it could erupt given the slightest nudge.

Sometimes, Evelyn allowed herself to imagine what life would be like for her mam if she divorced him once she was a woman in business. A woman of independent means. It wasn't that incredible an idea. These were modern times, after all. With this thought in mind, she trooped up the front steps of 46 Potter Street letting herself in the door.

Evelyn unpinned her hat and was about to shake her coat off when she froze. There were raised voices seeping under the parlour door. Cocking her head to one side, she recognised Violet's belligerent tone. It was a weeknight. *What was she doing here?* An iciness lodged in the pit of her stomach. Whatever it was that had brought her sister home, it couldn't be good.

Chapter Thirty

Evelyn stood in the passage with her hand resting on the door to the parlour. A movement at the top of the stairs distracted her, and she saw Beatrice and Nellie, white-faced, standing on the landing. 'What's going on?' she half-whispered.

'I dunno, our Evie,' Beatrice replied anxiously, her arm wrapped tightly around Nellie. 'Violet's in some bother. Mam's been ranting and raving ever since she got here.'

Instinctively Evelyn sought to reassure them. 'Don't be worrying now. You know what our Vi's like. It's bound to be something silly, and there's nothing that can't be sorted. D'you hear me?'

Beatrice didn't look convinced, but Nellie gave a slight nod.

'Evelyn, is that you?' Lizzie's voice filtered through the door. It was unnaturally shrill.

'Yes, Mam.' She flapped her hand, gesturing for her sisters to go to their room and gave them what she hoped was an encouraging smile. 'It'll be grand, you'll see.' She waited for half a beat to make sure they did as she'd said, then took a deep breath, her hand poised over the parlour's door handle.

The smell of meat and onions in the narrow passage on top of her trepidation about what was going on made her feel sick. Half of her wanted to walk back out of the front door and go in search of Ray at the lodging house she knew he bunked down in. It wouldn't change whatever had happened though, because it would still be there tomorrow. Better to face it now, she resolved, turning the handle.

Her eyes went first to her mam, who was grim-faced with her knuckles white, so tightly did she have her hands clasped. The purple satin she'd been working on was abandoned as she sat with her back to the sewing machine.

Evelyn turned her attention to Violet, teetering on the edge of the sofa with her head in her hands. Her cloche hat and matching wool, toast coloured coat with crush cuffs and collar would have cost half a year's wages, Evie thought, knowing full well Vi hadn't saved up for it herself. The battered old case she'd left home with was at her feet which didn't bode well, and she shifted from foot to foot, uncertain as to where to put herself as she lingered in the doorway.

'Come in and shut the door behind you, Evie,' Lizzie urged in a whisper, looking past Evelyn's shoulders as though she expected an audience to be gathered behind her.

Evelyn did as her mam said.

Violet raised her head once the door clicked shut, revealing her tear-stained face. Somehow, even with puffy eyes and a red nose, she still managed to look pretty, Evelyn thought.

'Sit down, for God's sake, Evie. I don't need you standing there in judgement of me 'n' all,' she snapped.

Lizzie made a clucking sound with her tongue. 'Don't you be giving out to your sister, miss. You're in no position to be giving out to anybody.'

'It's alright, Mam,' Evelyn said hastily, sitting down as far from Violet as she could manage on the small sofa. Her back hurt as she pressed it hard up against the wooden armrest.

'Go on then, Violet, tell her,' Lizzie said, her mouth settling in a hard line.

'Ah, Mam, don't make me repeat it,' Violet beseeched.

So, Evelyn thought with a stab of pity for her sister, the Birches had found out about Vi's carry on with her fancy man, and she'd been given her marching orders. It had only been a matter of time. In fact, it was a miracle it had taken this long. You couldn't gad about dressed like Vi was without people putting two and two together.

Lizzie leaned forward on her stool, her voice a strangled sob as she jabbed her finger at Violet, never taking her eyes off her. 'Your sister's in the family way.'

Violet flinched at Evelyn's sharp gasp.

'Oh, Violet!' she managed to choke out.

'Don't you be saying I told you so!' Violet spun in her seat as she decided lashing out was a better option than contrition.

'I wasn't going to!' Evelyn might not have been going to say it, but she was certainly thinking it. Her instincts that Violet was headed for trouble had been proven right, but she'd not seen this coming.

'You might be the older sister, Violet Ann Flooks, but if you'd an ounce of Evelyn's common sense, you wouldn't be in the mess you're in now. You'd have done well to listen to her.'

'She was always your favourite. Why do you think I couldn't wait to leave?' Violet sniffed.

'That's not true! Mam luvs us all the same.'

'No, she doesn't.' Violet got up from the sofa, unaware of the horsehair clinging to the back of her coat. 'I'm sorry I came here now. I should have known you'd not help me.'

'You sit back down this minute, madam.' Lizzie's bellow startled both sisters, and Violet fell back down onto the sofa as though her mam's words had pushed her.

'Where do you think you'll go if you leave here, Violet?' Lizzie demanded, two bright red spots of colour livid against her white face. 'The Birches certainly don't want you. It was the youngest son she was carrying on with,' she informed Evelyn. 'The stupid little fool thought he'd marry her. Only it's someone else he's after marrying. Course it is. He was hardly likely to wed his sister's lady's maid, was he?'

Evelyn didn't reply, even though the answer was evident to all except Violet, it would seem.

'And when your sister here went to Walter Birch and said his son had given her a promise of marriage and how she was in the family way, the younger Mr Birch denied it. He said she was a gold-digging scrubber who'd got herself with child and saw an opportunity to better herself by lying.'

'Mam, don't!' Violet cried.

Lizzie couldn't seem to stop though, as she spat, 'Not so high and mighty now, are you? You're a dirty little slut, Violet. Nothing more, nothing less.'

Evelyn got up then and went to her mam, wanting to stop the ugly flow of words. She grasped hold of both her hands and crouched down in front of her. 'Mam, shouting at her won't change things. It's happened, and now we have to work out what happens next.' Her words seemed to have a soothing effect as Lizzie's shoulders slumped. The fight had gone out of her.

Violet shot her sister a grateful look. There was hope in there too, Evelyn saw.

'There's only one way to fix this, Evie,' Lizzie said, her eyes latching onto hers, urging her to understand.

'How, Mam?'

Lizzie ruffled Evelyn's hair and kissed the top of her head. 'I'm sorry, Evie,' she said, getting up.

Evelyn straightened and watched as her mam went to her hiding place beneath the floorboard to unearth the tin.

'Mam, no!' Evelyn cried in horror, realising what she wanted her sister to do. She'd heard the stories of back street butchers whispered about at the button factory.

'It's the only way, Evie.'

Violet looked hungrily at the tin.

It dawned on Evie then, and her skin burned hot with the realisation there would be no dressmakers now.

She needed to put distance between herself, her mam, and Violet because she didn't trust what she might say otherwise. Her mam's cries fell on deaf ears as she staggered from the room and out onto the street. The shock of cold air galvanised her, and she began to run, uncaring she had no coat or hat on. What did it matter? What did anything matter anymore? She didn't consciously register her da weaving his way down the opposite side of the street, singing.

Liverpool, 1982

The pen fell from Evelyn's shaking hand. What came next was what she'd chosen to forget.

Part Four

Chapter Thirty-one

LIVERPOOL, 1982

Sabrina rested both hands on the ferry's railing as it docked, enjoying the briny air and her first up-close sighting of the Isle of Man. Rows of Victorian terraces lined Douglas Harbour in a wide-reaching arc, with the Manx capital's buildings smattered beyond the harbour giving way to rolling hills in shades of green and brown. A church tower punctuated the vista. As a ray of sunshine broke through the cloud cover her ring glittered, transfixing her, and she wondered if she'd ever stop admiring it.

Adam was resting his chin on the top of her head, his arms wrapped around her waist. They were jammed in like sardines on the boat with both riders and spectators for the TT heading to the island in time for Mad Sunday and the racing week ahead.

Linda, over to Sabrina's right, was making a song and dance about the seagulls spiralling overhead squawking their demands.

'She don't like birds,' Tim explained as she jerked about as though dancing to a beat only she could hear. He was on guard duty flapping his arms if they swooped too low. 'She's had a thing about them ever since she saw that film when she was a kid. You know the Hitchcock one.'

'*The Birds*,' Adam stated the obvious.

On Sabrina's left, Florence had spent the nearly three-hour journey seemingly mesmerised by the undulating waves whilst holding onto the rails with a vicelike grip.

'The boat's stopped moving, Florence. You'll be ahright now, kid,' Tony said, stopping short of rubbing her back.

It was just as well, Sabrina thought, watching out the corner of her eye. The mood Flo was in, she'd probably elbow him in the stomach was he to try.

Poor Florence hadn't handled their sailing to the island in the middle of the Irish sea well, despite the notoriously rough body of water being relatively calm beneath a sky that couldn't decide between cloudy and grey or sunny and blue.

Tony, who'd have made a good boy scout, had plied her with ginger biscuits in a bid to stave off nausea, but she'd been leaning over the rail, groaning for the best part of the journey, nevertheless.

'Thank God,' Florence muttered. 'Get me off this flamin' boat.'

Her wish was a step closer when a disembodied voice floated over their heads, informing them they could now proceed back to their vehicles.

'Did I tell you there's no speed limit on the island once you're past the town?' Adam asked Sabrina as they followed the surge of passengers down the stairs to the vehicle deck.

'No, you didn't,' Sabrina squeaked. She was pleased he'd not mentioned this in front of Aunt Evie, who would have gone spare. Or would she? Given how oddly she'd been behaving these last few days, Aunt Evie probably wouldn't have even registered what he'd said.

More than once, Sabrina had had to repeat what she'd said, even going so far as to wave her hand in front of her face and say, 'Earth to Aunt Evie.' But when she'd asked what had her so preoccupied, Aunt Evie had snipped she didn't know what Sabrina meant because she was perfectly fine.

'Don't worry. I won't let her rip with you on the back. I'll save that for the circuit tomorrow.'

Sabrina wasn't comforted in the least by this.

The diesel fumes in the contained space of the vehicle deck where motorcycles, cars towing caravans, and camper vans were nose to tail were threatening to give Sabrina a headache by the time the doors opened, and a roar of engines erupted.

They thundered off the ferry with Tim and Linda on the first bike navigating the way along abnormally busy roads, given the island's sleepy reputation, to the camping ground. There was a pitstop for a pint at a quaint pub with Tudor trim and a thatched roof before their convoy of three motorbikes bounced off the main road and through an open gate, coming to a halt in a field.

Sabrina hopped off the bike, easing the pack containing the tent, a few other bare necessities and the small bag she'd stuffed with what she'd deemed vital off her shoulders before taking her helmet off. She caught Florence's eye as her friend, who'd pronounced she was feeling much sprightlier by the time she'd downed a pint, mouthed, 'Have I got helmet hair?'

Sabrina gestured, fluffing her hair up, and while Florence titivated her spikes, she returned to her appraisal of her surroundings. The lads were already beginning to toss things out of their packs onto the grass.

When they'd said camping, she'd envisaged rows of static caravans, a common room and an ablution block. Nothing fancy but a proper camping ground. Not a field.

A sudden grunting, chuffing sound made her jump, and she craned her neck in its direction to see a bull. It was pawing the ground near the fence separating their field from his, and she hoped the fence was solid.

It wasn't an empty field either, with half a dozen other tents already pitched, rust-bucket cars parked nearby. A distinct herbal aroma was wafting over from the Kombi van with an awning attached to it parked near the gate they'd just ridden through. Sabrina blinked, not trusting her eyes as a man with long hair and as naked as the day he was born unfolded himself from a nearby tent. He waved over at them vigorously, causing everything else to wave, before disappearing out of sight around the back of the tent.

'Jesus,' Tony muttered. 'I can't unsee that.'

'I think everybody else is clothed,' Florence reassured him, clocking the hairy bikers guzzling cans outside one tent and the woman floating about in a long paisley skirt with a flower jammed behind her ear near another.

Adam stopped what he was doing and draped his arm proprietorially over Sabrina's shoulder. 'Oi, Tim, you didn't tell us you'd booked us into a flamin' nudist camp.'

Tim shrugged, 'The farmer didn't say anything about it. It's island life, man, anything goes, and it's not far from the circuit. The girls can wander up to the main road there and wave at us when we go past.'

Unusual sisterly solidarity passed between Linda, Florence and Sabrina as they silently communicated how thrilled they were at the prospect of two nights in a field just so they could wave at the lads showing off on their boys' toys.

'Well, did he say anything about a loo because that pint's gone right through me?' Sabrina hissed at Adam as the reality of their situation began to sink in. She knew accommodation would be at a premium over race week, but a field?

Tim overheard and, looking out from under his too long, dishwater blond hair, winked at her. 'It's wild camping, girl. We'll get the tents up in a jiffy, and you can duck behind them.'

Linda was standing in her painted-on leathers with her hand on her hip, looking decidedly unimpressed as Tim began to lay their tent out. Meanwhile, Sabrina flicked panicked eyes to Florence, who was also feeling short of breath as she realised what wild camping meant.

No shower, no hairdryer, but worst of all, no loo and where would they brush their teeth in the morning?

Tony rummaged in his bag and waved a trowel at her, 'I brought this. You can use it to dig a hole and bury, erm, you know.'

'C'mon.' Sabrina grabbed hold of Florence's arm. 'Let's find a tree to hide behind. I won't be needing the trowel, ta very much, Tony.'

There was a surprising lack of trees on the Isle of Man, Sabrina decided as she squatted down in a gully not visible from the road after a good fifteen minutes of searching for an oak, a sycamore, anything with a trunk and leaves.

Florence, a little way further down from her, did the same.

'We'll be ahright, queen,' she called over. 'So long as we lay off the pints, and we can always rub some toothpaste around our mouths.'

Sabrina couldn't help but smile at Florence's determined optimism, especially given how awkward she knew her friend was feeling around Tim. She turned beetroot every time he looked her way, which Tim being Tim was enjoying.

Linda must have noticed, she thought. But then again, she was more absorbed in who was looking at her to pay attention.

'How's Tony going to get in and out of those jeans of his in that tiny tent?' Florence shuddered as she jiggled, then stood up and pulled her jeans back up. 'Maybe he won't. Maybe he'll wear them all weekend and not change his—'

'Flo!' Sabrina cut her off, having no wish to think about whether or not Tony's hygiene was up to scratch. She sorted herself out, and they set off back towards the field.

By the time they returned, most of the tents were up.

'You two were gone ages. We were about to send out a search party,' Adam said, looking up from where he was hammering the last peg into the ground.

Sabrina didn't bother to answer as she opened the flap to the two-man tent. She hoped the damp wouldn't soak through the bottom of the tent because they'd no airbed to sleep on. 'It's only two nights,' she muttered, retrieving her sleeping bag and unfurling it. Poor Adam would have to sleep rough for seven whole nights. Mind you, given the company he'd be keeping, she was sure he wouldn't be feeling any pain by the time he staggered into bed.

'What was that, girl?' Adam asked, looking up.

'Nothing.' She smiled, taking a leaf from Florence's book and plastering a smile on her face because it wasn't all doom and gloom. She'd get to spend two delicious nights sleeping next to Adam; even if it were on rock hard ground, it would still make up for the lack of facilities.

Florence and Tony were engaged in erecting her pup tent and, straightening to watch what they were doing, Sabrina decided it was a case of too many captains and not enough crew.

Seeing the sideshow next to their tent, Adam stood up and brushed the dirt off his jeans before muscling in on the act. He had the tent pitched within minutes.

'You look like you're about to swoon and say, "My hero",' Florence said to Sabrina before chucking her sleeping bag and overnight things into it.

'Cheers, mate, but I had it,' Tony said to Adam.

Adam grinned. 'You sure about that? Listen, how about we go for a ride and see the sights.'

Sabrina and Florence nodded. The less time spent here in the field, the better.

Adam glanced over to Tim and Linda's tent. There was no sign of the couple, and Tim's bike was gone. 'I thought I heard a bike. Where've they disappeared too?'

'They were off to ride down the promenade,' Tony informed him.

Adam grinned, 'Good job it's overcast.'

Sabrina looked up. The sky had turned dull once more, but it wasn't raining and given their salubrious accommodation, that was something to be grateful for, she thought as a plane disappeared into the cloud.

Tony smirked, 'Yeah, wouldn't want Linda getting sunburnt.'

'You can still burn even when it's overcast,' Florence informed him.

'What are you two on about?' Sabrina was lost.

'I know what they're getting at,' Florence piped up. 'Dad told me he'd disown me if I went on the back of anyone's bike down the promenade. It's tradition to do wheelies down the prom, but you can ride out on it so long as you have a topless female passenger on the back.' She looked decidedly prudish as she added. 'I don't know what disturbs me more. That Dad even knows about it, or the thought of riding with me boobs out for all to see.'

Sabrina snorted while Tony's eyes lit up at the image Florence had planted in his head. She spied Adam wiggling his brows in her direction and told him he'd better not get any ideas because she was prone to burning. They all laughed.

The tents were zipped up, and the girls clambered on the back of Adam's and Tony's bikes, eager to see what the island had to offer.

Chapter Thirty-two

'I found out something interesting today,' Linda said, tapping her cigarette into the ashtray in the middle of the picnic-style table littered with glasses. She, Tim, Tony, Adam, Sabrina and Florence were squished around the table on a slope of grass out the front of The Mitre, the island's oldest pub in the coastal village of Kirk. If it hadn't been for the beer garden, they'd have had to have gone elsewhere because the tiny interior of the pub that smacked of history was heaving with enthusiastic TT riders and supporters alike.

The lads were happy with the seating arrangement because they could keep an eye on their bikes parked on the asphalt expanse off to the left of the garden while they supped their pints. Florence, who'd been bitten twice on the ankle, wasn't as enamoured.

'Don't scratch. You'll make it worse, Flo,' Sabrina said, swiping at a mosquito whining near her ear.

'They're always bad at dusk,' Adam said, making them all jump by clapping his hands suddenly before showing them the flattened insect.

'You're giving him that daft "my hero" look again,' Flo said, nudging Sabrina.

She wiggled her ring at Flo. 'That's because he is.'

Linda repeated her earlier sentiment, having not received the appropriate response thanks to the mosquito.

'What was that then, babe?' Tim asked with his arm draped casually over her shoulder. All heads swivelled in her direction.

How she'd managed to crimp her hair and look glam despite their lack of amenities was a mystery to Florence and Sabrina. They were feeling decidedly un-glam after their afternoon whizzing about exploring the island on the back of the bikes.

'The Bee Gee's are from Man. That arl fella from Manchester with the Harley we were talking to down at the prom this afternoon told me.'

'I hope she had her top on at the time,' Florence murmured from the corner of her mouth for Sabrina's benefit, earning a giggle.

Tony was disputing what she'd said. 'No, they're not. They're Australian. Everyone knows that.'

'Everybody *thinks* that, but Maurice, Barry and Robin were born here on the island.' Linda was adamant.

'I wouldn't have had that fella down for a Bee Gees man.' Tim sounded surprised. 'More AC/DC.'

'They're Australian and all,' Adam volunteered.

'You're not listening.' Linda pursed her shiny red lips, 'The Bee Gees aren't Australian. They were born here.'

'Actually, half of AC/DC is Scottish.' Tony added his penny's worth.

'Andy Gibb's my favourite, anyway.' Florence offered up randomly.

'Really?' Linda wrinkled her nose and looked down the opposite end of the table at Florence. 'I wouldn't say no to Barry.'

'Barry?' Tim spluttered into his pint.

'I like a man with a beard.'

Tim rubbed his stubble.

'Did we tell youse we saw a falcon?' Tony said, having had enough of the conversation.

'A bird or the car?' Tim asked, having decided to stop shaving.

'Bird.'

'Adam spotted it,' Sabrina said. They'd pulled off the road to admire the coastline, and he'd seen it keeping watch from a rocky outcrop. The bird of prey had held them transfixed with its hypnotic yellow eyes as it glared at them as if to ask what they were doing in his neck of the woods.

'It was a peregrine falcon,' Tony informed the table.

Sabrina, Adam and Florence were already privy to the falcon's particular species because Tony had volunteered it that afternoon. His insight into falcon breeds had seen the trio turn away from the bird to look at him in surprise.

'Me dad's a bird watcher, so I go out with him sometimes,' he'd explained.

'A twitcher!' Florence had exclaimed, causing Tony to stiffen indignantly.

'We don't like that term. It's bird watching.'

'Well, that's me told,' she'd muttered.

Now, nobody asked him to elaborate further on the bird as Tony and Linda began to drone on about the laugh they'd had down at the promenade.

Sabrina zoned them out as Adam got up to get another round in, leaving her to her thoughts.

It was lovely to have a break, especially from thinking about the wedding. Sabrina knew she was driving Aunt Evie, Flo and even Adam up the wall with the subject, but as a newly engaged woman, she couldn't help herself.

Adam was all for getting married sooner rather than later and keeping their day low key, which was all well and good, but the wedding wouldn't plan itself, nor would her dress design and sew itself.

She was driving herself demented doodling designs that weren't gelling.

As such, she'd decided not to mention or think about anything to do with weddings all weekend and the afternoon spent exploring had been a fun distraction. They'd enjoyed the tourist highlights, and the pretty stone Fairy Bridge and Peel Castle on St Patrick's Isle had been her favourite stops. The atmospheric castle had been built by Vikings and was connected to the town by a causeway. A half-moon bay nestled in alongside it. The island was a beautiful place; wild and windswept in parts, chocolate-box pretty in others. They'd learned the locals didn't class themselves as British but rather as Manx, which she and Florence had decided meant they could now officially say they'd been abroad.

The Snaefell mountain road connecting the towns of Douglas and Ramsey, Adam and Tony had insisted on taking to familiarise themselves with the next day's circuit had her worried, though. She was going to be a bag of nerves waiting for them to ride past the pub here where she, Flo and Linda had decided to spectate from.

Adam plopped her drink down, and the sounds of the jukebox wafted through the pub's open door. The temperamental sun, still hiding behind clouds as it dipped lower and lower, was turning the sky a soft purple. It wasn't cold, but still, Sabrina was glad of her jacket.

'Penny for them,' Adam said, clambering back over the wooden seat to sit down.

Sabrina shook her head. She didn't want him knowing she was worried about tomorrow. It wouldn't stop him riding, and Tim was only likely to tease her and call her a handbrake. And no way was she going to talk about the wedding.

It wasn't far off dark when they got back to the field. Flames from a drum flickered and danced near the other campers' tents.

'Might as well join them,' Adam said once they'd parked their bikes up, gesturing towards the small group gathered around the fire. The alternative was bed, and it was too early for that, so taking the cans they'd brought back from the pub, they wandered over to warm their hands over the drum. The others followed behind them.

The nudist was now clothed, and once they'd introduced themselves and room had been made around the fire, Sabrina cuddled in next to Adam.

The day's adventures had left her tired, and the murmur of voices sharing stories about where they were from washed over her.

By the time the flames had begun to die down and arrangements finalised for the ride in the morning, Sabrina was more than ready to snuggle down in her sleeping bag. First, though, she and Florence needed to spend a penny.

'Nobody's to peek around the tents,' Florence bossed, but the lads and Linda were too busy saying goodnight to the others to pay them any attention.

'I feel like one of Mrs James's next-door garden gnomes,' Florence muttered from her squatting position.

'Me too.' Sabrina giggled. 'Will you be ahright in your tent?'

'I'm that done in. I could sleep on a park bench.'

'It was a good day,' Sabrina said, straightening, job done.

'The best, ' Florence agreed before saying night, night.

Sabrina could see the glow from the torch inside her and Adam's tent, and unzipping it, she ventured inside. It was cosy in here, she thought. She could almost get used to this camping lark.

Adam, kneeling beside the sleeping bags, was wearing nothing but his underpants. He had the torch resting on their pack angled to see what he was doing as he wrested the zippers of the two bags together. The look of furious concentration on his face made her smile. Then, leaving him to it, she swished some toothpaste around her mouth with her finger before wriggling out of her clothes.

'There!' Adam was triumphant. 'Done it.' He looked up in time to see Sabrina sliding an arm inside her flannelette pyjama top. 'You're not putting those on, are you?'

'It might get chilly in the middle of the night,' she informed him. Flannelettes weren't exactly what she'd had in mind for their first full night spent together but, then again, tenting hadn't featured in the scenarios she'd imagined whereby she sashayed into their plush suite in saucy silk.

'I'll keep you warm, girl.' Adam grinned wolfishly and, opening the bag up, patted it invitingly.

Sod the pyjamas, Sabrina thought, discarding them as she clambered in beside him.

Somewhere in the darkness, a voice called out, 'Goodnight, John Boy.'

'Shurrup!' was the chorused reply.

Chapter Thirty-three

The bull was voicing his frustration, Sabrina realised, the foreign noise penetrating her sleepy brain. She rolled over and reached out, expecting to connect with Adam's bare skin, but his side of the sleeping bag, while still warm, was empty. Awareness that the ground was digging into her side and that her back ached began to sink in. How had she managed to sleep so soundly? she wondered, stretching like a starfish to ease the cricks. It must have been the ale and fresh air. A lazy smile spread across her face. That and what she and Adam had got up to before they'd settled down for the night!

Outside she could hear voices, Adam's and Tony's and their fellow campers in the distance, she deduced, opening her eyes. The light seemed overly bright, and it could have been anytime from five am to midday for all she knew. The tent was hot and stuffy, suggesting dawn had been and gone, and kicking free of the sleeping bag, Sabrina sat up.

It wasn't raining, so that was good, and she hoped the lads had managed to wangle a cup of tea from their fellow campers. They'd need to be on top of their game for the day ahead. She was gasping, and she was also naked, so first things first.

Digging around for her clothes in her overnight bag, Sabrina's hands settled over an envelope. Odd, she thought, frowning. It wasn't there yesterday when she'd zipped the bag shut, she was sure of it. She pulled it out to inspect it and smiled, seeing her name written on the white paper. Aunt Evie! It was her handwriting. She'd probably slipped in some 'just in case' spends as she used to when Sabrina went off on school camp as a child. Or, maybe it was a bon voyage card! She had been harping on about how she and Flo were going overseas all week. It felt too bulky to be a card though.

'Sabrina, are you awake yet? There's a brew here for you,' Adam called out.

Music to her ears, she thought, calling back, 'Coming!' She put the envelope to one side and hurried to get dressed. The spot on her chin would have to wait until later, she decided, clicking her compact shut in disgust before dragging the hairbrush through her knots. No way did she want to miss seeing Adam off. Herself, Flo and Linda were cadging a ride back to The Mitre with Katrina, the girl in the floaty skirt. She was going to watch her fella ride too. The lads would meet them back at the pub.

There was no sign of Flo, and Tim and Linda's tent was down, Sabrina noticed as she staggered out of the tent homing in on the steaming mug Adam was proffering. Tim's bike was gone too. *Strange.* - She blew on the tea before taking a tentative sip. 'Ah, that's luvly, that is. So where've they disappeared to then? I thought Linda was coming with Flo and me.'

Adam shrugged and cast a glance towards Tony, who was draining the contents of his mug. Both lads were clad head to toe in their motorcycle leathers and must be sweltering, Sabrina thought. She took in Tony's dishevelled appearance. His hair was sticking up on end, and his eyes bloodshot like he'd slept badly. His shoulders were tense too. She supposed he must be anxious about the day's riding. However, when he put his mug down on the grass and inclined his head towards Florence's tent, he looked decidedly unimpressed.

There was no sign of life inside the pup tent, so Sabrina assumed she was still asleep. She'd have to get her up in a minute; Katrina would want to get going to make sure they got a pew at the pub.

'You'll have to ask her,' Tony muttered, turning away and striding over to his bike.

Yes, there was a definite atmosphere. It was positively chilly, Sabrina mused, puzzled as to what had happened between everyone being chipper the night before as they headed off to their tents and the frosty vibe permeating off Tony this morning. Also, where were Tim and Linda?

'What's going on?' she mouthed at Adam.

'It's between them two,' he mouthed back, clearly not wanting to get into it.

Had Tony tried it on with Flo last night? Was that the problem? Sabrina wondered, her head beginning to clear as the tea worked its magic. Tony wasn't going to tell her. She'd wrangle it out of Flo when he and Adam had gone.

'Adam, mate, you all set?' Tony called over, pulling his helmet on. 'I'll see you later, Sabrina.'

She held her hand up in acknowledgement.

'Yeah, I'll just say cheerio to me girl.' Adam called back, turning to Sabrina. His dark eyes glittered with anticipation, and she could almost smell the adrenaline and testosterone building. 'Wish me luck then.'

'Is there any point in me telling you to ride safely? Preferably like an arl fella on a mobility scooter.'

Adam grinned, looking like an excited little boy. 'I won't ride like a lunatic, I promise.'

It would have to do, Sabrina thought, feeling very wifely as she put her tea down to give him a kiss and a cuddle goodbye.

'See you back at The Mitre later then.' He strode over to his Triumph.

'Yeah, see you there.' She watched them gun their bikes and gave them a final wave as they rumbled over the field and out onto the road beyond. She might not go to church with Aunt Evie on a Sunday, but she still raised her eyes heavenward and sent a quick prayer for Him up there to watch over Adam. She added in Tony and Tim for good measure.

'Have they gone?'

Sabrina swung around, nearly sloshing tea down her front, to see Florence poking her head out of the pup tent like a turtle emerging from its shell.

'The coast's clear. What's going on, Flo? Adam wouldn't tell me, but Tony's got a cob on, and there's no sign of Linda and Tim; their tent's gone and everything.'

Florence opened her canvas hidey-hole right up and eyed the mug in Sabrina's hand.

She held it out to her. 'Here, you can finish it.' Then she flopped down on the grass, sitting cross-legged in front of the opening with an expectant look on her face.

'Oh, that's better. I was gasping,' Florence said before fixing Sabrina with a mournful gaze. 'It was bloody Tim's fault, Sabs. I got up in the night for a wee, and when I climbed back inside me tent, I nearly died. There he was sprawled on me flamin' sleeping bag like I should be feeding him flippin' grapes.'

Sabrina tried to pictured Tim reclining like a shaggy-haired Greek God and failed.

'Oh my God, girl,' was all she could come up with by way of response. Then a horrible thought struck her, 'Flo, you didn't?'

'Of course, I didn't! I put a flea in his ear and booted him out, literally. I'm not going to be his bit on the side. Linda caught him climbing out of my tent though, didn't she and Tony heard her going off on one and came out to investigate.' Florence rubbed her temples. 'They both put two and two together and came up with five. It's all such a mess, Sabs.'

Sabrina could not believe she and Adam had slept through all of this. 'You should have woken me up.' She reached forward to hug her friend.

'I didn't need you and Adam involved as well, did I? We would have had the whole camp up.' Florence sniffed into her shoulder. 'I told Tony he had the wrong end of the stick, but he huffed off back to his tent, and I wasn't going after him. Why should I? If he thinks that's the sort of girl I am then he can bleedin' well sod off. I left Linda and Tim to it because I wasn't getting involved. I tell you, if looks could kill, I'd be dead. I had a lucky escape there, kid, have you seen the state of her fingernails? Lethal weapons those. I was awake half the rest of the night expecting her to storm me tent and scratch me.'

Sabrina nodded. She wasn't far wrong.

'She was too busy ranting at Tim though, and they upped and left as soon as it was light. With any luck, he'll be looking like he's survived a grizzly bear attack by now. Serve him right that would.'

'Yeah, it would.'

'And what I want to know is why is it always the woman who gets the blame for the man's bad behaviour?'

Sabrina shrugged. 'I dunno, Flo. Tony will get over himself though when he's had a chance to think it through properly. He knows you and Tim well enough to figure out which one of you was in the wrong. And, if Linda's got any sense, she'll pack it in with Tim. You get dressed, and I'll go and see what time Katrina wants to head to the pub. The sooner we get there, the more chance of getting a table. We can get some breakfast there and all.'

Florence still looked glum. 'I'd rather go home. I wish I hadn't come now.'

'What Tim did isn't your fault, Flo. Don't let him spoil what time we've got left here.'

'I s'pose you're right.'

'I am, so c'mon then, get yourself sorted, girl.'

The noise was phenomenal. Thousands of bikers and motorists were taking part in the free-for-all, all eager for a taste of what the professional racers endured.

'It's like swarming bees,' Sabrina shouted at Florence as every make of bike under the sun and a

Porsche, followed by a mini, careened past where they were standing. Their only protection, should one of the participants misjudge their manoeuvres, was the safety barrier, a collection of haybales and sandbags.

Katrina had disappeared in the melee somewhere, but Sabrina and Florence had their arms firmly entwined, determined they wouldn't lose sight of one another.

Florence had perked up after a full English breakfast and was now more indignant than upset over the night's debacle. Sabrina was both excited and very aware of the greasy bacon and eggs she'd wolfed down as she wondered how Adam was getting on. She wouldn't relax until this was over, she thought, wondering if any sound would come out if she joined in the cheering once more because her throat already felt raw.

'We should have worn hats,' Florence shouted over the droning and cheers.

Sabrina nodded. There'd be more than one case of sunstroke before the day was out. It was boiling with the sun beating down. The tents would be like pressure cookers when they got back to the campsite.

Both girls were dizzy from the sun, noise, people, and visual spectacle by the time the riders zooming past had begun to dwindle. They hadn't seen Adam or Tony whizz past, but that was hardly surprising given the volumes of traffic. The bottled water they'd managed to find had kept them going, but now they were keen to join the throng for something to eat and a cold drink. They fought their way into the tiny pub and began to inch towards the bar, doing their best to avoid hazards like the cigarettes and full pint glasses being waved about.

'I think I just saw Adam,' Florence yelled over the top of the cacophonous chattering and fog of smoke.

Sabrina stood on tippy-toes craning her neck and then felt all the knots inside her tummy loosen as she saw him waving out to her.

He made his way through the crowd towards them, and she was like one of those grinning funfair clowns by the time he reached them. It was only then she realised his expression was grim.

'What's wrong?'

'Tony came off his bike.'

Chapter Thirty-four

Sabrina felt cold, despite the stuffy heat inside the packed pub, but the colour had drained from Florence's face as she asked where Tony was.

'He's going to be ahright, kid. Sorry, I should have said that first. He's at the ozzy.' Adam reached out and laid a reassuring hand on Florence's shoulder. 'Don't you go fainting on us. Take some deep breaths.'

Florence did as she was told, listening as he again informed them that Tony would be okay.

'Before they carted him off in the ambulance, his main concern was his bike.' Adam gave a wry smile. 'It didn't look too bad to me. The tow truck was on hand, and they gave me the phone number for the mechanic's in Douglas where they've taken it.'

'What happened?' Sabrina asked with one eye on Florence, worried she might keel over. She had a feeling her friend hadn't moved past the word 'ambulance'.

'He came off on a bend not far from one of the villages we rode through. He was lucky, although he probably doesn't feel it at the moment because he didn't hit anything. He skidded off the road onto grass. It could have been worse; he was that far from a telegraph pole.' Adam used his hands to demonstrate how close Tony had been to a different outcome, making both girls shudder.

'If he's not hurt, then why's he at the ozzy?' Florence asked, the colour slowly returning to her cheeks.

'The medics checked him over on the roadside, and he's a nasty case of road rash, no broken bones or head injuries though. They wanted to take him in to be checked over for internal bleeding that sort of thing.'

Florence went white once more. 'So he's not out of the woods yet,' she stated flatly. 'Adam, will you take me to see him?'

'Course I will.' He looked at Sabrina.

'Don't worry about me. You two go. I'll catch a ride with Katrina back to the campsite. Go.'

Florence flashed a grateful smile at Sabrina, who gave her a quick hug before Adam steered her away.

Sabrina watched her friend's blonde spikes bob through the crush and couldn't help but think for someone who insisted Tony was only a friend, she'd had a pretty strong reaction to the news he'd come off his bike. Of course, as awful as it was hearing Tony had had an accident, he was going to be okay, and that was the main thing, but perhaps it had knocked some sense into Flo where he was concerned. Silver linings and all that she thought as she sought Katrina out.

The Noble Hospital was in Douglas on Westmoreland Road past the railway station, not that Florence noticed these details as Adam pulled in outside the entrance after a sedate journey from the pub. She clambered off the back of the bike with her eyes trained on the entrance.

'You go on in, I'll find youse both, once I've parked,' Adam said overtop of the Triumph's rumbling engine.

Florence didn't need to be told twice, and she strode in through the entrance to find a hospital as busy as any major city's A&E department, thanks to Mad Sunday. She was a woman on a mission though, to see Tony, and with the help of the harried admissions clerk and an orderly who was heading the way she needed to go, she found herself taking a hesitant step into the trauma ward.

She checked the beds filling the ward one by one wincing at the state of the bodies sprawled on them. Then, finally, her eyes settled on Tony down the far end. A nurse was talking to him, and he was focused on what she was saying, which meant he hadn't seen her. A pillow propped him up, and he had a hospital gown on.

Florence was suddenly shy, and she debated retreating to wait for Adam out in the corridor. *You're being ridiculous, Florence Teesdale. It's Tony.* She wagged a mental finger at herself because this was the fella she'd sat next to loads of times at the pub laughing with. The same fella who'd come to her rescue when she'd fallen over on the Bootle Tootlers maiden jog. Who called around with music tapes for her to borrow and laughed at her sisters' antics. It was him who'd cheered the loudest when she'd strutted down the red carpet at Esmerelda's.

And you, you stupid fool, she said with an extra big wag, have been so fixated on Tim you didn't see what was right under your nose all along. She'd refused to look beyond the tight trousers to see the lovely lad inside them despite Sabrina's best efforts. Mind, Mam said she'd always been a bit slow on the uptake. Well, she'd been a snail where Tony was concerned.

Hearing he'd come off his bike that afternoon had given her a short, sharp shock. Life was too short to spend it hankering after arses. She'd had blinkers on, and they'd been whipped off to reveal what Tony meant to her.

The nurse moved on to the next bed, and Tony turned his head slightly, catching sight of her. He raised his hand in greeting.

G'won, girl, Florence told herself with her heart racing. You've wasted enough time already. Seize the day! She told herself, marching down the middle of the polished floor towards him.

Tony pushed his head back into the pillows, startled as she descended on him. *Was she going to—?-* He felt the warmth of her breath on his face and an anticipatory flutter of something overriding his present discomfort as her lips, soft and tender, settled over his. *She was!* He might have abrasions running down the entire right side of his body, but this was a moment he was not going to mess up. He reached up and enfolded his arms around Florence, holding her tightly, so her body pressed down on his sore ribs as, uncaring, he returned the kiss with an urgent intensity.

'Excuse me. You're in the trauma ward. Not the honeymoon suite.'

They broke apart as though caught necking in the back seat of the car by Florence's dad.

The nurse had her hands on her hips, but her expression was nowhere near as stern as her tone. Giving them a wink, she turned away to carry on with her duties.

Florence's breath was shallow, her legs weak, and her heart still beating like the clappers. She couldn't believe what she'd just done or how right it had felt. 'I think I need to sit down,' she said sagging down on the chair next to his bed. Somewhere on the ward a man was moaning and as another began calling out for the nurse, she turned her head in that direction, alarmed.

'He's a bit doolally at the moment. It's the heavy-duty pain meds they've given him. The nurse said he'll be ahright though,' Tony reassured her, and trying to twist over to see her better, he grimaced.

'Lie still,' Florence ordered, shuffling her chair closer before reaching out and taking his hand; his fingers closed around hers. 'I was so worried.'

'I like that you were worried.'

The man had stopped shouting now, and the nurse's soothing tones drifted down the ward.

'Adam said something about road rash and checking for internal bleeding? All I heard was that you'd come off your bike. It all went in one ear and out the other after that.'

'I'm luckier than most,' Tony said, his expression grim as he inclined his head towards his fellow riders who hadn't got off so lightly. He lifted his gown to show her the white sterile dressings plastered all over his right side. I'm going to have some X-rays soon, that was what the nurse was talking to me about when you arrived, and they'll know more after that. They want to keep me in overnight. Do you know they had to cut me out of me leathers? Cost me a fortune they did.'

Florence squeezed his hand. 'You can get new leathers. But listen, Tony, that business last night with Tim being in my tent, I had nothing to do with it.' She needed to clear that mess up right now.

Tony held up a hand to stop her speaking, 'It doesn't matter.'

'But it does matter,' Florence said, and she told him about what had happened the night Tim had given her a ride home from The Swan and how he'd got the wrong end of the stick. 'Well, sort of,' she contradicted herself. 'I mean, I thought I fancied him, but I don't. Now I know he's an arse, and when I thought you were hurt, I realised it's you I erm—'

'G'won, say it,' Tony urged.

Florence swallowed. He could have been killed, but instead, he'd been given a second chance, and so had she. 'I erm luv. I luv you.'

Tony's grin lifted one corner of his mouth. 'So what you're saying is all I had to do to get you to realise I was the fella for you was come off me bike?'

'Yes, I mean no!'

'I don't care what you mean so long as I can have another one of those kisses. And I luv you too, Florence Teesdale.'

Florence checked the nurse was busy with her patient then homed in for another kiss. Neither she nor Tony was aware of Adam as their lips parted and new, unfamiliar, decidedly delicious sensations flooded them. He'd appeared in the doorway in time to see their lips lock.

About flamin' time, he thought. Smiling and turning on his heel, he went in search of the canteen. He'd leave them to it for now.

Sabrina was lying on her back on the sleeping bag. The tent's open flap allowed the gentle breeze in, and she was holding a sheaf of papers in her hand, a letter.

She'd been back at the campsite twenty minutes or so, not sure what to do with herself while she waited for Adam and Florence. But then, she'd remembered the envelope in her bag.

The letter from Aunt Evie folded inside it had taken her by surprise and bewildered, she'd begun to read it. She'd had to stop and close her eyes several times to try and absorb all that her aunt was revealing. She'd known nothing but the scantiest of details about her life before the bridal shop. Now she understood why Aunt Evie didn't talk about it.

She also suspected her aunt's words would take her into a story she wasn't going to like the ending of. But, she had to finish reading it, so she picked the letter up once more.

By the time she'd finished, Sabrina was reeling. A disconnect had occurred between her brain and her body. It felt like she was hovering slightly outside of it. There'd been so much of Aunt Evie's story she hadn't known, and she finally understood the bonds that tied her and Ray together. But why had she chosen to tell her now? Was she sick? Sabrina couldn't imagine her world without Aunt Evie in it. Or had she decided the truth needed to come out now Sabrina was about to marry Ray Taylor's son?

A shadow fell across the tent entrance and Adam crouched down, holding the flap back as he peered inside.

'Sabrina, you won't believe what I saw at the ozzy—'

Sabrina raised her head, the sensation as she tried to focus on Adam like she was in a pool trying to break the surface. She pulled away from her thoughts and reached out, wanting to check he was real. That she wasn't dreaming. He took hold of her hand.

'You're shaking, girl.' Adam frowned. 'Tony's ahright, you know. More than ahright. He and Florence were—' his words fell away once more as he saw a tear tracking down her cheek. 'What's going on?' He registered the letter on his side of the sleeping bag. 'What's that?'

The pieces of paper her aunt had poured the hidden part of her life onto rustled as Sabrina scooped them up. 'You need to read this.'

Adam took the sheaves of paper from her and scanned the first page. 'It's from Evelyn.'

'It's about her life when she was young. Read it, Adam.' Her aunt and his father had sat on their secret for too long.

Sabrina sat with her knees pulled to her chest as Adam learned what his father had done.

Chapter Thirty-five

EVELYN, LIVERPOOL, 1928

Evelyn woke with a start, listening out for a few seconds. The sounds were unfamiliar, footsteps running upstairs, doors banging, and even the busier road outside the window. Where was she?

She sat up, rubbing her eyes, aware her body ached from having lain in the same position too long. She didn't need a mirror to know her eyes were puffy, and she massaged her temples to try and clear her head.

The room smelled damp, she thought, breathing in, and she remembered then. She was at Ray's lodging house. It was where she'd run to the night before.

Ray had given the lad who had the room next door a few bob to distract their sharp-tongued, landlady while he sneaked her up the stairs to warm her up and calm her down.

Nothing had happened, of course, she reassured herself with a glance down at her dress. She was wearing Ray's jacket too. He'd put it on her to stop the uncontrollable shivering from having run through the streets with no coat in near-freezing weather and then had listened as, in between sobs, she'd told him about Violet and their mam's decision to give her the money for the dressmakers.

Of course, she felt sorry for Violet and horrified at what she would have to do. All of it was so unfair. The callous way her sister had been used and cast aside; Evelyn knew she'd never be the same after this. How could she be? Then there was the loss of hope. That money had meant freedom for her mam, Bea and Nellie. It would take forever to save up enough again.

The tears from the night before had left her depleted, but they'd also been cathartic and today was a new day. She refused to stay down for long because a new day meant new opportunities, and that was what she'd tell herself every morning until she and Mam finally opened their dressmakers. They'd get there. It would take longer than she'd thought was all.

Evelyn got up then and moved over to the window to peer out through the grime to the street below. Shadowy shapes were moving about, and she could hear the tram bells. What time was it? Alarm spiked at the thought of facing Mam, who'd be going mad with worry. She'd more than likely have called around to Ida's last night to see if she was there, so it was no good saying that was where she'd been.

The door creaked open then, and Evelyn froze, only relaxing as Ray's familiar shape filled the doorway. The hallway light was behind him and she caught a glimpse of his dingy lodgings.

'I'm saving up for better things,' he said, reading her mind as he shut the door. 'I brought you up a piece of toast.' He held it out, but Evelyn shook her head. She wasn't hungry. Ray shrugged, 'No point wasting it.' He sat down on the end of the bed and began to eat it.

'What am I going to do, Ray? Everything's such a mess.'

He finished the toast, standing up to brush the crumbs off his waistcoat before moving towards her. 'C'mere, girl.'

Evelyn sank into his embrace, wishing she could stay there in his arms forever, but already he was pushing her away.

'You've gorra go home, kid, and sort things out with your mam and sister.' He reached inside his waistcoat, retrieving a roll of notes from an inside pocket and thrusting it towards her, he said, 'Here. Take it. I've more where this came from. Use it to open your shop.'

'No.' Evelyn shook her head, her voice firm. 'We've talked about this before, Ray. You know I can't accept it.' He'd offered her money each time she'd mentioned how grim life was with her father and how the business was a way out, but she'd given him the same answer each time.

He swore under his breath and mumbled something about her being too stubborn for her own good. 'It's not only yourself that pride of yours is hurting, girl. What about your mam and sisters?'

'No, Ray.' She held firm, her chin tilted proudly. How could she explain she'd made a vow to herself as solemn as any nun's? She would never be indebted to any man, not even Ray. Only that way could she be sure she'd never wind up trapped like her mam. If they were going to run their own business from a proper shop, they needed to do it under their own steam. It was the way it had to be.

They eyeballed one another for a long second before Ray looked away. He knew he'd met his match in Evelyn, and he stuffed the money back in his pocket.

Evelyn could feel his annoyance, but she couldn't worry about that now. She needed to get home and get herself off to work because she wouldn't be packing in the button factory any time soon, not now.

'How am I going to get out of here without your landlady collaring me?' The thought of what the old wagon would have to say if she caught Evelyn skulking down the stairs made her feel hot despite the chill in the room. She shouldn't have come here.

It was foolish and selfish. She could have got Ray kicked out, still could, but she'd needed him.

Ray wasn't prone to sulking, and his crinkled brow softened as he gave her a rakish grin and a wink. 'Gotchya in, girl, we'll get you out.'

He was true to his word, Evelyn thought, feeling conspicuous as she hurried towards home, still wearing his jacket. Her head thumped at the prospect of the fibs she would have to tell her mam, and she kept it down, not making eye contact with any passers-by. But, as she drew nearer to Potter Street, the angst she was feeling at facing the music changed. It was replaced by that same feeling of something terrible reaching out towards her family like bony fingers. She'd thought it was down to Violet's news the day before, but this now was different. Something wasn't right at home. She knew it!

Evelyn's footfall echoed in the misty morning as she quickened her pace so she was half running, half walking in her desperation to get home to her mam and sisters. She stopped short at the top of her street. Through the wisps of fog, she could see the outlined figures of people huddling together on the cobbles and something bulkier.

She began to walk towards them, aware of the heavy smell of smoke weighing down the fog. The smell grew worse the closer she got to the group gathered outside the row of houses where hers sat, and the bulky shape she registered belonged to a fire truck.

The puddles of water she'd splashed through had soaked her feet, and her mind refused to comprehend what this all meant.

Potter Street residents, with coats thrown on over nightwear, watched as the firemen wound their hoses up. Evelyn saw Mrs Murphy from next door conversing with a policeman who was taking notes. Her neighbour had buttoned her green coat up to her chin, and her white nightgown peeked out of the bottom, at odds with the sturdy leather shoes on her feet. Mrs Murphy looked past the bobby and spotted Evelyn, staring in disbelief at number 46.

What had been her home less than twelve hours earlier was a gaping brick shell. The windows were black holes like a mouth open, ready to scream, and the door was ajar, revealing the charred passageway. 'Mam!' she cried out, running into the crowd, oblivious to the danger of the slick cobbles as she frantically scanned faces. 'Mam! Violet!' She pushed the people she'd lived alongside her whole life out of the way, refusing to acknowledge their sombre, pitying gazes. 'Nellie, Bea!' The cloying smoke made her throat raw as her cries grew more panicked.

Mrs Murphy appeared in front of her, blocking her way as she wrung her hands. Her face was pinched beneath the headscarf knotted beneath her chin. 'Oh, Evelyn, luv, where've you been? It's a terrible, terrible thing.'

She knew then they were gone and felt strong arms haul her upright as she crumpled towards the wet cobbles.

'Take her inside. I'll make a pot of strong tea,' Mrs Murphy was saying. 'Her da will look after her. Eee, poor mite.'

Evelyn allowed the unfamiliar hands to steer her into Mrs Murphy's parlour, where her father was sitting at the table with his head bowed.

''Ere you go, queen. You sit yourself down,' a man's voice she didn't recognise said, and she did as she was told, not trusting her legs to hold her weight.

Mrs Murphy loitered in the doorway. 'Your da's been asking for you, haven't you, Jack?' she said before bustling off to make the tea, glad to be put to work.

Jack raised his head, his bloodshot eyes trying to focus on her. 'Evelyn. They're dead. They're all dead.'

Evelyn put her hands to her ears, not wanting to hear it.

Chapter Thirty-six

ONE MONTH LATER

For a blissful moment each morning, when Evelyn opened her eyes, she would think everything was as it had been. She was in her bed at Potter Street. But then, she'd realise the spidery cracks in the ceiling were different and that it was Ida and her sister Agnes, sleeping next to her. Not Bea and Violet. Nellie's little feet weren't pressing into her back because they were gone. Her mam, her sisters, all gone as a result of smoke inhalation from the fire that had engulfed their house shortly after ten on that fateful Thursday night.

Her disbelief that she'd never see their faces again or hear their voices hadn't lessened any, and she'd grown thin despite Ida's mam's extra helpings of stew she could ill afford to dole out.

The Mercers had taken her under their wing, suggesting she stay with them for the time being until she got her head straight, a kindness she was grateful for given their already cramped living space.

Ray had helped her shoulder the burden of grief by listening to her talk and holding her tight when the pain knifed through her afresh day after day. He wanted them to get engaged. 'Make it official, like,' he'd said. 'I want to look after yer.'

Evelyn had asked him to give her time. A part of her was desperate to say yes and to get wed. She wouldn't have to think about her future, and what she would do now her father was the only family she had left. A bigger part of her knew that wasn't the right reason to marry someone, and even now, she remembered the vow she'd made to herself never to be dependent on a man no matter how tempting the prospect was.

She refused to examine her feelings too closely, knowing the guilt she felt at not having been home that night would swallow her whole if she did.

Her father was staying in a doss house, and she hadn't seen him since the funeral. The service was held three days after the inquest had ruled accidental death. A gas lamp had started the fire in the parlour, igniting material her mam had been working on that evening.

Mrs Murphy had reported hearing shouting earlier in the evening. Around nine, which wasn't out of the ordinary, she'd confided in the young policeman. It had gone quiet by ten, however, and she'd thought no more about it supposing Mr Flooks had gone back out or to sleep.

Her father had corroborated this with the policeman saying he had indeed gone back out and how sorrowful he was he had. If he'd stayed home, perhaps they'd all still be here. Or failing that, he'd be up there with them now, in heaven, which was preferable to the living hell he found himself in.

It was around eleven thirty, Mrs Murphy said when splintering glass woke them. Upon rushing outside to investigate, they'd seen the flames, and Mr Murphy had attempted to enter number forty-six, but by then, it was an inferno. It was a miracle the fire hadn't spread and that their house had been spared, she'd stated.

As for Evelyn, she'd told the truth of where she'd been, and Ray had backed her up.

The day of the funeral had been fittingly bleak with sleet blowing in and out. Evelyn had thanked Mrs Mercer for lending her a black coat and dress, uncaring that they hung off her like a sack. She'd heard someone whisper she was a bag of bones as Ray in his overcoat with a black armband led her into the church.

The pews were packed with their neighbours. Some of the men would have taken a day off work to attend. No small sacrifice as they'd be docked a day's pay, and this had touched her. The women, wrapped in their black shawls, were the same women who'd sneered at her mam for thinking she was better than them, but Evelyn knew their horror over what had happened to Lizzie Flooks and three of her daughters was real. They needed to pay their respects.

Her father's frame was skeletal inside his jacket as he sat hunched over. His face was grey, and despite his efforts to scrub up, he still stank of stale booze. Only the two of them were left, but Evelyn couldn't find it within herself to offer him comfort because while she could forgive the neighbourhood women for their treatment of her mam, she couldn't forgive her father.

She'd told him as much as they'd sat at the table waiting for Mrs Murphy to bring them in some tea that awful morning. All the pain had spewed forth, and Mrs Murphy had to shake her to stop as she screamed out, 'I wish it were you was lying in there dead!'

It had taken all her strength, but she'd forced herself to look over at the four coffins in the hope that knowing her mam, Violet, Bea, and Nellie were in God's arms now would give her peace.

At the back of Evelyn's brain tickled the knowledge there was something else. It was something she knew she needed to remember about that night. But no matter how hard she tugged at the tantalising threads, it wouldn't come to her.

That particular morning as she stared up at the cracks in the ceiling, she remembered it was Sunday, and after church, she and Ray were going to go back to the house. She'd not been strong enough to set foot in Potter Street, let alone return to number forty-six before. But, since the landlord had made it known demolition work was soon to begin, she had no choice.

She needed to go back for her mam's ring.

Evelyn was glad Ray was by her side as they made their way down Potter Street. She hadn't known how she'd feel returning.

The familiar chanting of girls playing jumping rope in the street made her catch her breath as the memory of playing the same game with her sisters when they were younger burned fresh. A little ways farther down the street, three small boys attempted to play whip and top with a turnip top on the cobbles. She could see Ma Kenny sitting on her front step smoking her clay pipe and Mrs Jones and Mrs O'Brien from across the way deep in conversation outside their front doors. They paused to greet her and ask how she was getting on, giving Ray a frown of disapproval. Evelyn could almost hear them whispering as to how young Evelyn Flooks had fallen in with a bad-un once they'd carried on their way.

There was no sign of Mrs Murphy, which was a relief. Evelyn didn't want to get waylaid by her old neighbour, knowing she'd press her as to how she and her dad were faring. She too, would shake her head over the company she was keeping.

People's minds were narrow, Evelyn had come to realise. They rarely took the time to examine their prejudices, let alone question them.

Ray wasn't perfect. He was human, and he'd been hurt. That was why he ran with the Lime Street Boys. But, if you scratched beneath the surface of those women, Evelyn was confident she'd find they all had their reasons for needing to be part of something bigger than themselves. It was why they went to church.

She pulled her eyes away from her old neighbour's house. Her mam had had the measure of Mrs Murphy. In a very un-Mam-like manner, she used to say that the woman had a gob on her the size of the Mersey tunnel.

'This is it,' Evelyn said, coming to a halt and staring at the house she'd called home. It was a shock seeing it with boards over the windows and front door, and for a moment, she was frozen where she stood as she absorbed the enormity of what had happened.

Ray laid a hand on her arm and looked at her questioningly. 'Are you sure you want to do this?'

'I'll be ahright.' It didn't matter how grand or poky a house was, Evelyn thought, it was the people inside it who made it home, and this wasn't her home. Not anymore. 'How will we get in?' She'd no wish to linger any longer than she had to.

'Don't worry about that, girl. I can get into anything, me.' He glanced to his left and right and, seeing no one in the immediate vicinity, went up to the front door and began to work on dislodging the middle wooden panel.

Evelyn watched him work, aware the eyes of the street were on them both. No one would say anything though, just as they hadn't said anything when her father's fists had flown.

Her feet tapped as she tried to stop herself dwelling on what Ray's throwaway comment had meant because she was sure one of these days that cockiness of his would land him in hot water.

At last, there was a splintering sound, and the boarding gave way, leaving a black hole big enough for them to clamber through.

Ray rubbed his hands together. 'I'll go in first and check it's safe.'

Evelyn clenched and unclenched her hands as she waited for him to reappear. It felt like forever instead of a minute or two before he finally poked his head through.

'I don't reckon it's safe to go upstairs, but you'll be ahright down here, girl.' He had a black smudge on his cheek.

Evelyn knew she'd be giving the neighbours something to talk about as she lifted her leg in an unladylike manner and stuck it through the gap, feeling it connect with the floor on the other side. Then she bent down to ease the rest of her body through, managing to snag her stockings along the way.

Ray took hold of her hand to steady her as she emerged in the dank passage.

It took a moment for her eyes to adjust to the dim light, and when they did, a nightmarish scene of blackened walls and timber greeted her. The stairs were in a state of collapse, and the questions crowded in. Had her mam or sisters woken up and tried to get out of the house? Had the stairs been on fire trapping them? If so, why hadn't they jumped from the window?

'Don't, Evelyn. It won't help,' Ray said quietly, reading her mind. 'The what-ifs don't help.'

However he knew this, he was right, and she focused instead on trying to conjure the sounds of her sisters' laughter or her mam's sewing machine, but the only noise was a steady drip from the rafters overhead. It was no good being fanciful. She'd come here for a reason, and so she determinedly moved into the space that had been the parlour.

'The fire started in here,' Evelyn said, knowing Ray was right behind her. The floorboards were scarred in places and eaten through by the fire in others. They groaned ominously beneath their feet. The smell of smoke was worse, and she dug her hanky from her coat pocket, pressing it over her nose and mouth.

'Mam's sewing machine,' Evelyn murmured, seeing the cast iron machine lying on the floor. She crouched down to touch it, and the emotion that swelled up threatened to drag her down into the damp earth alongside her mam and sisters.

Ray's hand settled on her shoulder. The warmth of it through her coat was solid and real. It gave her the strength she needed to stand back up and pick her way over to the corner of the room where her mam's hidey-hole had been.

Her foot connected with something and looking down, Evelyn saw the money tin. The lid wasn't on, and even knowing it was empty, she picked it up anyway.

It clattered and rolled away as she dropped it to the floor.

As she drew nearer to the wall that connected their house to Mrs Murphy's, she saw the fire had barely touched the boards here.

'It's around here somewhere.' Evelyn got down on her knees and ran the palm of her hand over the timber until she felt a groove that told her this was the one. She dug her nails in and lifted the board.

Ray's lighter rasped and flared, illuminating the cavity where the floorboard had been.

It was empty.

Evelyn frowned. 'I don't understand,' she said, reaching down and patting around, but there was nothing there. She looked up at Ray, whose features were underlit spookily by the flickering flame. 'How can it be empty?'

Ray shrugged and let the flame die, his finger too hot to hold the flint down any longer. They plunged them back into the gloom and the memory that had been hovering out of Evelyn's reach since the night of the fire came crashing back.

She rocked back on her heels, moaning softly.

She knew her dad had come to the house the night of the fire because Mrs Murphy had said she'd heard shouting and thudding. What she'd been unable to recall though, was that she'd seen him heading to the house as she ran from it. He'd been singing.

It was much earlier than Mrs Murphy had placed him there—than he said he'd come home. Her brain raced, trying to connect the dots. Had he walked in on Mam and Vi and seen the tin? If he had, he'd have wanted to know where it had come from and what else Mam had been squirrelling away. He wouldn't have been happy. Did he take the money and the ring?

Other questions refused to stay silent.

Was it him who'd knocked the lamp over that night? Had he come back in a drunken stupor having already squandered what he'd taken at the bookies, convinced there must be more?

Evelyn wanted to scream, knowing she'd never find out the truth of what had happened, but instead, she told Ray what she suspected. 'I need to know where me mam's ring is, Ray.' Sobs wracked her body. 'I've nothing else left.'

He helped her to her feet and pulled her into him. She clung to him as her body shook with sorrow and hatred.

'You've gor me, girl. I'm here, and you leave it with me. I'll sort it.'

Chapter Thirty-seven

'I'll see you later then.' Ida squeezed Evelyn's arm before pulling hers free to wave over to Ray. He was leaning against the wall, smoking.

Ida joined the crowd of workers, eager to put distance between themselves and the factory for the evening while Evelyn hurried over to him. He flicked his cigarette onto the ground before greeting her with a smoky kiss, and his expression as they broke apart was unusually solemn.

'What is it?' Evelyn searched his face for clues.

'I always keep me promises, girl. Remember that.' He reached out and caressed her cheek.

The leather of his glove was soft against her skin, and she watched as he delved into the pocket of his overcoat to produce a red velvet pouch.

'Mam's ring,' Evelyn breathed. She stared at the pouch, oblivious to the factory girls surging past them as, instead of thanking him, she uttered a string of 'but where and how, did he have it?

'He'd pawned it,' Ray said with a sneer of disgust. 'The only thing left of his wife, and he pawned it.'

Evelyn wasn't surprised. It was the drink and the bookies that ruled her father, not his heart, and she didn't care if she never saw him again. So far as she was concerned, he was dead to her.

Her eyes shone as she took the pouch from him, eager to peek inside it at the ring. Having this with her would mean her mam was always by her side. 'Thank you, Ray,' she finally managed to say, her voice breaking as she added, 'This means everything to me.'

'Now, will you marry me, Evelyn Flooks?' All traces of his usual cocksure demeanour disappeared, and he looked almost childlike in his uncertainty.

Evelyn bit down on her bottom lip. Ray had never let her down. He was always there for her, a solid and dependable presence without whom she'd have been lost.

Ray, sensing she was wavering, took her hand and dropped down on one knee, uncaring of the damp cobbles or the curious stares of the passing girls as they slowed, pausing in their chatter to watch the scene unfold.

'Ger up, Ray,' Evelyn urged, mortified by the spectacle he was making of them both.

'Not until yer give us yer answer.'

Evelyn pulled away from him, panic swelling at being put on the spot. 'Don't push me. I asked you to give me time.'

Reluctantly he got to his feet, brushing his trousers off. 'A man can only wait so long, Evelyn, remember that,' he sighed. 'I've something else for you. I was going to wait until we got there, but...' He shrugged. The wind had gone out of his sails at her refusal to either reject or accept his proposal. The stalemate they were at was driving him mad.

Evelyn stowed the ring away in her coat pocket, looking up in time to see the flash of navy silk as he opened his overcoat to retrieve an official-looking document from the inside pocket.

''Ere.' He held it out to her.

Taking it, she untied the ribbon before unfolding the stiff bond paper. Her eyes skated over the formal typed wording, trying to understand what it meant. She looked at Ray questioningly.

'It's a property deed in both our names.'

'It says the premises are on Bold Street.'

Ray nodded. 'There's room for yer business downstairs and a flat for yer to call home upstairs.'

Evelyn was speechless, still not fully comprehending what it meant.

'You can open your shop, and you'll have a gaff of your own. It's not a gift, mind. I knew you wouldn't accept it if it were. The deed's in both our names, which means I own a half share. It's an investment for me. The first property in me portfolio.'

'Ray, I—'

'Don't say anything, Evie, girl. It's done. That there is legally binding. It's yours to do what you want with so far as I'm concerned. I'm a silent partner.'

'Can we go and see it?' For the first time since the night of the fire, Evelyn saw a glimmer of light where there'd only been darkness.

Three nights later, still thrilling over the fact that she was to open her shop and on prestigious Bold Street no less, there was a knock on the Murphys' door. The family had only just sat down for their tea, and Mr Murphy hauled himself up with a sigh, announcing he'd see to it.

Evelyn, lost in her thoughts as to how Ray had said he'd loan her the money she'd need before she could open the doors to the business she'd decided to call Brides of Bold Street without the interest a moneylender would demand, was unaware Mr Murphy had returned until he cleared his throat.

'Evie, there's a policeman to see you,' he said, addressing her.

'To see me?'

Mr Murphy nodded but didn't enlighten her about why a bobby would want a word with her. 'He said he needs to speak with yer.'

Evelyn put her soup spoon down and pushed her chair back, excusing herself from the table. 'It must be about Mam and me sisters,' she mumbled, half to herself.

'Do you want me to come with yer?'

'No, ta, Mr Murphy, I don't want your soup to get cold.'

The policeman peering out from under his custodian helmet was po-faced as she greeted him warily at the door.

'Miss Evelyn Flooks?'

'Yes?'

'I'm sorry to have to inform you we pulled a body from the Canning Dock this morning. Fellow dockworkers identified him as Jack Flooks, yer father.'

Evelyn leaned on the door frame for support. 'What was he doing in the water?' She thought it was a stupid question, knowing the likeliest scenario was that he was staggering about drunk and lost his balance.

The officer looked uncertain whether he should impart the grisly details to the frail young woman in front of him, but she was the deceased's only relative, and he had a job to do. 'He'd been beaten before being thrown in the water.'

The policeman seemed to sway back and forth as bile rose in Evelyn's throat, and she kept a tight hold of the frame. Her shock wasn't over her father's death. That had only ever been a matter of time. It was for Ray because he'd killed her father, and he'd done it for her.

Evelyn decided right there and then, as the policeman reached out to steady her, that she'd never breathe a word of it, not to Ray or anyone.

Chapter Thirty-eight

LIVERPOOL, 1982

An insect's high-pitched whine was the only sound in the tent as Adam looked up from the letter he was clutching. His forehead was creased as he turned to Sabrina, still next to him with her legs pulled up under her chin. 'I don't understand, Sabs. She says me dad killed her father. That can't be right.'

Sabrina reached for him, the ring on her finger taking on added meaning as she laid her hand on his arm. 'Aunt Evie wouldn't have made it up, Adam, your dad did it for the right reasons.'

Adam shook his head. 'But why tell us this now? What's she got to gain from it?'

'Nothing, except I suppose she felt we should know before we get married. She must have been weighed down by it since we met. We'd have found out one day because the deed to Bold Street Brides and the flat is in your dad's name as well as Aunt Evie's.'

'Jesus!'

Startled by his outburst, Sabrina moved her hand away as Adam tossed the letter aside and ran his hand across his head. 'Me mam said she thought he luved someone else but your aunt Evie? Jesus, Sabrina. I can't take it in.'

Sabrina didn't say anything. Subconsciously, it hadn't come as a shock because she'd known it all along. 'What do we do now?' she asked tentatively.

'Go home and talk to them. I dunno.' He turned towards her, his eyes flashing. 'We can't unknow it now, can we?'

'Adam, it doesn't change anything.'

'Yeah, it does.'

Fear stabbed at Sabrina. 'I meant it doesn't change us.'

'I can't get me head around it. I need to hear it from me dad.' He began manically tossing things into the pack.

He hadn't answered her question, but Sabrina knew not to push him. 'What about Flo and Tony?'

'We'll swing by the ozzy on our way to the ferry. C'mon pack yer things.'

Sabrina longed to talk to Florence about the letter and what Aunt Evie had divulged, but her friend was full of Tony as she fussed around his hospital bed, and she hadn't wanted to dampen her glow. Nor had Flo picked up on anything amiss, taking Adam's explanation that they hadn't seen the point in hanging about now and they were due to catch the last sailing back to Liverpool.

Florence had informed them she'd move into a B&B on the island near the hospital until Tony was discharged and could go home.

Sabrina had clung to their hug goodbye, and Florence had broken away with a laugh. 'Steady on, girl. You'll see me again in a few days.'

Adam was distant on the ferry crossing and Sabrina opened her mouth to say something more than once as he stared out to sea. But she'd closed it again. He needed to process what Aunt Evie had revealed. So did she, and she'd passed the time trying to absorb all she'd learned about her aunt's life.

Adam's kiss goodnight as he'd idled the bike outside the Wood Street entrance to the shop had been chaste and he'd followed it up, saying they needed to get his dad and Aunt Evie together in the morning to hear what had happened all those years ago straight from them.

Nine o'clock had been agreed upon and as she closed the door behind her and heard his bike reverberate up the street, she'd leaned against it shutting her eyes until she couldn't hear it anymore.

THE SUMMER POSY

Then, padding over to the stairs, she stared up at them, pondering how to play things with Aunt Evie.

Having made her mind up to keep her cool, she banged into the flat demanding to know why she'd had to tell them and why she couldn't have let the past lie?

Evelyn, who'd been expecting Sabrina home late Monday afternoon, dropped the biscuit she'd been dunking into her tea and, once she'd recovered from her fright, suggested Sabrina sit down instead of hovering over her like an avenging angel.

Sabrina did so, biting down on her bottom lip. Everything was so normal; the television playing in the background, the tea on the side tray table, the distant honk of a horn and siren wailing drifting in through the window, but her world felt out of kilter as she waited to hear what her aunt had to say.

'Ray and I kept secrets all our adult life, Sabrina. It was time to wipe the slate clean for your and Adam's sake because one day you'd want an explanation, and I wouldn't be there to give it to you.' Evelyn picked up her tea, then, spying the soggy biscuit bits floating in it, put it back down. 'You and Adam would want to know why Ray's name is on the deed to this,' she waved her hand vaguely about. 'And how we came to that point. I wanted you to hear it from me.'

Sabrina nodded slowly, the tense set of her shoulders softening. It made sense, but she was struggling to put this familiar Aunt Evie with her glasses, grey curls and soft cheeks with the young woman of her letter.

'I'm tired of hiding from my father too. I hid from him when he was alive, and I hid from the truth of what happened to him in the years since he died. No more, Sabrina. It's time to look forward to the future, yours and Adam's without secrets festering in the background.'

'I never knew what it was like for you, Aunt Evie, and to lose your mam and sisters, but...' Sabrina's voice fell away. She couldn't say the words, but Evelyn knew her almost better than she knew herself and understood the struggle to accept what Ray had done.

'My father was a brute, Sabrina. Ray was looking out for me in a way Dad never did because he luved me. I'd have been lost if it wasn't for him because it was the shop that helped me heal.' She gave an ironic smile. 'When I was a girl, I made a vow to myself never to marry. I'd never be reliant on a man like my mam was, I decided that way I'd never be trapped. I would stand on my own two feet. I might not have married Ray, but I still wound up tied to him.'

Sabrina stared down at the ring on her finger. She knew now the heavy price both Ray and Aunt Evie had paid for it.

Her head was thumping, and she needed to lie down in the quiet of her bedroom. 'Adam and Ray are coming over in the morning at nine o'clock.

Adam wants to hear it from both of you.' She stood up then and slid the ring from her finger, placing it on the tray table.

'It's yours, Sabrina.'

'I'm not sure I want it, not knowing what I know now.' She turned away.

Evelyn watched her go, thinking how weary and sad she'd sounded. Had she done the right thing? She hoped she hadn't acted selfishly. As Sabrina closed the bedroom door behind her, it felt as though a chasm yawned between them.

Chapter Thirty-nine

They made an awkward tableau seated around the table in the flat. A pot of tea and a plate of Malted Milk biscuits in front of them. Outside it was business as usual on Bold Street, but the shop hadn't opened, and if the people who passed by it every morning thought it strange, they didn't falter in their strides, having things to do and places to be.

Evelyn, who was in civvies, not her Monday shop coat, was also smoking in blatant disregard to her one a day rule.

Sabrina was pleating the hem of the tablecloth. Her finger felt naked without the ring, and she was trying to get Adam to look at her, but his expression was inscrutable and he looked like he hadn't been to bed, let alone slept in his crumpled shirt and jeans.

Ray, by comparison, was dapper in his suit and tie with his hair combed back and a heavy helping of aftershave. He'd been chipper upon arrival despite his working day being eaten into by an impromptu meeting. However, now he eyed the trio around the table with apprehension, having been told it wasn't the wedding he'd been summoned to discuss when he'd sat down and helped himself to a biscuit.

'It's still going ahead, isn't it?' He brushed crumbs off his shirt front and looked to Sabrina and Adam for reassurance. Finally, receiving no response, he turned to Evelyn. But, just as Adam was avoiding making eye contact with Sabrina, Evelyn dipped her head and, grinding her cigarette out, began to fuss with the tea things.

Sabrina didn't know what to say. She wanted to burst into tears or kick Adam under the table and make him tell his father that, of course it was, but this Adam coiled tight with pent up emotions was one she didn't recognise. And he hadn't noticed the ring missing from her finger either.

'I don't want to talk about me and Sabrina, Dad. I want you to tell me whether this is true.' Adam pulled the envelope Sabrina had found stowed in her bag the day before out of his jacket pocket and thrust it across the table.

'What's this?' Ray's brow furrowed as he took it.

Adam turned to Evelyn, who had her fingers curled around the teapot handle. 'Would you like to tell him, or shall I?'

Sabrina didn't like the gruffness in his voice because this wasn't her Adam. Evelyn, too, looked startled. She released her grip from the teapot and pushed her glasses back up her nose, fixing her stare on Ray. 'I told them, Ray. It's all in there.' She gestured to the envelope.

Ray sighed, sitting back in his chair and loosening his tie. 'You always did know your own mind. And you're the most stubborn woman I have ever met, Evelyn Flooks. Now, are you going to pour that tea or is a man going to die of thirst waiting?'

Evelyn was glad of something to do with her hands.

'I don't need to read it, son,' Ray said.

Adam glared at him expectantly as Evelyn clattered with the cups and saucers. 'Is it true that you killed her father?' His voice was hoarse.

Ray's head snapped back. 'What are you talking about?'

'It's all in there.' Adam stabbed at the envelope Ray had put down on the table and Sabrina wanted to snatch it up and tear it into tiny pieces. She wished she'd never opened the flaming thing now and that she could put the lid back on all that it had released.

'Evelyn, what's he on about?' The bewilderment was plain to see on Ray's face.

'Jack, Ray,' Evelyn said. Her eyes were soft, but they hardened as she turned to Adam. 'I told Sabrina last night, young man, and I'm telling you now. Jack Flooks was a monster to his family and what your father did seeing him off like that, he did for me. He'd hurt enough people. There was no one to mourn him except the bookies and the publicans.'

'Evie, girl, I don't understand what you're talking about? Me and the lads, we roughed him up a bit. We gor 'im to tell us which pawnshop we'd find your mam's ring in and told him to keep away from you if he knew what was good for him, but we didn't kill him. That wasn't our style.'

'He was fished out of the water at Canning Dock, Ray, three days after you gave me the ring back.'

Ray's jaw, clean-shaven unlike his son's, dropped. 'But you never said. Why didn't you tell me?'

'I drew a line under it then and there.'

'Because you thought I was behind it.'

Evelyn nodded, feeling the years peel away until she was that scarred young woman trying to find a way through her grief once more.

'I thought you knew me, Evelyn. I was hot-headed and quick to throw a punch back then, and I talked a good talk but a murderer?' He shook his head. 'I was never that.'

Ray was many things. He'd done many things and sailed close to the wind; Evelyn knew that. He'd never lied to her in all the years she'd known him, though, and without his help, she'd never have opened Brides of Bold Street, her lifeline. At a loss as to what to say, she simply said, 'I'm sorry, Ray.'

'Is that why you wouldn't marry me? Because of what you thought I'd done.'

The atmosphere was suddenly charged as they faced one another across the table. Both were searching for answers to a past that had derailed somewhere along the line. They were oblivious to Sabrina and Adam, seeing themselves as they had been when their lives had stretched ahead of them. A fork in the road they were on had separated them, with Evelyn going one way, Ray the other. But their paths had kept entwining thanks to the shop.

'You're right. I knew you weren't a murderer, but I thought I'd pushed you into it. You'd gone too far. I asked you to get Mam's ring back; therefore, it was my mistake. I knew you'd see his face every time you looked at me. What kind of life would that have been? I already owed you so much, my home, the shop. It was too much, Ray, too much.' Evelyn's eyes glistened dangerously. Too much, and then he'd married Laura, breaking her heart. Evelyn didn't say this, though that too was her fault. He'd waited long enough for her to trust him, and it was too late when she finally had. She'd made her choices. 'I'd always promised myself I'd stand on my own two feet. I didn't bank on how lonely that would be, but then Sabrina came along.'

Ray's eyes narrowed. He'd taken Evelyn's story about her being an orphaned niece with a pinch of salt and had never questioned it. He wouldn't do so now either.

Aunt Evie was not a woman prone to tears, and seeing her on the verge of them now, Sabrina didn't hesitate to reach over and take her hand.

What had happened back then didn't matter. Aunt Evie needed her.

'It wasn't your place to decide everything, Evelyn.' There was sadness in Ray's voice.

Adam butted in, having heard enough his face was dark as he turned on his father. All the anger and hurt he'd felt over his mam's death and the long-ago conversation he'd overheard spilt out into one loaded question. 'Did you ever luv me mam, Dad, or was it Evelyn all along?'

Ray dragged his eyes from Evelyn and looked to his son. 'Of course I luved your mam. She was me sun, moon and stars but—'

'There was always Evelyn,' Adam finished for him, and Sabrina's heart ached, seeing the anguish in his eyes. She was desperate to reach out to him, but Evelyn squeezed her hand, understanding this conversation between father and son needed to be had.

Ray didn't answer, and it was answer enough in itself.

'She knew you luved someone else. I heard her talking to Auntie Jean about it once.'

Ray splayed his hands out flat on the table and stabbed at the thick gold band on his ring finger. 'See that there, son. That symbolises the promise I made your mam when we wed, and I kept it.'

'You weren't there when she needed you most!' His Adam's apple bobbed up and down as he fought to keep himself in check.

'And it was wrong of me. You were a lad. I let you down, and I'm sorry for that, son. I've never been frightened of anything in me life, but I was terrified when Laura got sick, and I crumbled. To see her suffering and not be able to do anything about it.' He shook his head. 'I've always been able to fix things, you see. When I was young, it was with these.' He held up his fists, his gold cufflinks glinting as his jacket sleeves slid up his arms. 'Then when I got older, money talked, but I couldn't fix her. You should never have had to shoulder that alone.' Ray bowed his head and swiped his cheek with the back of his hand, but they'd all seen the tear trickling down it. His voice was pleading as he locked eyes with his son. 'I need you to forgive me, son. Can you do that?'

There was no sound apart from their fraught breathing and the distant noises of everyday life wafting in through the open window.

Sabrina pulled her hand from Evelyn's and, getting up from the table, she put her arms around Adam and held him tightly. He sagged against her.

'I luv you, Adam, and I want to spend the rest of me life with you. I want to be Mrs Taylor more than anything. But, you have to let this go. We've no chance of happiness while you're holding on to so much hurt and anger. You need to forgive.'

Releasing Adam, she turned to Evelyn. 'I'm sorry, Aunt Evie, about last night.'

Evelyn didn't reply. Instead, she got up and, opening the sideboard drawer, retrieved the red pouch.

'Could I have that, Evelyn?' Adam asked, and she dropped the pouch into his outstretched palm.

The clock on the mantle ticked the seconds; then, he raised his head to look at his father. 'I forgive you, Dad.'

Adam untied the pouch's ribbon and tipped the ring from it before taking Sabrina's hand in his.

'Sabrina Flooks, will you do me the honour of becoming me wife?'

Evelyn was ready with the box of tissues as Sabrina sniffed, 'Yes.'

Chapter Forty

Two Months Later

Somehow, Sabrina had pulled it off. Organising a wedding in two months was no small feat, but she'd done it with Florence's and Aunt Evie's help. A glance down at her dress reassured her all was in order and she swallowed the Opal Fruit she'd been chewing. All the initial agonising over the design of her wedding gown had disappeared when Adam had told her she'd look beautiful in a sack and would she hurry up and marry him.

It had dawned on her, the dress didn't matter. The vows they'd exchange and the promises they'd make to one another were what mattered, and feeling like a princess in her fairy tale silk taffeta dress was the icing on the cake.

Today she'd become Mrs Sabrina Taylor and she couldn't wait.

An elegant room with seats festooned by silk bows lay beyond the engraved timber double doors in front of her. Friends from the past she'd stepped back to along with friends from the present filled them. They'd all come on this, the happiest day of her life, to see her and Adam wed. Ida, Esmerelda, the Bootle Tootlers and Bossy Bev, Mickey from The Swan, Linda and Tim who'd patched things up, Mystic Lou they were all in there.

Fred's sister Betty was a marriage celebrant, and when the wedding invite had arrived in the post, she'd telephoned Sabrina to insist she be the one to conduct the ceremony. It was only fitting, given all Sabrina had done for her and Fred, she'd said.

Sabrina hoped she wasn't wearing tweed because she'd cook given the beautiful late summer's day outside. She couldn't wait to see Fred, who Betty had informed her was doing well with only a few whoopsies along the way. He attended regular meetings to help with his tippling problem and he'd joined a local theatre group, having recently performed the lead role in a production of *Romeo and Juliet*. Betty had trilled her brother made rather a long in the tooth Romeo, but then Mrs Seymour as Juliet was no spring chicken either. Sabrina had put the phone down on that call with a huge smile on her face.

It was an honour to have Patty, Davey and Lee here, given they'd flown from Australia; Bernie and

Jane too would be excited to see her walk down the aisle to meet Adam.

She fizzed with anticipation knowing he was there now waiting on the other side of those doors for her with Tony, his best man alongside him.

There'd been a wobble earlier that morning over knowing her mother and siblings would never share in her and Adam's life. Only Flo had been privy to it as they'd sat having their hair done by John-Paul and Penny.

Sabrina had accepted that part of her life wasn't to be, but that didn't mean there wouldn't always be a piece of her who wished she'd had the chance to know her mother and her half-brother and sister properly. Fate had different plans, however.

Florence had soon had her smiling by telling her she was taking Tony shopping come the weekend for new jeans.

'Ready?' Evelyn asked, holding her arm out for Sabrina to take.

Sabrina took it holding her glorious summer posy of wildflowers, carefully chosen to include soft pink daisies the exact shade of Aunt Evie's two-piece suit and hat along with Florence and the twin's dresses, in her right hand. Bubbles of happiness bounced inside her.

It wasn't conventional having your aunt give you away, but then neither was arriving at the registry office on the back of a Triumph Bonneville! The looks their wedding party had received from startled pedestrians and motorists alike had been priceless.

Aunt Evie had refused to ride pillion, so Ray had chauffeured her and a disgruntled Shona and Teresa who'd wanted to go on a motorbike to the registry office. They'd snapped out of it once they'd arrived though, because, clutching their baskets of petals, they were model flower girls.

Mrs Teesdale had already taken hundreds of photos because it wasn't often her youngest two looked like butter wouldn't melt or wore such pretty dresses.

Sabrina took a deep breath. Tonight she and Adam would sleep in their new home, gifted by Ray. Aunt Evie wouldn't be on her own either because Ray was around keeping her company every night. At first, Sabrina had been worried as to how this would make Adam feel, but he was as eager for his dad not to be alone as she was her aunt.

Happiness was contagious and forgiveness healing.

Florence tweaked the bow at the back of her dress and then twiddled with Sabrina's veil.

It wouldn't be long before it was her and Tony's turn, Sabrina and Adam reckoned. Her friend looked beautiful in the flowing A-line chiffon gown with a ruffle top over her bust. She'd chosen it herself. Tony had all but drooled when he saw her in it.

You're all set, girl,' Florence announced, satisfied with her titivations.

Sabrina took a deep breath, smiled at Aunt Evie and as the doors swung open, she stepped forward to greet her future.

The End

Also By Michelle Vernal

The Cooking School on the Bay
Second Hand Jane
Staying at Eleni's
The Traveller's Daughter
Sweet Home Summer
When We Say Goodbye
Series Fiction
Isabel's Story
The Promise
The Letter
The Guesthouse on the Green
O'Mara's
Moira Lisa Smile
What Goes on Tour
Rosi's Regrets
Christmas at O'Mara's

A Wedding at O'Mara's
Maureen's Song
The O'Maras in LaLa Land
Due in March
A Baby at O'Mara's
The Housewarming
Rainbows over O'Mara's out on July 28, 2022. Pre-order here: https://books2read.com/u/3yKy0J

About Michelle

Michelle Vernal lives in Christchurch, New Zealand with her husband, two teenage sons and attention seeking tabby cats, Humphrey and Savannah. Before she started writing novels she had a variety of jobs:

Pharmacy shop assistant, girl who sold dried up chips and sausages on a hot food stand in a British pub, girl who sold nuts (for 2 hours) on a British market stall, receptionist, P.A..

Her favourite job though is the one she has now – writing stories she hopes leave her readers with a satisfied smile on their face.

Printed in Great Britain
by Amazon